Aqua Bay

By Casey Fae Hewson

Cover design by Lynn O'Shea
Freshfields Graphic Design
Info@ffieldsdesign.co.nz

ISBN: 978-0-473-41256-2 (Softcover)
ISBN: 978-0-473-41088-9 (Epub)
ISBN: 978-0-473-41089-6 (Mobi)
ISBN: 978-0-473-41090-2 (ibook)

To Bob Boze

For showing me the true meaning of being a writer

People protect what they love.

Jacques Yves Cousteau

Chapter 1

Nerissa sped down Cottage Row as she had done many times before. She was familiar with every section of the road, which bends required careful slower manoeuvring in the van and straight stretches where she could drive as fast as she dared.

Tomorrow skirted around the fringes of her mind. Scott, her fiancé, would be arriving in Aqua Bay tonight and they would have one night together before heading back to the city tomorrow to attend Frances, her seven-year-old niece's birthday party. But first she needed to get to Dolphin Eco-tours, where she worked as a tour guide. She sang along to Train's "Hey Soul Sister".

She stuck her head out the window and laughed as her hair whipped round her face in the summer breeze. Salt air lingered; it was a smell she never tired of. To her left the sun shimmered across the half-moon inlet of Aqua Bay. Beyond, the colour deepened to green as the bay gave way to the ocean. Would the dolphins be out playing and cavorting in the bay? To her right the rugged mountains rose up hugging and protecting the small township.

The early morning sun threw its full force into her eyes. In the distance, a grey Range Rover grew larger and began drifting over to her left. She slowed down. This wasn't a main road, but was quite often frequented by campervans and rental cars out tiki-touring.

The outline of the Rover grew larger and it was making no attempt to move over to their side of the road.

Nerissa dropped her speed down. The Range Rover charged towards her.

She jammed on the brakes, slammed on the horn and swerved too late as the Rover clipped the side of the van and came to a halt. She pulled the steering wheel hard left to avoid a telephone pole.

"For the love of…" Metal crunched on metal as the van came to a stop on the grass verge. She drew in a shuddering breath. *That had been close. Too close.*

Nerissa climbed out of the van and peered at the Rover. Long, tanned, muscly, male legs emerged first, followed by long arms and the rest of him.

He strode over to the van and knelt down inspecting the slightly crumpled bumper bar. "Is there much damage?" He didn't wait for an answer. "Not too bad." He straightened up towering over her at six feet. His T-shirt was a good fit and outlined his tight chest muscles. His long black, wavy hair had an 'I've-just-got-out-of-bed' look about it. Something pulsed within her.

Walking round to the front of the van, she examined the damage.

"Hmm. A bit of a dent," he said, rubbing his jaw.

"You were across the centre line," she said.

"Yeah. I think I drifted a bit," he drawled.

An American accent. *Great. He must be a tourist.*

"You need to be more careful." She rubbed her wrist which thumped with pain. "And, by the way, I'm fine."

"I only dinged the front of your car. It wasn't like it was a head on collision."

She glared at him. *Arrogant.*

"You look fine to me – or should I call an ambulance?" His deep brown eyes had a devil's smile in them.

"There's no need to be sarcastic." This guy was pushing her buttons. Why couldn't he just acknowledge that he had been in the wrong? "How about paying more attention to the road?"

"Yes, ma'am." He mock saluted her.

"Oh!" She opened up the driver's door and pulled out her cell phone. "You'd better give me your contact details. This dent will need some panel beating."

"You won't have trouble finding me."

"Oh yeah, how's that?" She peered up at him. His broad shoulders and arms looked like they had enough power in them to push her van all the way into town. She tucked a wave of hair behind her ear.

"It won't take you long to figure it out."

"Look, man of mystery. I haven't got time to chase you all over the place."

He laughed, rough and loud as he walked back to his Rover.

"What are you doing? You're required by law to give me your number." Nerissa shouted.

The only response was the gunning of the Rover and a cheeky wave as he drove past.

She threw her cell phone into her bag and jumped into the van, muttering under her breath as she continued to town driving the narrow coastal road that led round to Aqua Bay.

Arriving at work, she drove into the allocated parking space smiling at the dolphin logo on the banner above the building. The dolphin's eyes twinkled back at her.

She gathered up her gear and strolled into the front entrance. "Sorry I'm late."

"I knew you wouldn't be too far away," said Katey, Nerissa's childhood friend, as she attached the latest sea conditions to the noticeboard.

"You wouldn't believe it. Some American guy clipped the van on my way here."

"Are you all right?" Katey asked.

"I'm glad you asked, which was more than he did. Yeah, I'm fine but the van will need some panel beating. He was really evasive about giving me his details saying that I wouldn't have any trouble finding him and he'd be in town for a while." She shook her head. "As if I have all day to go hunt him down."

"It would be some tourist trying to squirm their way out of it."

Nerissa pulled the calendar for the day's tours off the printer. "How many people have we got this morning?"

"Ten."

"Great. Just as it should be for the summer."

The excited babble of the eagerly-waiting tourists on the boat, *Seabird*, drifted through the window.

"Are we still on for drinks at The Crab and Apple tonight?" Katey asked. She pulled on her jacket which had the words *eco-tour guide* printed on the back.

"Sure thing. We'll meet Scott there."

After Nerissa waved off Katey and the passengers on the tour, she spent the next couple of hours analysing the latest financials. Figures bored her. She would much rather be out on *Seabird* proudly showing off the beautiful coastline and its abundant sea life. As she stared out the window, the waves churned up onto the beach and the tang of seaweed lay heavy in the air. The never-ending mournful cry of the seagulls drifted in through the windows. She sighed. She would miss all of this when she left Aqua Bay at the end of summer.

She picked up the upcoming bookings sheet. They looked good. Most of the tours would be booked out by the end of next week.

Time dragged as she counted down the hours to when she and him would meet up at The Crab and Apple. She hadn't see

Scott for two weeks. He normally drove up after work every Friday, but last week there had been an eleventh-hour crisis at the accounting firm where he worked. Not only did he pull an all-nighter but worked Saturday as well, making it impossible to make the trip.

Nerissa twisted her engagement ring round her finger. She'd suggested to Scott that he didn't need to drive up to just stay the night and then make the trip back with her into the city tomorrow, but he had insisted. She smiled to herself. That was the kind of guy he was. There was nothing he wouldn't do for her.

The hours slowly passed by and at 4.30, *Seabird*, chugged back to the jetty.

She strolled out to the boat.

Captain Peter Haffrey, who was in his late 50s, threw her the ropes and she tied them securely to the bollards.

The passengers chatted to each other still high on the thrill of their adventure and she helped them disembark, taking photos for those who wanted a permanent memory of their day out.

Katey picked up the bucket and hose to begin washing the outside of the boat, but Peter offered to do it.

"It's Friday. You young things go and enjoy yourselves."

"Thanks Peter," Nerissa and Katey yelled out.

"What have you got planned for this weekend?" Nerissa asked Katey as they walked inside to the changing rooms.

"Not a lot, although I thought I'd go over all the course information for this accounting degree I've kind of convinced myself I should start doing."

"You don't sound very enthusiastic." Nerissa pulled a long summery dress over her head and zipped it up at the back.

"I know. I've been putting it off but if I want to move up, focusing on management qualifications is the way to go. I've just been procrastinating at the thought of all that study."

"I think it's a great idea. That's something I probably should be doing, but I just don't think it's the right time."

"Of course not," Katey replied, rummaging round in her handbag. "Besides, you have a wedding to plan soon."

Nerissa stared at herself in the mirror. She ran a brush through her long, curly, blonde hair then tied it back so it flowed in loose waves down her back. Yes, that's right. Her marriage to Scott. The love of her life. A date had to be set first. Then a venue booked, invitations sent, cake, flowers, a dress... A chill swept over her. It happened every time someone brought up the wedding.

"Nerissa?" Katey broke into her thoughts.

"Oh. Sorry, yes, yes, the wedding. That'll certainly keep me busy."

Katey narrowed her eyes. "That didn't sound at all like an excited bride-to-be."

Nerissa leaned her hands on the washbasin. "Yes. I need to get on with the wedding. It's just that..."

"Pre-wedding nerves. Everyone gets that, right? Maybe it's because there's a lot to plan."

"I suppose so. I'm just being silly." Nerissa sighed. But somehow it wasn't that. She was a good planner so why was making that first step of even setting a date proving to be an obstacle as tall as a mountain? Did it have something to do with whether marriage would fulfil her?

"I'm happy to help. That's what bridesmaids are for. Let's get together next week and start working on it." Katey whipped a comb over the wisps of her short brown hair.

"That would be great. You're the push I need to get things started."

"I'm glad I'll get a chance to see Scott tonight. I wanted to get his advice about what papers I should consider if I'm going to be studying."

"I'm sure he'll be more than happy to help."

After putting on the final touches to their make-up they walked along the esplanade chatting about work.

They entered The Crab and Apple, the quaint bar popular with both locals and tourists.

The air was full with heady wine, beer fumes and fried food.

"I'll get the first lot of drinks." Katey made her way to the bar, while Nerissa grabbed their favourite table in the courtyard.

She'd just sat down when Scott Maindonald wandered through the front door throwing her the smile she loved so much, the one that radiated from cheek to cheek and sent tingles down her spine. Even after a 1 ½ hours' drive his pale blue shirt and dark blue trousers still looked crisp and clean on his slim runner's build. She waved to him as he weaved his way through the jovial crowd.

"Hey," he said.

She stood up to receive his kiss. "I didn't expect you as early as this."

"I'm trying to make up for last week. In fact," he paused for a moment. "I've bought you a wee something." His hands were hidden behind his back.

"What have you got me?" She reached playfully behind him.

"Oh, patience." Scott teasingly pulled away from her.

Nerissa's hands continued to flounder blindly searching for her gift. "OK. I surrender."

Scott's hand appeared in front of her, holding a box of chocolates. It was one of many gifts he was always surprising her with. "For you, my love." He planted another kiss on her lips. "I've missed you."

"I missed you too." She held his soft gaze, the love reflecting back in his hazel eyes. All she wanted now was to wish everyone away so she could have him all to herself.

"Come on you two lovebirds," Katey said, placing the drinks on the table.

Scott grinned boyishly and gave Katey a hug.

"Where are *my* chocolates?" she teased.

"I'm sure Nerissa will share."

"Yeah, right."

"You'll just have to wait for your own knight in shining armour," Nerissa replied. She took a sip of wine.

"I'll be waiting a while I think." Katey sighed.

Scott ordered a beer and then they were swapping the week's stories.

They eventually ordered food and as the night wore on the bar got louder with conversation and laughter. Some groups were watching a cricket match on the big screen and a deafening cheer would erupt occasionally when someone was caught out.

"Must be my turn for the last drinks order," Nerissa said.

She smiled as she passed some of the regulars. It was a busy night and she waited patiently for her turn to be served at the bar. She tapped her foot to David Bowie's "Modern Love" which blared from the juke box. She studied the memorabilia sprinkled round the walls – old nautical maps, barometers, flags and a huge net draped over the ceiling that was secured by a number of boat anchors.

"Nerissa, what can I get you?"

"Hey, Sam. One OJ and two sauvignons."

"How's your day been?" Sam, part owner of The Crab and Apple asked. He poured a large glass of orange juice.

Nerissa scowled. "It was my turn in the office today so not the most exciting."

"The weather's looking good." Sam turned to the fridge, grabbing a bottle of wine.

"We're in for some solid bookings. You must be pleased with the crowd you have here tonight."

"It's perfect for a Friday night."

There was an outburst of raucous laughter from the group beside her and a male voice let out a loud whoop.

"Thanks, Sam. See you later," she said, carefully picking up the three drinks.

Suddenly a large elbow jabbed at her hand sending wine and orange juice slopping over the sides of the glasses.

Nerissa gasped as the liquid dribbled over her hand and splashed onto the front of her dress.

"Hey," she yelled above the noise. "Can't you be more careful?"

The tall figure turned round, still laughing. "Well, I'm mighty sorry ma'am."

It was the American who had collided with her earlier on in the day and there he was bumping into her again. His tanned face was flushed from the heat of the day.

"Are you always banging into things?" she asked.

He tilted his Stetson up with his beer bottle. "Only when you keep getting in my way." A mischievous grin spread across his face.

15

"I keep getting in your way? You should be more careful."
She pinched her lips together as her breath caught in her throat.

"How about I pay for some more drinks?" he offered, his
voice husky and deep.

"No, it's OK." Nerissa looked down at the glasses. "I think
I've managed to save most of it." She licked the back of her
hand where the wine had begun dripping.

"Your dress might need a wash." His eyes travelled down
to her breast where the wine had soaked in. He bent down
towards her, hot breath close to her ear. "See. I told you you
wouldn't have any trouble finding me."

Not even so much as an, "I'm sorry." My dress 'might'
need a wash! And now he thinks I was looking for him! Heat
tingled in her chest and her eyes narrowed. "Not only are you
arrogant. You haven't even apologised."

"Oh, you're still mad at that?" His eyes had a playful glint
in them..

Nerissa huffed. Everything was just a big joke to him.

The front of the bar was crowded with people jostling and
swaying. The only way back to the table was past him. She held
the glasses close to her body to prevent further spillage and
glared at him as she brushed past.

He laughed uproariously and turned his back on her.

Scott and Katey were deep in conversation as she put the
glasses down.

"Sorry it's a bit wet," Nerissa said. "You wouldn't believe who was at the bar."

Deafening laughter erupted causing Scott and Katey to turn round.

"Sounds like someone's having a good time," Katey said in amusement. She peered hard at the tall figure with the Stetson. "And someone stands out like a sore thumb."

"That's the American who collided with me today."

"What?" exclaimed Scott.

"He was on the wrong side of the road and went wham! into the front of the van."

"Heavens. Are you hurt?" Scott touched Nerissa on the arm.

"My wrist aches slightly from wrenching the wheel over to the side when the Rover impacted against the van." She rubbed her wrist. "It was only a ding really but there will need to be some panel beating. You know, he was really evasive when I asked him for his contact details." Nerissa swirled wine round in her mouth savouring the rough gravelly sensation against her tongue.

"Do you want me to go over and talk to him?" Scott asked, frowning in the American's direction.

"No. No. I'll sort it out on Monday."

The American was saying his good-byes and thumping people on the back.

"It doesn't look like it's taken him long to make friends," said Nerissa.

"Well, well, well," Katey said.

All eyes were on the American, unsteady on his feet, who was leaving hand-in-hand with a woman.

"Isn't that Tanya?" Nerissa lifted her head to get a better look.

Katey nodded as her eyes followed the American and the attractive buxom blonde, who was draping a pink sparkly scarf across one of his shoulders.

"He doesn't waste any time," Scott said.

Nerissa swallowed the last of her wine. "They'll be very well-suited."

Neither Nerissa nor Katey had any time for the town's 'loose woman'. Tanya was flighty and used her feminine charms to try and lure every male in town into her life.

"Hey, babe. We'd better get going," Scott said, getting up from his chair.

After Nerissa and Scott dropped Katey off at her flat in Forest Road it was only a further five-minute drive down Cottage Row, to home.

Scott pulled up in the driveway and Nerissa hopped out of the car. She dug round in her handbag for the cottage keys. The air was heavy with jasmine and honeysuckle, which added to the alcoholic fuzziness in Nerissa's head. She opened the front door to the cottage and switched on the lights.

Scott carried in his overnight bag and placed it on a stool by the small breakfast bar.

"It's warm in here." Nerissa blew out her cheeks in the dense atmosphere. She threw open the blue French doors that led into the garden letting out the smothering heat, and lifted her head to greet the cool breeze.

"Gosh, Nerissa. Were you hit by a hurricane?" Scott raised his voice.

Nerissa turned back towards the open plan lounge and kitchen. She looked round. There was stuff everywhere – clothes, clean and dirty, towels, linen hanging off the back of the couch, plastic glasses, magazines, books, her easel and paint pots and photos strewn across the kitchen table. She would've tidied up if she'd had the time.

It was a standing joke between them. Scott hated mess; she couldn't keep anything tidy and in its place for more than five minutes and he complained he was always picking up and straightening after her.

"I don't know how you can find anything," Scott said, glancing at the pile of clothes on the couch.

"I do. Eventually."

They both laughed.

"I'll do a quick tidy up now. It won't take long," Nerissa said. She reached out to pick up a pair of jeans and T-shirt, but Scott gently grasped her arm.

"Oh no, you don't. We have some catching up to do. I haven't driven all this way to watch you fold up clothes."

Scott pulled her towards him. He kissed her and a warm intensity rushed up in her as their lips touched.

She had missed him and the two weeks he had been gone increased the longing.

"Let's turn in now," he murmured against her neck. "I'll take a quick shower."

She reluctantly drew back from him.

Scott wandered down the hall and within a moment the shower was running.

Closing the French doors and switching off the lights she made her way into the bedroom.

She loved to sleep with the drapes open waiting for the colours of the landscape to change at the break of dawn. She stared out the window. The chicken coop down the bottom of the garden bathed in the light of the full moon.

"You look beautiful."

Turning round, Scott stood in the doorway watching her. His lower half was covered in a big white, fluffy towel.

Nerissa held Scott's gaze as he walked towards her.

He pulled the tie from her hair and she shook her head freeing the curls. He cupped the back of her head in his hand and gave her a soft, lingering kiss that radiated sparks through her.

She wrapped her arms round his back drawing him closer, breathing him in – soap, shampoo and damp hair.

Scott unzipped her dress and lifted it over her head. He unclasped her bra and slipped off her underwear. She stood completely naked.

"I love you," he whispered.

"I love you too." She could no longer control the anticipation. She untucked the towel that was the barrier between them and pressed her body against him. They fell onto the bed. Nerissa stretched out and Scott's warm lips glided over her mouth, breasts and stomach.

Nerissa let out a soft moan and strained against him. Her breathing signalled a rapid, urgent need. She placed her hands on his shoulders, pulled him in closer and wrapped her legs round him.

His hands caressed her head and she melted into his touch.

They began to move as one, slowly at first and then quicker until their desire was released.

Scott gently rolled off her and they climbed under the sheets. She turned on her side as Scott cuddled into her. She sank back against his body. The solid, secure beat of his heart, steadied her breathing, her breath.

Sleep called to her, entwined with images of lovemaking and wedding dresses.

It wasn't Scott in her dream but a tall, husky-speaking, cheeky American.

Chapter 2

Nerissa stretched out in the bed. From the kitchen, came the sound of plates clashing together. She sniffed the air: Bacon, tomatoes, mushrooms, toast and eggs.

She held onto the covers just a moment more tracing her hand over the pink flowers on the duvet cover. In the bathroom she splashed cold water on her face, cleaned her teeth and ran a brush through her wayward curls. She looked in the mirror. Her blue eyes were almost the same colour as the sea.

"Morning." Nerissa greeted Scott in the kitchen. She kissed his cheek. His freshly shaved skin was smooth and hinted at his sharp and citrusy cologne.

"Morning sleepyhead." He handed her a full plate minus the bacon. "Just in time for breakfast."

Nerissa carried her plate over to the table.

Scott pushed open the French doors, which squeaked on their hinges. In the distance, the sun's early morning rays penetrated through the mist surrounding the mountains. "I'll get some oil for those squeaky hinges."

"I've been meaning to do it..." She glanced round the room. Scott had tidied up and the lounge floor was clear once again.

Her attention turned back to Scott who was flicking through the morning's newspaper. He was reading the business section, but then turned over the page chuckling at the cartoons. He screwed up his nose, a movement she found weirdly sexy, reminding her of when they'd met three years ago. On her weekly business trip to the city, Nerissa had dropped off some financial papers to the accounting offices of Maindonald Jones Crowley. Lou Maindonald had introduced Scott to Nerissa. Scott had just rejoined his father's firm having returned from working for four years in various accounting positions in London. He was a smart and hard worker, conscientiously working towards his ultimate career goal – a partnership in the firm.

It was Scott's calm and steady nature that attracted her to him at first. When they first started dating he would shower her with flowers, chocolates and jewellery. The fact that he lived in the city and she in Aqua Bay hadn't deterred him. He drove up every Friday night to spend the weekend with her and be the handyman constantly painting, rewiring, planting and fixing things round the cottage. He ate healthily, exercised regularly and drank moderately. She was overjoyed when he'd proposed to her six months ago. Even Katey had said, "Good catch, Nerissa. Never let him go. I want a man just like him!"

Nerissa rubbed her wrist.

"Still sore?" Scott folded up his newspaper.

"A bit tender. I should probably put some ice on it."

"Do you think it needs bandaging?" He gently picked up her hand, inspecting it.

"No. I don't think so. I'll try the ice first."

"Hmm. Dangerous tourists. They shouldn't be allowed on the roads."

Nerissa cleared the plates from the table and popped them into the sink.

After the dishes were done and she'd packed her overnight bag they were on the road arriving in the city two hours later.

Scott pulled into the driveway of the modern two-story two-bedroomed apartment he rented. He carried his and Nerissa's bag up the stairs and unlocked the door.

Nerissa set her handbag on the kitchen table.

The apartment was spotless, as always, just like a scene in the latest home magazine. *Such a contrast to me.*

The lounge was minimally furnished with a grey couch and dining table and a solitary abstract painting hung on the wall; its straight lines, cold and clinical. A pile of photography magazines lay neatly stacked on the coffee table.

She wandered into the bathroom, unpacked her toiletry bag and haphazardly placed items in the cabinet next to Scott's. All his toiletries were lined up side-by-side, like soldiers standing to attention, with the labels facing her.

Nerissa grabbed a towel and flannel from the linen cupboard. The pile of towels was folded with their creases against the wall. Every time she was in the cupboard she wanted to rearrange the towels, mess with the perfectionism.

"Would you like to drive out to Surfboard Point on the way to the party?" Scott asked.

"Great idea."

They had lunch and soon were back out on the road. As they drove further round the estuary, they hit heavy traffic and it was a stop-start affair.

"We've had every red light along this road." Scott tapped the steering wheel impatiently.

The cross signal came on accompanied by a blip-blip-blipping and Saturday shoppers darted across the road hurrying to get to the next summer sale. A woman wheeling a pushchair yelled at her toddler trailing behind her to hurry up.

The light turned green and a bus spewing out diesel fumes pulled out in front of them. Nerissa coughed and closed the car window.

Gradually they left the traffic behind and Scott drove the car round the hilly, narrow, suburban streets parking outside a vacant, grassy section.

Nerissa climbed out of the car narrowly avoiding the 'For Sale – Section' placard with the big red 'Sold' sticker slapped sideways across it. Her hand fell into Scott's and they walked towards the back of the section.

Below them were the roofs of the houses occupying Surfboard Point. The houses dotted the hillsides, skirting the estuary and the main road leading into the suburb. Boardsailers skimmed across the water. In the distance, the mountains peaked upwards.

"This was a great choice of land," Scott said, hugging Nerissa from behind.

"The views are amazing." Nerissa tucked a curl behind her ear.

The day they had bought the land had been edged with excitement as it cemented another step forward as a couple. They had talked endlessly and long into the nights on their plans. Scott had it all worked out. He earned more than her and had a secure career. After they married Nerissa would quit her job, leave Aqua Bay and move to the city and hopefully babies would soon follow. They would live together in Scott's apartment until the house was built.

Scott swung Nerissa round so she was facing the opposite way.

"Here is the kitchen," Scott said, leading her to the imaginary kitchen. "The lounge here... main bedroom here..." He continued walking her through the various rooms. "And here, we will have two bedrooms." He grinned. "One each for a little boy and a little girl."

Nerissa smiled shyly. "You're pretty sure you can arrange it so it works out like that?"

"Absolutely."

Nerissa turned away from him. Although it was a warm, sunny day the cold easterly wind had a bite to it. She shivered, pulling her cardigan round her. This was not a new conversation between them. It was typical of Scott to conjure up the perfect family. One boy, one girl as if it could be ordered on demand. *But is the city the best place to raise a family?*

"Is everything OK?" Scott asked.

"We'd better get going. We don't want to be late."

The route to Erin's took them back through the city. Brakes squealed and horns tooted angrily. They stopped at what must've been the one-hundredth red light. Even though the windows were closed the jackhammer at the construction site across the road vibrated through her like thunder. She clasped her hands until her knuckles turned white. Right now she'd give anything to be back in the peaceful and unhurried surroundings of Aqua Bay. *How will I cope when I have to live here?*

'You're quiet. You seem a little distracted," Scott commented as they halted at another red light.

"Just tired." She checked her cell phone. "I can't believe Frances is eight today."

"Seems like only yesterday she was starting school," Scott said. He accelerated quickly as the lights turned green.

Ten minutes later they had arrived outside her older sister, Erin's house, easily identified by the pink and white balloons tied to the letterbox.

Nerissa braced herself, ready for the onslaught. Girly laughter and screams rang out indicating the party was in full swing. She held Scott's hand as they walked up the driveway.

"Hey, we're here," Nerissa announced above the noise.

"Aunty Nessy!" Frances yelled. She ran towards her aunt and wrapped her arms round her waist. "It's my birthday today!"

"Happy birthday, pumpkin." Nerissa kissed Frances's forehead and placed a large package wrapped in pink paper and secured with a big pink bow in her hands.

Frances tore at the paper revealing a cute pink dress with matching hair clasps. She squealed in delight. "Thank you! Thank you!"

Nerissa laughed.

Frances held the dress up against her, twirling round.

"Darling, you've arrived."

Nerissa looked up as her mother, Gail, greeted her first and then Scott. "How are you?" She hardly had time to respond before the rest of her nieces descended on her – Lauren, Erin and Ian's five-year-old daughter, and her middle sister, Danielle's two girls, Emma and Chloe.

"How was the trip down?" Danielle asked, jiggling two-year-old Abigail, on her hip.

"Good. Not much traffic until we hit the city, of course."

"OK. Who wants to play musical chairs?" Erin yelled out.

Excited girls all chorused at the same time, "Me! Me! Me!"

Erin waved at Nerissa from across the room before being swamped in a blur of party hats and running feet.

"Where are all the guys?" Scott asked.

"Oh, I think Ian, Jonathon and dad are firing up the BBQ down the back. Did Nerissa tell you, your parents will be here later?" Danielle asked.

"I wasn't sure whether dad would've been able to get here today. We're pretty full on at work at the moment."

"I think he promised he'd try to sneak away for a couple of hours."

"How about you go and join the guys? I'll have a chat to mother," Nerissa said, as she followed Gail into the kitchen.

"Nerissa, what have you been eating? You look like you've put on weight." Gail's critical eye scanned Nerissa's figure.

"I've been eating fine." The balloons, streamers and 'Happy Birthday' banner bounced against the walls in the light breeze. Did her mother stop to think what a thoughtless comment that was?

Gail placed a string of small sausages into a pot of boiling water. "Here, can you put these bowls on the table?" Her hands moved glacial-like as she handed Nerissa the chips and dip.

Loud music and squealing erupted from outside.

Nerissa set the bowls on the table, then opened up packets of plastic forks and plates, laying them on the Barbie tablecloth.

"Nerissa, sweetheart."

Nerissa looked up. "Dad." She moved towards her father, Andrew, kissing him on the cheek.

"How's my girl?"

"Great, thanks."

"I've come looking for a poker," he said, rummaging round in the kitchen drawer. "I'm sure Erin will have one somewhere."

Nerissa set out plastic cups next to the plates.

"It shouldn't be too long before the next family celebration," Gail said, pouring lollies into glass bowls.

"Who's the next birthday?" Andrew asked.

"I wasn't so much thinking of birthdays," Gail replied, touching her perfectly blow dried, short, brown hair.

"Oh, what then?"

"Nerissa's and Scott's wedding."

A plastic cup slipped through Nerissa's fingers bouncing a few times as it hit the floor.

"Have you discussed a date yet?" Gail asked. "A December wedding would fit well in the social calendar. We were married in December, weren't we, dear?"

Andrew nodded, retrieving the poker. "Nice time of year."

"You know that's a busy time for work. Autumn next year would be better," Nerissa replied.

Gail pursed her lips. "That's getting too late. Besides you'll be giving up your job once you're Scott's wife and moving to the city." Her eyes narrowed. "The dolphins will get by quite happily without you. You'll be able to get a real job in the city." Her voice screeched like metal grating against metal.

"They'll set a date when they're ready to," Andrew said, throwing his daughter a weak smile.

"I'm not a fan of long engagements. Erin and Danielle didn't move in with Ian or Mark until after they were married," Gail said. She frowned and the lines on her forehead intensified.

"I'm not living with Scott," Nerissa argued.

"No, but you are... sleeping together." Gail hurried over the last two words flapping a hand in the air.

Nerissa swallowed hard. She wasn't about to discuss her sex life with her parents.

"No one in our family has had a baby out of wedlock," Gail said. She shook a bottle of cream and poured it into a bowl.

"Is that all you're worried about? What the neighbours would think if I turned up tomorrow with a baby and no hubby?" Nerissa's stomach tightened and she stepped back from the table.

Andrew's eyes widened. "Are you pregnant, love? It would be nice to have another grandchild."

"No!" Nerissa snapped.

Andrew averted his eyes.

"There's no need to be rude." Gail whipped the cream vigorously.

Nerissa sucked in her cheeks.

"I thought you'd want to get this settled," Gail continued as though she was referring to a business arrangement. "You've always talked about getting married and having children."

"And I do. I just don't feel the need to rush the wedding." Nerissa screwed up the empty packets and placed them in the rubbish tin.

"I'm sure Nerissa and Scott's wedding plans are still a priority. It's early days yet." Andrew placed a soothing hand on his wife's shoulder.

Gail let out an exasperated sigh. "I just don't know how I'm supposed to plan ahead."

The doorbell rang.

"I'll get it." Nerissa hurried to the door, pulling it open.

It was Scott's parents, Sharon and Lou.

"We made it," Lou said, walking inside and hugging Nerissa.

"Hello darling." Sharon planted a kiss on Nerissa's cheek.

Nerissa led Sharon and Lou into the kitchen and within moments the women had paired up swapping greetings and "you look lovely" comments, the men were shaking hands and making small talk about the weather.

The vibration of stamping feet ricocheted through the floorboards as a blur of girly dresses, long streaming hair and screaming voices descended inside.

"I won the musical chairs, Aunty Nessy," Frances yelled, as she plonked herself down at the table.

"Wow!" Nerissa exclaimed. "I bet it's because you're eight now."

Chairs scraped on the floor as ten girls bumped and elbowed for seats at the table.

"You'll have all of this to look forward to," Sharon commented in Nerissa's ear.

Nerissa twirled the bangle on her wrist. Why did everyone keep bringing up the wedding? Her parents' beliefs and ideals of how an engaged woman was supposed to behave no longer held true for her. Her upbringing had been strict and littered with rules and guidelines driven by her mother. The pressure was like a big, heavy cloak, stifling her, preventing her from breathing. Moving to Aqua Bay had partly helped her escape the rules she was supposed to live under. But that temporary reprieve would be ending soon.

Yet a month ago she would not have had such a strong reaction to these comments. And circling in her mind was that Scott was an only child, and the hints Sharon and Lou were dropping around grandchildren.

"How about we wash our hands first?" Erin yelled above the noise. Chairs scraped back again amongst moans and

34

groans. A blur of long hair, red, hot faces and legs stampeded to the bathroom. Scott, grinning, was caught in the middle, diving and ducking against the swarm of girls.

Suddenly there was a loud crash as Chloe tripped over a chair leg and landed with a thump on the floor.

There was a moment's silence and then an outburst of crying that gained quickly in crescendo.

"Oh, Chloe." Scott bent down and untangled the chair from the little girl's legs. He encircled Chloe into his arms. "There, there," he soothed, patting her on the back. "Where does it hurt?"

"My ankle." Chloe sobbed in between hyperventilated breaths.

Scott carried her carefully over to the couch. "Maybe we can get Mummy to put some magic ice on it. Would that make it better?"

"Hmm." Chloe nodded, her hands still firmly clinging to Scott's neck.

Nerissa's heart melted and her spine tingled at the tenderness with which Scott had lovingly embraced his niece. There was something about it that made him look vulnerable and she was completely turned on by it.

"He'll be a great father," Danielle said, as she stood beside Nerissa.

"I know," Nerissa replied. "He can't wait to have kids."

"Mummy," Chloe yelled, as she spotted her mother.

"Here I am, honey."

Scott passed Chloe over to Danielle, kissing the top of her head.

"Well, you saved the day, Prince Charming," Nerissa said, as Scott joined her at her side. She grabbed his hand and turned towards him.

"Poor thing getting knocked over in the rush," he said.

They watched Gail pass a packet of frozen peas to Danielle. Chloe flinched at the coldness, but then erupted into giggles as her mother launched into a story about *The Princess and the Pea.*

Any creeping doubts that had been niggling away at Nerissa dispelled at that moment. She was unclear as to what had caused her worries over the past few days, but she didn't want to spend her life without Scott. *If it meant she had to live and raise her family in the city then, hey, we all make sacrifices in relationships, right?* She squeezed Scott's hand and he glanced at her, smiling.

The girls had returned from the bathroom all sparkly clean and the party resumed. Little hands popped cupcakes with sticky pink icing into their mouths. One scoop of ice cream was not enough for one girl while two others giggled as they rolled the orange coated chocolate jaffas off the table. "I'm a Barbie Girl" blared out from the stereo and someone let off a party popper.

"Have some food." Sharon offered Nerissa a plate of savouries.

She took one and bit into it.

Lou appeared from outside. "Did Scott mention we won the contract?" he asked, clapping Scott on the back.

"No, no, he didn't." Nerissa flicked the hot pastry round in her mouth to prevent it from burning her tongue. "That's great news."

"We won it because of Scott's reputation for delivering results on time. His innovative ways have proven clients' businesses grow but overheads are kept low," Lou said, and smiled the proud smile of a father. "It will mean having to juggle a lot of the current workload amongst the staff. But Scott will be our account manager for this new client, Drill New Plymouth. It'll be a great account for you and it'll really get your name out there. You'll be one step closer to a partnership." Lou winked at Scott.

"It will mean a heavier workload. May not be so many weekend trips down to Aqua Bay." Lou directed his comment at Nerissa. "Have you thought about moving to the city sooner?"

"We've just been having the very same conversation," Gail piped in, sweeping another disapproval look in Nerissa's direction.

"It looks good if Scott has a partner beside him supporting him. The clients like that. It shows a solid character. Scott can't keep going to client functions by himself," Lou said.

Nerissa bit her lip. What could she say? It was such an old-fashioned way of thinking in this day where a man still had to have a woman by his side to represent a complete package. She didn't want to be just someone's wife – a plus one.

But nobody even waited for her comment as Gail wiped up runny ice cream from the table and Scott and Lou began discussing the new client in depth.

Nerissa refused to say what she really wanted to say. She tilted her chin up and turned her attention back to the happy party scene - her sisters, her parents, her nieces and their friends. She wanted this too. And she would marry Scott and move to the city; she was just as keen as he was to have children. But she wouldn't be railroaded by others.

She would do it when she was ready.

Chapter 3

Peter slapped the local rag, *Aqua Bay Brief*, on the counter. "I wondered how long it would be before this happened."

Nerissa looked up from reading the day's weather report to see Peter scratching his head furiously.

"What do you mean?"

"Here, have a read." Peter pushed the paper into Nerissa's hands.

American Oil Company sneaks into town for fracking

Taxxoil, the giant American oil exploration company, arrived in town last week ahead of their drilling ship, Perspeculor, which will begin seismic surveying in a month's time.

A local, who did not want to be named, witnessed a vehicle unloading storage boxes and furniture into an office in town on Thursday. They had maps and all sorts of gear with them."

Unease has been mounting in the Aqua Bay community for the last 18 months after the government announcement to tender for offshore blocks for oil and gas exploration. Taxxoil's brief will include drilling, seismic mapping and the controversial procedure of fracking.

A spokesperson for Taxxoil, Jackson Darnell, confirmed that a number of staff had arrived ahead of Perspeculor to undertake preparatory work.

He declined to comment on the number of staff that would be based here or what their roles would be.

"We are looking forward to beginning our work and getting to know the locals and community."

"What a cheek!" Peter thundered. "How have they managed to get their office set up and nobody had any inkling they were here?"

Apprehension trickled through Nerissa's veins. This was not going to be good. The government had borne the wrath of the Aqua Bay community when it announced that Taxxoil would have the opportunity to undertake seismic testing of Aqua Bay's coastline despite little research of the impact on the marine eco-system. Initial protests had obviously not been enough to persuade the government that any activities associated with deep sea oil drilling were a no-go. It was the words 'seismic surveying' that made her nerves jangle. Seismic surveying was a technique that bounced waves off the ocean floor in an attempt to reveal gas packets and oil deposits. The soundwaves could be a danger to the dolphins, whales and other marine life from causing hearing loss to disrupting mating and feeding patterns.

"I don't like this one bit." Peter grabbed the paper from Nerissa. His eyes darted back and forth across the article again.

"I don't understand how they can just turn up. 'Sneak into town' is quite appropriate," Nerissa said.

"We need to find out more about exactly what's going on here. I'm going to make a few phone calls." Peter stormed off to his office.

Nerissa re-read the article, her hand crumpling the paper. She jumped up out of her seat. Sitting never achieved anything. Movement helped her to problem solve and right now she needed to move. She grabbed the keys to the van. "I'm going into town to do the banking," Nerissa shouted out to Mavis, Peter's wife, who was working in the office.

As she drove the van into town, her mind whirled. Any deep sea oil drilling could – would – have serious consequences on the pristine beauty of Aqua Bay. Not to mention the many people who the sea provided food and work – the divers, the fisherpeople, and, of course, tourism. Businesses like Dolphin Eco-tours.

She arrived in town which was buzzing with the January holiday crowd. Tourists in shorts and T-shirts, licking ice creams, strolled leisurely down the streets stopping at the souvenir shops. A little girl bent down in front of a large basket and scooped up a paua shell. The iridescent gem-shaped greens and blues caught the sunlight and danced in the air. Nobody was in a rush to go anywhere as if walking slowly would prevent time moving forward and ending the peaceful holiday feeling. She took a deep breath. Nothing, absolutely nothing, could compare with the fresh unpolluted salty air of Aqua Bay.

She parked the van, and did the banking. As she walked down the main street, a vehicle on the other side of the road caught her eye. It was the Range Rover that had collided with her on Friday.

Nerissa hurried across the road and stopped beside the vehicle. Who was this mystery American who had been flashing intermittently through her mind all weekend? Should she wait for him to come back? That could mean a while and she didn't want to loiter. Maybe he was in one of the shops or cafes. She glanced behind her into the foyer of a small two-storied office. A number of boxes with Taxxoil blazoned across them stood in the corner. She should definitely check this out.

She strolled up the stairs and pulled open the swing doors, which opened out to a small open-plan office.

Marine charts of Aqua Bay lined the walls. In the middle of the room was a large conference table littered with manuals, drawings, specifications and books.

A man was crouching down on the floor, deep in concentration and peering intently at a map.

"Hello?" Nerissa said.

The man looked up. "Well, hello there, ma'am." His knees cracked as he stood up.

Nerissa watched as his full tree-tall height unravelled. It was the American who had collided with her on the road last week.

"Ha!" he said, with an easy grin. "You again."

"I saw your Rover parked outside," she stammered.

"You trying to hunt me down?" The devil twinkled in his eyes.

Nerissa cleared her throat. "We haven't resolved the work that needs doing to the van."

"Before you take me to court and sue me for everything I've got, the least I could do is introduce myself properly." He shot out his hand. "Jackson Darnell, ma'am."

"Nerissa Taylor." She offered her hand which was almost engulfed by the strength in his rough and hardened hand. Numerous tattoos ran up and down his arm.

She wandered over to the table. "What are these?"

"This stuff is for some work that I'm doing here," Jackson replied. He closed a couple of folders.

"Which is what exactly?" Nerissa queried, her suspicions increasing.

"I'm an exploration geologist." His brown eyes held her gaze for a beat too long.

She dragged her eyes away. "And what does that mean?"

"I look for the presence of hydrocarbons in rocks."

He was deliberately being vague, but she wasn't going to make this easy for him. "Why?"

"You sure do ask a lot of questions."

"I'm interested in knowing what it is that you're really doing here. Are you from Taxxoil?"

Jackson stepped closer towards her. "Ah-ha. The secret's out."

"That would explain why there's no name on the address board downstairs."

"We've only just got here."

"And you've certainly made your presence known. You've already spoken to the media, dinged my van and, by the way, how did it go with Tanya?" Nerissa could've kicked herself.

"Tanya was very welcoming. She's made me feel right at home." Jackson's eyes teased.

Heat rose in her cheeks.

"Why are you so interested in what I did on Friday night?"

"It's not what you did. It's who you did. She's bad news," Nerissa snapped.

"If you could recommend someone more suitable…"

She clenched her jaw. "So these rocks and hydrocarbons, this is where the oil is?"

"That's right. We're doing some prep work before the *Perspeculor* arrives."

"Your job here is not going to be easy. The Aqua Bay community doesn't want oil exploration. It would destroy a lot of people's livelihoods."

Jackson's face hardened. "I've done this kind of work all around the world for a while now so I kind of know the feelings among communities when the Americans come in and take control. Nobody seems to like that, but we've developed a pretty thick skin."

Nerissa smothered a smile. So he knew Kiwis could be anti-American. This guy had done his homework.

"Anyway, how do you know the community here is opposed to deep sea exploration?" Jackson asked.

"Oh, I know. Take a look outside. Who'd want to destroy all of this?" Nerissa pointed to the rocky peninsula in the distance that reached into the dazzling aqua sea.

Jackson frowned. "Are you really sure the people here are against deep sea exploration? Have you tested that theory?"

"I don't need to," Nerissa responded. "Everything in this town revolves round the ocean. Everyone feels the same way."

Jackson closed another folder. "It doesn't help to see things through rose-tinted glasses."

"I'm not–," Nerissa started to argue.

"You need to look at things from both sides."

"You're getting defensive."

"And you're annoying!" A sneaky grin curled up round Jackson's lips.

Nerissa half-smiled. Here was a guy who didn't take himself too seriously.

"Maybe we should talk about something else," Jackson suggested.

"How about the van? It needs panel beating." She wasn't going to let him get out of this.

"Yeah. How about you take it to the panel beaters and we'll reimburse you back?"

"Why do I have to do all the work?"

"You'll know the best place to take it to."

That was true. "Fine. It's going to be inconvenient to have the van out of action though."

"Maybe we can arrange it so that you can use the Rover if you need a vehicle."

"I'm sure we'll get by. Why doesn't the Rover have the Taxxoil logo on it?" Nerissa asked, peering through the window.

"Pretty obvious I would have thought. I've lost count the number of times I've been driving and had rocks thrown at me."

"Ouch!" Nerissa sympathised.

Jackson stood beside her at the window.

She turned to face him swamped by his towering frame.

"I guess we'll be seeing more of each other round town then."

Nerissa touched her lips as his eyes bored into her. "Yes, I guess so." She looked away quickly.

"Well, seeing as you have a low opinion of the females that hang out at The Crab and Apple, how about you join me for a drink tonight?"

The cheek of it. "Thanks, but no thanks." She wiggled her finger with her engagement ring in front of his face.

"Oh, a pity." Jackson's shoulders slumped. "So the guy you were with on Friday night is your fiancé?"

Nerissa nodded. "What about Tanya? Are you going to work your way through the whole town's female population?"

"Won't take very long I'm sure."

"Oh!" she fumed. "You're infuriating!"

The hearty laugh mocked her as she turned and flew down the stairs.

One person who would know exactly what Taxxoil was doing in Aqua Bay was Rachel Wheeler, the reporter who had written the newspaper article. Nerissa had met Rachel on her first day of work at Dolphin Eco-tours. They socialised occasionally together, but their association seemed dependent on her connections to the news story of the day. And if you didn't have a connection to a good news story, then Rachel almost didn't want to know you. Her manipulation skills at getting what she wanted was legendary. Rachel wouldn't be her first point of contact by choice, but she needed to get more information on what these Americans were up to.

She strolled down to the Aqua Bay Brief's offices in the next block. She opened the front door, almost colliding with Rachel.

"Oh, oops, sorry," Nerissa apologised.

"Nerissa. How's things?"

47

"Good, thanks. I was actually coming to see you. Do you have a minute?"

"I was just on my way out," Rachel said, pulling her black framed sunglasses off her head. "Bother. I've left my cell behind. Walk with me to my desk and we can have a chat."

Nerissa followed Rachel through the open plan office. Reporters on phones tapped away at computers and the air held the sense of urgency as the inevitable production deadlines loomed.

"What's up?" Rachel asked, rummaging round on her overladen desk for her phone. Paper collected everywhere along with plastic water bottles and a half-eaten biscuit. Coffee-laced steam drifted out of a half-drunk cup.

"How much do you know about this Taxxoil thing?"

"The phone's been ringing red hot this morning. In fact, Peter called me just a minute ago giving me an earful. The interest has certainly peaked. This is going to be a hot topic." Rachel continued searching for her phone.

"I've just had an interesting conversation with one of Taxxoil's employees," Nerissa said, moving to the side as two men in suits walked past.

"Oh?"

"Do you know they've set up an office just a block down from here?"

"No. I didn't. I only spoke to Jackson on the phone."

"I just had a chat with him. He dinged the van last Sunday and left me with rather loose arrangements regarding the repair job."

"Ah, here it is." Rachel pounced on the missing phone as it reappeared from under a stack of papers. "I'm just off to an appointment at the council. They think it would be a good idea to get this out in the open. I'd like to suggest to them that we could arrange some kind of debate night round the pros and cons of deep sea oil drilling." Rachel headed towards the front door, Nerissa following.

"Sounds like a good idea," Nerissa agreed. Both women stepped out into the warm sunshine.

"Let's stay in touch over this, now that I have you as an inside source." Rachel winked at her and then hurried off in the direction of the council offices.

Nerissa headed down the narrow alleyway. The big trees cast deep shadows across her path. She walked quickly. What was Taxxoil up to? Any oil exploration in the area would not be good for the community. Hers and others' lives could be threatened by this move. How could anyone in Aqua Bay possibly support such a thing? Yet Jackson didn't seem to think that the community's views would be so clear cut. Something would need to be done. Maybe a community debate would be good.

She left the alleyway and walked through the tunnel that led back up to the footpath that would take her to the van. Her shoes squelched through puddles of water that never had a chance to evaporate. Dank and moss chilled the air and she shivered.

A strong arm grabbed her from behind and encircled her neck. A scream thundered out of her.

"Don't move," a gruff male voice said, as his hand covered her mouth.

Oh no, not again. Nerissa struggled trying to pull away from him. Her heart stopped and her blood chilled as she choked against the dirty hand.

"Don't move," he repeated, louder this time.

The cold steel point of a knife pressed against her neck. A mixture of stale cigarettes, alcohol and rank body odour overwhelmed her and she gagged.

"Drop your bag."

Fear took a stronghold in her chest and nausea pummelled her. Memories of another time and place, another knife, flooded her mind. She wouldn't let this happen to her again. The adrenaline kicked in. She pulled her elbows back and thrust them forcefully into her attacker's body, yelling at the top of her voice.

The man lost his balance. She pulled away hard from him, but the strap of her handbag caught in the man's arm pulling her sharply back. In a commotion of arms and legs, the knife slashed against her hand. She winced in pain. The man tugged harder on her bag wrenching it off her shoulder. The force was so strong she stumbled back losing her footing on the slippery concrete. Her head slammed against the tunnel wall and she fell to the ground.

Footsteps ran away from her… Footsteps thundered towards her. A pair of strong, tanned arms enveloped her and scooped her up. She moaned in pain and then gave herself up to the warmth of her protector as she sank into a swirling blackness.

***

Her eyes fluttered open. Where was she? Why was she in bed? Her eyes blurred, but she could make out the fuzzy silhouette of a man sitting in a chair close to her.

"Scott?" she murmured.

"No. It's Jackson."

"Jackson?" Who was Jackson? "Where am I?"

"You're in hospital."

"Hospital. Why…"

"You were attacked." The lazy American drawl penetrated through her fog.

Nerissa's vision cleared. She looked down at her hands. One had a big plaster over the top. She stared at her other hand which was covered and swamped by Jackson's.

"I'm sorry," Jackson said. He slowly removed his hand.

Was he sorry for what happened to her or that he had been holding her hand? She shifted uncomfortably in the bed.

"What happened?"

"Some low-life scum pulled a knife on you. Seems he was after your handbag. You were knocked out."

That would explain the thumping headache. "How did I get here?"

"I must've been two minutes behind you in the alleyway. I heard a woman screaming and found you. I called an ambulance."

There had been flashing lights and loud sirens, but she kept blacking in and out of consciousness. Everything was so fuzzy.

"Thirsty," she croaked.

Jackson poured some water into a plastic cup and handed it to her.

She reached for it with a shaky hand and swallowed the cool water relieving the parchness in her throat.

"Someone has called Katey, and Scott is driving here," Jackson said. "You kept saying, "no, not again". Has something like this happened to you before?"

Tears stung her eyes and she nodded. "It was when I was walking back to my car one night at uni and I was assaulted. God, it's almost déjà vu. A guy held a knife to my throat and demanded money. He took off with my bag." She touched her head in an effort to relieve the pain.

"Did he hurt you?"

"No," she said wearily. "But it took me a while to recover mentally. I wouldn't go anywhere by myself for ages."

"Did they get him?"

"Yeah. Campus security were onto it pretty quickly."

Scott and Katey appeared at the door.

"Nerissa, baby." Scott rushed to her side. "Are you OK?"

She fought in vain to keep the tears in check, but as soon as Scott touched her bandaged and stitched hand she could no longer hold it in. She sputtered and started sobbing.

"It's OK. It's OK," Scott soothed, giving her a hug and then pulled back. Strain pulled down on his face. Dark pools of worry filled his eyes.

"How's the hand?" Katey asked.

"It's my head that feels like it's about to explode," Nerissa replied, wiping the tears away. "Have you met Jackson?"

"Jackson?" Both Scott and Katey asked in unison.

Jackson had retreated to the back of the room and stood watching, alone. "She's meaning me."

Scott and Katey turned round.

"Apparently he's my hero," Nerissa attempted a joke.

Jackson introduced himself and filled Scott and Katey in on what had happened. They didn't get very far before the doctor on his rounds made an appearance.

"How are we feeling?" Dr Waiton asked Nerissa, studying her chart.

"Sore."

Dr Waiton looked up at her over the top of his glasses. "That's understandable. You've had a lucky escape. We'd like to keep you in overnight for observation."

"Really? I'd much rather go home."

"You've been concussed. You've a rather nasty bump on your head. We'd like you to stay here as a precaution."

"It would be a good idea." Scott squeezed her hand. "I'll stay here with you tonight."

"Me too," Katey chimed in.

Nerissa looked at Jackson. He remained silent and it was the first time since she had met him where there was no cheeky grin lighting up his face.

"It's for the best. The police will be here soon. They will want more info from you so they can find the guy and arrest and charge him," Scott said.

"No. No," Nerissa said. Her breath rasped in her chest. "Scott, please."

Scott put his arm round Nerissa's shoulders. "It's all right."

Wracking sobs shook Nerissa's shoulders and she held her head in her hands. More memories of the night she was attacked on campus engulfed her.

While the attack had been traumatic, what happened afterwards was worse. Her attacker was a student who had an expensive high class drug habit. Initially her parents had been keen to press charges, but they quickly changed their tune when they discovered that her attacker was their close friend's son,

Dominic. A hastily arranged meeting between Dominic's and Nerissa's parents resulted in some 'hush money' exchanged for Nerissa's silence. It would not do for Dominic's held-in-high-esteem-in-society parents to be submitted to such a scandal.

Nerissa had been horrified when Gail and Andrew, who only days before swore black and blue that Dominic would face the law, did a complete about face and coerced her to drop the charges. Feeling the pressure of upcoming exams and still recovering from the attack, this sudden turn of events sent her anxiety levels soaring. Where she had thought her parents, especially her mother, were her advocates instead, they had chosen to support their close friends. She went through the whole ordeal alone and was eventually convinced that she should never have gotten the police involved.

Why should she pursue this latest incident? She didn't want to go through all that again.

"We don't need to make any decisions now. You're tired and upset and you should get some rest." Scott's voice soothed her and she leant back onto the pillows. If the drums in her head would just stop beating.

Dr Waiton scribbled on her chart. "Good. You're in the best place for us to look after you. I'll be back soon." He nodded at Nerissa and scurried out of the room.

"I'd best be going," Jackson said.

"Jackson, thank you." Nerissa attempted a weak smile.

"You just get better, ma'am."

Scott thrust out his hand. "Thanks for what you did. We owe you."

Jackson shook Scott's hand, nodded towards Katey, and then he was gone.

A silent whisper from deep inside of her said, *Stay.*

"I'll go back to the cottage and pack some stuff for you," Katey offered.

"Thanks, Katey." Scott handed her the keys and she was out the door. He sunk down wearily in the chair and placed both hands over Nerissa's.

"I'm so glad you're OK. This could have been much worse." Scott sighed. "If anything had happened to you…"

"I'll be OK, "Nerissa assured him. She swallowed hard. Twice in a life-time. How unlucky could someone be? "I feel so much better since you're here."

"I can stay as long as you need me. Dad has given me some extended leave. In fact, there're some possible business opportunities here he wants me to check out."

Nerissa raised her eyebrows. There wouldn't be many accounting opportunities Aqua Bay would hold for Maindonald Jones Crowley. But she didn't have the energy to question Scott further. By the time Katey arrived back with her bag she was ready for sleep. Scott kissed her and settled into the chair he would be sleeping in tonight.

The incessant banging in her head worsened. She called the nurse who gave her a painkiller.

She laid her head back on the pillow and squeezed her eyes shut tight. Was she about to relive the nightmare of ten years ago all over again? The sterile hospital smell brought back so many unwanted memories. Memories she'd rather leave buried.

Chapter 4

Nerissa was discharged from hospital mid-afternoon, a bundle of nerves after a restless night. Scott drove them home – past the campground and seaside beaches - and when they arrived back at the cottage, Katey was arranging roses, daisies, carnations and dahlias into vases, their sweet scent drifting through the air.

"They've been arriving all morning," Katey said. There were cards and flowers from many people including Sam, her aunt, Peter and Mavis ('come back to work only when you're ready.').

"Oh, your Mum rang," Katey added.

Nerissa rubbed her stiff, sore neck. She'd talk to her mother later.

"Come and sit down," Scott said, pulling out a chair.

"I'd love to stay, but Peter needs me for this afternoon's tour," Katey said, snipping the end off a carnation and arranging it with the others in the vase.

"This will make us short staffed," Nerissa said.

"Don't you worry," Katey replied. "A double shift is not a big deal. Actually, the extra money will be good. Oh, I've made a casserole for you. Just pop it in the oven tonight."

"Thanks, Katey. You're a honey."

"I'll see you later. Rest up now."

She watched Katey walk down the garden path. How many summers had they spent together in Aqua Bay? They'd met at the playground when they were ten-years-old, Katey's family sharing the picnic table with Gail and Andrew, her and her sisters. Then every summer holidays, day after day, they were inseparable, swimming in the pool, playing in the playground, out on Katey's parents' boat, barbecuing, or helping look after sick or hurt seals.

They shared their Barbie dream houses, swapped colourful and glittery butterfly clips and combined their Furbies into a fluffy animal zoo.

By the time they were thirteen, they were trying to grasp the horror of 9/11, and comparing notes on *Harry Potter and The Philosopher's Stone*, *The Lord of The Rings* and *Planet of the Apes* movies. They sang along to Avril Lavigne's "Complicated", Jennifer Lopez and Pink (coinciding with Katey dying her hair pink, which somehow turned orange). Sparkly shoes, embroidered and sequined tops reigned.

Three years later they discussed *Harry Potter and The Goblet of Fire* and *The Chronicles of Narnia* movies and developed a girl-crush on Christian Bale after watching *Batman Begins*. Gwen Stefani and Kelly Clarkson songs ruled and Nerissa's taste shifted to Keith Urban, Garth Brooks, Carrie Underwood and LeAnn Rimes. While Katey dressed in denim jackets, crop tops and cargo pants Nerissa explored vintage clothes and made jewellery from wood, sea shells, glass and seeds.

Nerissa's love of the ocean and the dolphins grew stronger with each passing summer and after days of hanging round Dolphin Eco-tours and pestering Peter with endless questions, he gave in and soon she had a summer holiday job helping out on *Seabird*. There was no question about what she'd do for a job – a career – so after she'd completed her Bachelor of Tourism Management, Peter offered her a job as an eco-tour guide. She was ecstatic – to do what she loved and be paid for it. Katey could never settle on what road to take so she too joined eco-tours "to fill in time until a handsome stranger whisks me away to his Mediterranean villa."

And here they were now, for however flighty Katey was, she was making sure her best friend was all right.

"You're on the front page," Scott said, holding up the newspaper.

She half-heartedly glanced at the headline: *Local Tour Guide Knifed in Daylight.*

"Not the kind of thing you want on the front page. It will frighten the tourists away." Nerissa skimmed the article. "They've named me. Shouldn't I've been asked about this? Typical Rachel."

"Don't let it worry you," Scott said. "You just concentrate on getting better."

Nerissa idly flicked through the paper stopping at a public notice announcing a community debate night on Saturday. "That'll be interesting. Jackson seemed to think that some of the community would welcome deep sea oil drilling."

"He may be right."

"Really?"

"It's an idea worth testing."

"You don't honestly think that anyone in Aqua Bay would support such a crazy idea as oil drilling?"

"We don't know that. We shouldn't be too quick to knock the concept. At the moment you're just guessing what other people are thinking."

Nerissa tilted her head. How could Scott not see how dangerous letting the Americans anywhere near Aqua Bay could be? "I'm sure if we-"

There was a knock at the door and Scott let Rachel in.

"How are you feeling?" she asked, juggling a bunch of flowers and a stack of papers. She handed Nerissa the flowers.

"They're lovely, thank you."

"What a nasty thing to happen." Rachel sat down at the table while Scott filled up the jug.

"Did I have to be on the front page?"

"Did you read the bit about the debate?" Rachel asked, ignoring her question.

Here it comes. Subtlety was not Rachel's strongest point. "Yes?"

61

"Someone told me you were a star debater at uni. How about being on the team – the against side, of course?"

"Oh, I don't know, Rachel. Uni was a long time ago and I haven't done any debating or public speaking since," Nerissa protested. "I think there would be others who would offer more than me. How about Peter? He's pretty vocal."

"I have asked him and he's all go. I need one more person, and female, to balance it up."

"I don't think Nerissa's really up to it at the moment," Scott said. He balanced a tray with steaming cups.

"The timing's not great." Nerissa frowned.

Rachel sipped her coffee. "Fair enough. We do need a chairperson for the debate though. Would you consider that instead?"

"Perhaps Nerissa could think about it and let you know in the next day or two," Scott suggested.

She glared at Scott. She was capable of making her own decisions, but this was Scott just being Scott – over protective and even more so since her attack. And now Rachel was chipping away at her until she got what she wanted. Even still, Nerissa did want to be involved somehow - the issue was too important not to.

"Actually I think I wouldn't mind being the chairperson. I could do that."

"Are you sure, honey? You probably should be resting," Scott said.

"I know all the debating rules and it won't be onerous to get up to speed. Besides it will give me something to do until I'm back at work." She swallowed a mouthful of her favourite chocolate drink, Milo.

"Excellent!" Rachel exclaimed. "Here's some background papers round deep sea oil drilling. Even though you're not actually debating it may help you with your preparation. They're all referenced to reputable websites. Let me know if you need anything more. Thanks guys for the coffee. I'll ring you later in the week." She breezed out the door.

"Why do I feel like Rachel had an ulterior motive in visiting me?"

"That's Rachel," Scott replied. "*She* should be on the debating team."

Nerissa thumbed through the stack of papers. What had she'd let herself in for?

Another knock at the door imitated the knocking in her head. "It's like a railway station." She sighed.

"It's the police," Scott said. He let two female police officers inside.

She didn't want to do this now. She wanted to push the incident to the recesses of her mind and forget about it.

"Nerissa, I'm Senior Constable Valerie Appleton and this is Constable Win Harrow."

Nerissa stood up and shook their hands.

"How are you feeling?"

"Sore, tired," Nerissa said, pressing her fingers to her temples.

"That's understandable," Valerie empathised. "We'd like to get some details from you about what happened yesterday."

"Have a seat," Nerissa offered. She put down the lukewarm Milo.

"I'll make some more coffee. I'm playing barista today," Scott joked.

Valerie pulled a notebook out of her pocket and flicked it open to a blank page.

"Now, can you tell me what happened?"

"I was walking through the tunnel when I was grabbed from behind." Nerissa gulped. Sweat clamped at her palms and her breathing snapped in her chest. The presence of the women in blue closed in on her. Her hands flicked faster and faster through the stack of papers that Rachel had left as the questioning became more intense. Up and down, up and down - blind to the pain in her injured hand.

In the corner, her half-finished painting of part of Aqua Bay beckoned to her, inviting her to melt into the blankness and just disappear.

"I don't want to do this," she blurted out. "Just do what you need to do, but I won't be pressing charges."

The two policewomen looked at each other.

"We know this is difficult for you, but we need as much information from you as we can so we can locate this guy and then charge him," Valerie said.

"I can't do it. I don't want to go through it all again," Nerissa said, shaking her head. She took another sip and once more set down the lukewarm Milo.

"What do you mean you don't want to go through it again?" Win asked.

Scott abandoned making the coffee and hurried over to Nerissa. He placed his hands on the back of her shoulders, rubbing them.

"Could we not do this now?" Nerissa asked, biting a nail.

"The longer we wait the more difficult it becomes. If you don't help catch him he'll do this to other women," Valerie explained.

"It's been a long day for Nerissa. Maybe we could leave it for a day or two and she might feel better about it then," Scott offered.

Valerie closed her notebook. "OK."

Nerissa rested her hands on top of the papers.

"You might benefit from some counselling. You're understandably shaken up, but we do encourage you to make a full statement so we can successfully convict," Valerie said.

"I know. I've had a nasty experience in the past and I'm not keen to repeat it."

"Have a rest Nerissa and we'll come back in a couple of days. We've made a good start."

"I'll see you out," Scott said, escorting Valerie and Win out the door.

Nerissa searched for the Panadol buried under the pile of papers.

Scott returned the dining area. "I'll get you a glass of water. You know, Valerie has a good point."

"What's that?"

"Getting some counselling. It might help you deal with what's happened."

"Please, let's not talk about it now." She took a gulp of water and swallowed the Panadol which left a bitter aftertaste in her mouth.

Scott's arms enfolded around her and she snuggled into his chest inhaling his familiar scent that meant safety and security. If she made herself as small as she could, then maybe everything would go away and she wouldn't have to deal with it. What would counselling solve? Talking about it with someone wouldn't change what had happened in the past – other people had decided what was best to save face for the sake of appearances. She hugged Scott harder. No, counselling wasn't the answer to help her get through this. But what was?

Chapter 5

She stood in the shower and soaped over her hand, careful not to get her stitches wet. The spikes of biting bullets in her head diminished as the warm water sent relief into the tight spots.

Scott stuck his head round the door. "I've cooked you breakfast, baby."

"Thanks. I thought I'd go over all that information Rachel left for me and start revising what I'm supposed to be doing as chairperson for this debate."

"Don't wear yourself out. I'm just popping into town to get some groceries. I'll be back later." Scott blew her a kiss.

Out in the lounge the salty morning breeze drifted through the French doors.

The sun streamed into the cottage and she watched the bell flowers, corabells, daisies and delphiniums hypnotically swaying back and forth like mothers rocking their new-borns.

With her plate of eggs, tomatoes and toast in her good hand, she used the other to switch on the lap-top.

She plumped up a cushion, crunched into her toast and spread out the stack of papers on deep sea oil drilling.

There were heaps of documents, newspaper items and proposals and she flicked over occasionally to a website to check something out, constantly writing notes. Deep sea oil drilling was a topic she'd touched on only briefly when she added a Diploma in Eco-tourism to her qualifications.

She glanced down at what she'd written:

Offshore blocks released by the government for tender for possible oil and gas exploration

possible methods to be used: seismic mapping, drilling, fracking

Taxxoil to undertake initial drilling in summer 2016,

the Perspeculor to arrive next month to prospect by permit, Aqua Bay community had no opportunity to comment.

She'd drawn a heavy underline under the word 'no'.

How could the government get away with not consulting people, the ones that this was going to affect the most?

She jumped at a knock at the front door. "It's open," she yelled.

A mass of black moved through the doorway and into the kitchen.

"Oh, Jackson." She'd been expecting anyone but him. She touched her face. *I would've put make-up on if I knew he was coming round.* "How did you know I lived here?"

"Ah-ha. I have hero status now. People will tell me anything."

Nerissa laughed. His southern charm was just what she needed.

"The town-folk were quick to tell me you like chocolates, so here you are." Jackson held out a box of boutique chocolates secured with a red bow.

"The way to a girl's heart," Nerissa said, taking the box. Her fingers brushed against his and a bolt of electricity ran up her arm tickling her stitches.

"Where's Scott?" he asked, peering into the lounge.

"He went into town."

Jackson's smile beamed wider.

"Can I get you a drink?"

"A Coke, thanks."

"Mmm, sorry, I don't have Coke. That stuff will rot your insides. I can give you fruit juice, lemonade and um, that's about it," Nerissa said, looking in the fridge. It was a good thing Scott had gone to the supermarket.

"Lemonade will do just fine."

"Where are you staying while you're here?" she asked.

"In a cottage, very similar to this, just down the road."

So that's where he had been coming from the day they first ran into each other. He was staying at the cottage that was rented out to tourists over the holiday season.

"What's this?" he asked, noticing the documents on the table.

"I'm sure you are aware of the debate on Saturday night. I've been asked to chair it."

"That's an interesting position to be in given your job as a tour guide."

"I'm sure I will be able to keep my personal feelings in check and be impartial, maybe. Will you be attending?" she asked casually.

"Are you wanting to write my death certificate?" he joked.

"It was you who seemed to think the community may not be sure it knows what it wants. Surely you will want to hear the case for why Taxxoil should be allowed here."

"It's not really up to the community to decide that. I'm already here."

"We can get rid of you."

"It won't be easy."

"Don't underestimate us."

"Remember we're Americans. We rule the world."

Nerissa spluttered. "With such arrogance, too."

He obviously liked to spar. She could give as good as she got. The twinkle gleaming in Jackson's eye suggested the same.

Tiredness seem to hit her like a sledgehammer and she rubbed her eyes.

"You all right?" Jackson asked.

"Yeah. Mental exhaustion from trying to get my head round you lot." She picked up a pen and clicked it. "I'm glad you dropped by. I want to thank you for what you did the other day. There could've been quite a different outcome." She dropped her head.

"Anyone would have done the same. I just happened to be there first. See us Americans do have our uses." He touched her shoulder. "Pray the Lord it wasn't worse."

Nerissa moved away. Why did everything pulse inside her whenever she was near him?

"So, you will be there on Saturday night?" she asked again.

"I may have big plans for Saturday night."

"Tanya again?"

He let out a hearty laugh. "Does it have to involve a female?"

"Oh," Nerissa mocked. "A male then."

His laugher boomed. "Now there's a thought."

"Have a chocolate," she offered, untying the bow.

"Mmmm." Jackson bit into a mint chocolate. "You guys make great chocolate."

"I'll take the compliment quickly." Nerissa selected a chocolate shaped as a love heart. Sweet strawberry liquid filled her mouth. "Have you tried our chocolate fish?"

"Your what?

"Chocolate fish."

Jackson screwed up his nose. "Not sure that I want too."

"It's not a real fish covered in chocolate. It's a kiwi thing. Pink marshmallow covered in chocolate in the *shape* of a fish."

"Oh, well, that sounds much better. I'd definitely give that a go." He looked at his Timex dive watch. "I'd better be off. Coffee maybe later?"

"Did you forget? I'm engaged."

"You're still allowed to have coffee though? Or will you be one of those wives who'll be dictated by what her husband says she can do."

She licked the chocolate from her lips. "Hardly, but you're persistent."

"Definitely. I'll see myself out."

"See you Saturday night then?"

His only response was the teasing laughter that trailed behind.

***

Scott continued to stay on to look after her. While she researched, he disappeared for a couple of hours each day.

By Friday Nerissa had reviewed the rules and guidelines round debating and she was more confident about her chairing role. Her neck wasn't as bothersome and the bump on her head had subsided.

Community interest had been steadily growing all week.

Rachel dropped by on Friday afternoon to go over the logistics. "The topic will be, 'That the community opposes any deep sea oil drilling in Aqua Bay', fairly simple. And Scott, you're speaking last."

"You didn't tell me you were going to be on the team," Nerissa said.

"Rachel twisted my arm only half an hour ago," Scott said sheepishly.

"You didn't take too much convincing," Rachel reminded him.

"You'll put up a really good argument against deep sea oil drilling," Nerissa said.

"Actually I'm speaking for the negative team."

"What? You're kidding." Nerissa squeezed her eyes tight as a cold wave swept over her. "Why would you support this?"

"I think this is something that really needs to be considered. There's a heap of potential here that we need to explore properly."

"At a cost to the environment. I don't think so," Nerissa said, raising her voice.

"Oh, um, I'll leave you guys to discuss this." Rachel picked up her keys. "I'll see you tomorrow night."

Nerissa and Scott sat in awkward silence.

"I thought you were on my side," Nerissa said.

"I am on your side. This isn't about taking sides."

"That's exactly what this is. That's why it's called a debate."

"I'm sorry. Please let me explain," Scott said. "You know how we've just won this big contract at work?"

Nerissa nodded.

73

"The organisation we'll be working for is called Drill New Plymouth, DNP. They're a joint venture company who were set up to provide mechanical and technological services for the off shore drilling and production sectors in New Plymouth. When the government released the tenders, they saw the potential for getting into the market down here. DNP wanted to be the first with their fingers in the pie if the way is paved for future drilling. Dad sent me down here to get a foot in the door with Taxxoil. He thought it would be a good idea for us to push DNP's case and all the other economic benefits that could come out of this."

"That's what you've been doing in town this week?"

"Yes."

"So the real reason for coming up here wasn't to be with me."

Scott shifted in his chair. "No, that's not true. I drove up as soon as I heard about what happened to you. Dad caught whiff of Taxxoil being in town and thought we could kill two birds with one stone."

Why did he look like was struggling to convince himself that he would be advocating for something she was adamantly opposed to?

"Look," he said, taking her hands in his and caressing them. "I didn't mean to upset you. Let's just see how this plays out. It's just a debate after all."

"You're trying to downplay not only the debate, but your role in it," Nerissa persisted.

"Let's not argue." Scott wandered out to the kitchen and took a glass from the pantry. "Chocolates. I didn't see them before. Another get well gift?"

"Yes. They're from Jackson."

"Oh. He was here?"

"He dropped round a couple of days ago to see how I was," Nerissa said, as she watched Scott's reaction. "So you won't need to worry about me when you go back to the city."

Scott raised her eyebrows. "That's unfair."

Nerissa ignored the comment.

Scott chose his usual, a scorched almond. "Do you want one? What about the strawberry ones you like?" He handed the box to her.

"I think I'll try something different." She picked up a mint chocolate and popped it in her mouth. The mint exploded and she swung her tongue round the invigorating freshness. Different was definitely good.

***

Nerissa and Scott arrived at the old brick town hall an hour before the debate was to take place. Scott wandered off to have a last minute discussion with his team.

The hall was humming with people and there was a sense of anticipation in the air.

"Nerissa!" Rachel waved from the front of the hall. "Thank goodness you've arrived. We've got a problem. Edward did his back in this afternoon. He won't be able to take part. That makes us an affirmative team member short. You'll have to go on."

"What? No, Rachel, I can't." Chairing was OK, but debating was not what she signed up for. A chill ran down her spine. The last time she debated was at university and she was attacked that night. "Can't somebody else do it?"

"No. There's no one else we could think of who's done recent research and who could do it at such a short notice."

"I'll try to find someone else."

"There's no time."

Nerissa wavered, overwhelmed with dread. "Who'll chair if I speak?"

"I'm going to. Come on, Nerissa. You'll be great out there."

Scott appeared at Nerissa's side. "What's wrong? You look stressed."

"The affirmatives are a team member short. Rachel wants me to go on."

"Is that a good idea? You're not looking well."

"I think it's just nerves." Nerissa wiped away a few beads of perspiration from her lip. She took a few calming breaths. *Stop thinking about yourself and think about how important this is for the community.* "I'll give it a go."

"Hey, that's a girl." Rachel gave her a quick hug. "You're a lifesaver."

Scott turned to Nerissa. "Are you sure?"

"Definitely." She pushed her shoulders back. Determination stirred inside her. This could be interesting going up against Scott.

Nerissa found her other team members, Peter and Henry, who ran a scuba diving business. Nerissa rearranged her chairing notes to the back of her folder and moved her other notes to the front. They had a quick strategy meeting and given her previous debating experience it was agreed that she would speak last. She quickly scrawled some notes based on the information she'd read earlier on in the week.

The clock ticked closer to 8 pm. A buzz reverberated throughout the hall as the chairs filled up and it became standing room only. Nerissa glanced over the hall. There were heaps of locals, fishers wearing their white gumboots, tourist operators, the old couple who ran the best fish and chip shop in town, council staff and the collective groups of locals who sold crayfish from caravans up and down the coast. There was Ginny, the Marine Mammal Emergency Centre manager, Yvette, the barista from the Blue Penguin Café, Harold the Hermit and, thank goodness, the MP for the Marlborough region, David Douglas.

Rachel opened the debate with some comments and outlined the rules and Peter began the debate. Then the first speaker for the other side was up.

Nerissa focused on the speakers while both sides of the argument heated up. Scott hadn't yet spoken for the other team, which meant she'd be going up directly against him.

"For those who don't know our next speaker, please let me introduce you to Nerissa Taylor who's making a good recovery," Rachel announced.

Everyone broke out in loud clapping and cheering as Nerissa made her way to the centre of the stage and turned on her lapel microphone. She opened her mouth, but no words came out. Her throat was as dry as the desert.

Peter handed her a glass of water. She took a few sips. The cool liquid flowed down her parched throat.

Through her blurred vision, a sea of faces swam in front of her. People looked at her in anticipation. Some shuffled in their seats. A baby cried out.

Her knees trembled like jelly. Could the audience see them knocking together? Butterflies trembled in her stomach sending small waves of panic through her and her heartbeat roared in her ears.

She spotted Katey in the front row.

"Go on," Katey mouthed, gesturing subtly to the cue cards Nerissa held.

A bit of encouragement and a familiar face was all she needed.

"During this debate we have demonstrated that we do not support deep sea oil drilling in Aqua Bay. The other team tried to point out that the possible growth in the economy could be an extra $1 billion over the next 20 years and would create 1,000 jobs. Unfortunately, what they didn't mention was that information released last month challenges those figures. New jobs and new businesses will require more infrastructure putting more pressure on the economy." She twisted a strand of hair round her finger. People leant forward and moved their head to the side, straining to hear.

She raised her voice to project out across the hall. "The second speaker argued that major operators are attracted to New Zealand's stable political climate. Do they not know there's an election this year? A new government may look at things quite differently."

She wavered for a moment, but people were nodding, signalling for her to continue. She had them engaged. Memories of her university debating days were returning and how much she enjoyed public speaking - the rush and thrill of adrenaline at facing an audience.

"The royalties of four percent of net revenues with favourable tax treatments – once again, this could be all up in the air with a change of government."

There were so many points she could dispute. "The team mentions the statistics of a poll recently undertaken that 24 percent of people support oil exploration, but they failed to mention that 70 percent do not.

"Yes, 60 percent thought we should do more to explore our mineral resources but 80 percent said we needed to do more to protect the environment."

She strode over to the left of the stage so she could be closer to the audience. "Under law in Ghana, residents can own up to five percent in an oil drilling company. If such a scheme happened here, how would it be administered? How much extra in admin costs would this be? How much tax would a person have to pay if an oil company's dividends go into a pension fund?"

Stopping, she made a dramatic sweep of her hands. "There is little evidence to support that allowing more oil companies into New Zealand will increase our political nous. Our isolation means we shouldn't rely on just one type of energy resource and we would be foolish to cut ties with major players."

She stepped out over to the right side of the stage ensuring everyone was included in her message. She focused on various people making strong eye contact with them, holding their attention. "As the government opens up more areas for drilling, where will it stop? There is currently no limit on how many permits can be granted. Do we really want our coastline dotted with oil rigs ad infinitum as is the case in some countries?"

She lowered her voice so the audience really had to hear what she said. "The team tried to say that there have been improvements in technology and better government oversight, which has made drilling safer. However, they forgot to point out that many local operators on the Gulf Coast will tell you it did not help them after approximately 4.9 million barrels of oil were leaked. "The risks of deep sea oil drilling far outweigh the benefits.

"Our team has proven that allowing deep sea oil drilling would come at a great cost. The most important thing to remember is that we want a future for our children that directly reflects what we have now or even better. It is our responsibility to protect our environment for our children's and their children's future so they can enjoy what we have here today.

"We *want* to continue to be part of this country's 'green' reputation and we *embrace* our eco-tourism industry. We *do not want* this town's life blood – the sacred whales and dolphins, birds, crayfish – threatened or killed because of harmful pollutants or an oil spill.

"We do *not* support deep sea oil drilling in Aqua Bay in any shape or form."

The audience erupted in cheers and clapping. Some people were on their feet, yelling "hear", "hear".

Nerissa wiped perspiration from her forehead. She'd done all she could to put up a persuasive argument. She took a bow and walked back to her seat.

"That was pretty inspiring," Peter said, patting her on the knee.

"I'm glad that's over with." Her hands trembled slightly. This time it was from exhilaration and not fear.

"You did a great job," Henry agreed. "Well said."

"Now please welcome our next speaker, Scott Maindonald," Rachel announced.

Scott rose from his seat and started the closing arguments for his team. Part of his sentences washed in and out of her mind, "...threatening 13 marine mammal species in the area is unproven...", "...no research round the suggestion of engaging New Zealand in unstable boom and bust economies..." He finally ended with, "We would like to reaffirm that we support deep sea oil drilling."

Nerissa folded a corner of her notes back and forth.

The threat of deep sea oil drilling was real. Very real. This could happen to Aqua Bay, the place where she belonged and it hit her like a freight train. Her team's arguments and her own arguments had added conviction to her beliefs. She wanted her children to grow up in Aqua Bay, not in the city. And there was no way she would let anyone or anything destroy its beauty. She frowned, focusing on the doors at the back of the hall. How could Scott not feel the same? Was he using Aqua Bay to further

82

his own career? It certainly looked that way. He wasn't standing by her, supporting her. He was working against her.

"...the team's claims are void..."

One of the doors at the back opened and a tall figure slipped through. It was Jackson. *So, he had decided to check it out. Brave of him.*

He stood, hanging back, choosing not to sit with the crowd.

Her neck muscles tensed. Jackson and Taxxoil represented a change she didn't want. The possibility of destroying what she held dear. She shifted her attention back to Scott and with a defiant lift of her chin she made a silent commitment that she would do whatever she could to ensure oil drilling in Aqua Bay didn't become a reality.

Subdued clapping broke out. Scott had finished, but no-one had risen to their feet at the end of his speech.

"Well, there you have it everyone. There was certainly some food for thought in those arguments and I think we achieved what we wanted tonight - to raise awareness of this serious issue and get all sides out in the open. I think most people will agree with me that despite this debate being an informal forum for the community to air its views, we are opposed to oil exploration," Rachel concluded.

"Where do we go from here?" A voice came from the middle of the hall. "How do we progress this further?"

"Good point. We'll have a think about that and we'll certainly keep you informed. I'd like to thank everyone who contributed tonight particularly Nerissa who stepped in at the last minute."

Everyone clapped again and gradually the crowd drifted out or gathered in small groups to chat.

Nerissa turned to Peter. "I'd like to come back to work on *Seabird*."

"This is a bit sudden, isn't it? What about your hand? You still have stitches in it."

"I will have to be careful as they don't come out for another week. Maybe light duties?"

"OK. Perhaps we'll start you off on reduced hours and see how you go."

"Thanks Peter."

Nerissa looked round the hall for Scott finally spying him talking to a group of men. She walked down the aisle. The men were wearing the same clothes. Some kind of uniform. She could make out a logo on their T-shirts and underneath the logo were the words, *Drill New Plymouth*. This must be the company Scott was referring to that supported oil exploration.

"Hey," Scott said. "Great speech under pressure." He gave her a quick hug.

"You weren't so bad yourself," Nerissa said.

"Look. I might be here a while. Do you want to drive back and I'll get a lift with one of the guys?'

"Um, yeah, sure," Nerissa said, as she scratched her neck. "I'll see you later then."

She walked to the back of the hall, which had now pretty much emptied out. She scrambled in her bag for her car keys. Outside dusk had given way to the encroaching darkness.

Remembrance of another time and place flashed through her mind. The dark of night, the university car park, the debate, rough hands yanking her handbag intermingled with the recent attack – more rough hands, a glint of a silver knife, blackness.

She froze. There was no way she would be able to get to the car. Her feet were glued to the ground, but all her senses were yelling at her to run and run fast! *Oh God. I think I'm having a panic attack.* Light headedness overwhelmed her. Was she about to faint? Her limbs shook and she gasped for air. She gripped the side of the hall wall. A scream threatened to burst from her mouth.

"Nerissa, are you all right?"

Someone touched her arm and she jumped.

"I...I..." she stumbled.

"It's OK. Just breathe deeply," Jackson said.

Nerissa panted then took a couple of long breaths as the panic subsided.

"Where were you heading?" Jackson asked.

"I was just trying to get to the car. This awful feeling of dread just came over me. All I could see was a knife and a horrible man." She placed her hand on her chest to still the thumping.

"Let me drive you home."

"Oh no, no," she protested. "I'll be OK."

"You don't look OK," he said doubtfully. "Come on. It's not far. You can't drive in this condition."

"How will you get home?" Nerissa asked.

"It's a nice night for a walk. I'll collect the Rover tomorrow."

Why was it that it had been Jackson who had seen and realised her state? She hesitated. But she didn't want to wait. Not out here by herself. She handed him the keys and pointed to the Holden.

Jackson guided her to the car, his hand on the small of her back. He unlocked her side of the car and she climbed in.

"Better?" he asked, turning the keys in the ignition.

She nodded pressing the window button to let in fresh air.

"Now, I'll try to stay on the right side of the road. I mean the left side of the road, which is the right side of the road. Aw, you know what I mean."

Nerissa smiled. He was keeping the situation light with humour. Her breathing had slowed. She gripped the seat; the solidness of the car somehow reassuring.

The CD had switched on automatically and Keith Urban launched into "You'll Think of Me". It was the perfect song for cruising.

Jackson pulled up outside the cottage and turned off the engine.

Nerissa sat for a moment and stared out the window. "Thank you – again. I'm not always the damsel in distress."

"Well, you do kinda seem to need rescuing regularly."

"This stuff only happens when you're around" she said.

"Hmm, maybe." The corner of Jackson's mouth upturned in a way that seemed to be mocking her.

"What do you mean by that?"

"It could just be a catalyst for something."

She shook her head. "You're speaking in riddles."

"You put up a good argument tonight," Jackson said. His body seemed to fill the whole of the car.

"You came in after my speech," she challenged.

"I heard some of it from outside before I came in. You were so busy concentrating on your points you didn't see me."

"I wasn't supposed to speak. It was all last minute. I didn't really want to. I'm still feeling a bit..." - she searched for the words - "...sensitive. Which team do you think won?"

"Oh, I think both sides had valid points."

Did he not want to support the 'for' team? That's what he was here for.

"You know, I used to be so sure what I wanted in life. Now I'm not so sure." Her lower lip quivered and she bit on it hard. Every bone in her body ached from exhaustion. She didn't want to cry in front of Jackson, to show any weakness. "I should have been more careful."

"What do you mean?" Jackson asked.

"I shouldn't have gone through the alley by myself." She tapped the heel of her hand against her forehead.

"Nonsense. It was true daylight."

"If I hadn't taken the short cut back to the van I wouldn't have been attacked," Nerissa spluttered. Her shoulders slumped forward.

"You can't blame yourself," Jackson said. "It could've happened to anyone."

"I just don't feel grounded any more." Tears fell silently down her cheeks. "I'm sorry..."

Jackson shifted in his seat. His hand hovered over the gap between them dropping to clasp her hand, covering it completely. The street light threw a faint glow across his long fingers. The skin brushed rough against her own. His hands were clean but the engrained dirt in his fingernails indicated that no amount of scrubbing would ever shift the tell-tale signs of his job.

Somehow that little gesture, her small hand captured in his, steadied her, prevented her from cracking. Desire started in her stomach and crept over her.

"I'm sorry," she said again. One part of her wanted to withdraw her hand; it wasn't right. The other part of her yearned to be touched more by this complex man whose hot breath was so close to her, stifling her.

She sighed and wiped her tears away. "I never felt so strongly about the need to safeguard anything in my life, but how can I do that when I can't even look after myself?"

Jackson looked away. "I think you are more strong-willed than what you give yourself credit for. You'll find a way."

The weight of Jackson's hand lay heavy, scorching her skin. She started to reluctantly pull her hand away, but Jackson tightened his grip.

"I like you, Jackson but you represent danger to me."

Jackson gasped. "I'd never hurt you."

"That's not what I meant. You have the potential to destroy what I need to save from harm. I think its best that we stay away from each other."

"Oh." Slowly he released her hand. "If that's what you want."

It wasn't what she wanted, but she didn't know how else she could separate her growing physical attraction towards Jackson plus, he was a potential threat to her Aqua Bay.

They both climbed out of the car.

"Thanks for dropping me off," she said. "Are you sure you'll be OK to walk home?"

Jackson lingered, running a hand across the car bonnet. "No worries."

He doesn't want to stay away from me. His reluctance to leave her said everything.

The silence hung heavy in the air.

"I might see you round. Stay out of trouble," Jackson said over his shoulder.

"Bye." Nerissa watched as he retreated into the darkness, his boots crunching on the gravel.

She walked past Maisie, her trusty, reliable Ford Anglia and let herself inside the cottage.

All she wanted now was to be alone. The seesawing emotions of the last few hours had finally caught up with her, sapping her energy.

Watching the shadows of the leaves dance in the moonlight on the wall, she could just make out the outline of one of her crystal dolphin figurines on the shelf above the fireplace. She put out her hand to touch it. Its solidness was real, but in a careless move the dolphin could be knocked to the ground and shatter into tiny pieces.

She stared at the dolphin. *Don't worry. I won't let anything happen to you.* The need to guard the safety of the dolphins was so strong it made her heart ache. She couldn't bear it if something happened to them that compromised the sea that was their playground.

But was this just fool's talk? A passive person's thinking? How on earth could she begin a crusade if she couldn't even protect herself, or let other people decide her fate?

Her first attack had happened a long time ago. And she'd been easily swayed by her parents, particularly her mother, Gail, to do what they wanted, what they believed was right. She wasn't so naïve now. She could take a stand against her mother. The right thing to do would be to press charges against the man who'd assaulted her when he was found. She hadn't rung her mother back, not wanting to hear how in some way the attack would've been her fault. If she hadn't been walking alone... in an alleyway... in Aqua Bay instead of the city...

She folded her arms across her chest, Jackson was right; she was determined. She'd devote all her time to saving the dolphins and watch out anyone who got in her way.

She frowned. Scott hadn't supported her tonight. He'd been speaking for the other side. It was like a betrayal. They should be standing on this issue together. And then he'd left her to come home alone when he knew she was still feeling unsafe.

And Jackson. He was on the other side too, but compassionate enough to see her home safely. Scott, Jackson, merging together to send her into the land of confusion.

Chapter 6

Nerissa folded up Scott's T-shirts. She looked out over the jagged peaks of the mountains that filled the view from the French doors. The same jagged peaks seemed to spike the morning atmosphere within the cottage. She'd not told Scott of her panic attack and that Jackson had brought her home. She wasn't sure why she needed to keep it a secret. That Scott had chosen to stay behind after last night's debate left a bitter taste in her mouth.

Scott was hammering a nail into the wall for one of her paintings she'd been meaning to hang up. He popped the painting on the nail, stood back to see that it was level and made a few adjustments. "How about you come down to the city this weekend? We need to start looking at building plans for the house."

A trip to the city was the last thing she wanted to do. Noise, pollution, traffic, being closed in.

"Could we leave it a couple more weekends? I'm not feeling ready to tackle something that big yet."

"O-Kaay," Scott said.

She caught the reluctance in his voice.

"I just thought it would be good to get something underway so we're not trying to do that and plan a wedding at the same time."

Yes, the wedding. Wasn't she supposed to be excited? *What is wrong with me?* This is every woman's dream yet she couldn't even envision herself in a wedding dress.

"Maybe we should look at a wedding date first. We'd originally discussed building the house, getting married and then moving straight in. But if you have other ideas we could look at those," Scott suggested.

"No, you're right," Nerissa conceded. "That's what we decided to do." She threw some old newspapers next to the wood on the fireplace.

Scott walked over to her and took her hand. "I know you've been going through a tough time, but I feel like I'm in limbo here. We do have to get things moving. Timing is really important otherwise we may end up living with my parents if the house isn't built in time. Or yours."

Nerissa screwed up her nose.

"I thought so." Scott smiled.

"I'm sorry. I know I've been dilly-dallying about the date. I promise I'll give it some thought."

"Maybe Katey could give you a hand. Isn't that what bridesmaids are for?"

Nerissa nodded. Katey would be a great help. She'd be in there planning it as if it was her own wedding.

"I might make an earlier start back to the city this afternoon," Scott said.

"How come?"

"Some stuff I want to get a head start on before tomorrow."

"Does this have anything to do with the people you were talking to last night?" Nerissa asked. Her breath quickened.

Scott fumbled round in his overnight bag. "Yes."

No other explanation was forthcoming. So he was putting work first rather than spending time with her. She let it go. "Are you leaving now?"

"I can avoid the weekend traffic that way."

"Makes sense." Nerissa hung her head.

"Will you think about coming down this weekend?"

"Sure."

"Good. If I get a head start on work today hopefully I won't have to do anything over the weekend and I'll be 100 per cent devoted to you."

Nerissa couldn't resist Scott's school-boy charm, the charm that made her smile, the charm that made everything all right.

"Here's some T-shirts you left behind last weekend. All washed for you," Nerissa said, handing them to him.

"You're going to make a great wife."

What started out as a cringe she disguised with a half-smile.

94

"Come here," Scott said, holding out his hand.

Nerissa moved into his arms cocooning her from the world.

"I love you," Scott whispered.

"I love you too." Their lips came together and she embraced Scott harder savouring the moment and keep the memory till they'd be together again.

"Be careful," Scott said. "Please don't walk anywhere by yourself."

Nerissa nodded. She didn't need any convincing. She drew in a deep breath. "When they catch this guy, I'm pressing charges."

"That's a good decision. It'll help save other women and bring closure for you, for both times these awful things have happened. What made you change your mind?"

"The handling of what happened after I was attacked at the uni was all wrong. I wasn't strong enough then to realise I shouldn't have been convinced to not take it any further. But this time I'm going to do what's right. This time I'll make my own decision about it and not be talked out of it by my mother for her reasons, but please don't mention anything to Lou. He'll tell Sharon and Sharon will tell Mother and then she'll try and talk me out of it."

"Don't worry. I won't say a thing, and I'm proud of you."

Nerissa and Scott strolled out to his car.

"Don't work too hard," Nerissa said, giving him a final kiss on the cheek.

"Ditto. I'll text you."

"Drive safely."

Throwing his bag in the boot, Scott jumped in his car and headed down the road.

Nerissa watched until the car had disappeared. She rubbed her wrist. A silent voice cried out, *Scott, come back.*

Down the road a bright red VW with the 'Aqua Bay Homes' logo on the side pulled up to the grass edge. Angie Thomson, her landlady, stepped out of the car.

"Nerissa, hi," she said, as she waved. Her gold hoop earrings glinted in the sun.

"Hi Angie. Is it time for an inspection? Didn't we just do one recently?"

"No, no. I'm not here for an inspection. Can we go inside?"

"Sure."

Nerissa made Angie a cup of coffee with freshly roasted fair trade coffee beans and a Milo for herself. She plated up some cheese and crackers.

"I heard you gave a pretty good speech last night," Angie said, entwining her perfectly painted red fingernails round the cup.

"I don't know about that." Nerissa brushed away the comment. "I probably said what anyone else would've said."

"Maybe so, but not everyone would have got up on that stage and put themselves out there especially after what happened to you. How are you feeling?"

"Good. Stitches come out this week." Nerissa popped a cracker in her mouth.

"I've got some news to add to your day. The owners want to put the cottage up for sale."

"Oh." A brief flutter of panic beat deep in her stomach. Her attack had unsettled her. All she desperately wanted now was for time to stand still so she could gain her balance.

"I hope this isn't the start of people wanting to sell up because of the threat of oil drilling," Angie pondered.

Nerissa looked round. She had lived here for four years and had loved every minute of it. The cottage held some great memories – one's she'd had alone, one's she'd shared with others. Like the late night girly sleepovers with Katey or the one's with she and Scott.

"Don't worry, hon." Angie patted her on her uninjured hand. "The owners aren't ready to kick you out, but they want to put the cottage on the market immediately."

A crazy idea stirred in the back of Nerissa's mind. "How much do they want for it?"

Angie opened her black portfolio folder and pulled out a flyer. "280,000 or near offer."

Nerissa studied the flyer with a photo of the cottage on it. Why had she asked what the price was? What was she thinking? She couldn't afford to buy it, and why would she anyway?

"You were only planning to stay until the end of summer, weren't you?" Angie asked.

Nerissa nodded. "Yeah. I'm supposed to be moving to the city to be with Scott. Well, that was the plan."

"Have things changed?"

"No, not really." Nerissa sighed. "I didn't realise that time was coming round so soon."

"It might be a good timeframe to work towards. If I can sell the cottage by the end of summer then you won't have to move twice. There's not a lot of rental accommodation available in Aqua Bay at the moment."

Angie chatted on about the general state of the property market, but the words washed over her. Everything seemed to be pushing her towards leaving Aqua Bay.

After Angie left, she spent the rest of the afternoon tidying up inside. She always had the best intentions of keeping the cottage tidy during the week but by Friday somehow stuff had accumulated everywhere. It never used to be like this. Up until a few months ago, she'd always been tidy. Maybe she was just getting lazy.

That night as she ate her dinner - an omelette made from freshly laid eggs she had collected from the chickens - she studied the easel set up in the lounge corner facing the garden.

With everything that had happened recently she hadn't had time to do any painting. She ran her hand over the half-finished scene – a picture capturing the purple wisteria framing the wooden doorframe of the back door. She frowned at the painting; the colour of the wisteria wasn't quite right. It was too pale and watery and needed more depth.

Her phone rang. It was Scott.

"You obviously got home OK," she said.

"It was a good idea starting early. I missed an accident by about half an hour, which closed the road for a while."

"Have you managed to get some work done?"

"All set for tomorrow. It's a relief to get my head round some of the tricky parts of this contract."

"Angie popped round just after you left."

"What did she have to say?"

"The cottage is up for sale." Nerissa glanced down at the flyer on the table.

"That's very sudden."

"Angie's worried that this oil drilling might be scaring people away from Aqua Bay."

"An overreaction I'd say."

"It got me thinking."

"And?"

"Why don't we buy it?" Nerissa rushed on. "It would be a great place for us to have as a holiday bach and when we have children we can bring them here for weekends and holidays." A picture of two blonde littlies romping round on the beach, digging for shells and building sandcastles, squealing as the tide rushed up to nip at their feet formed in her mind.

"Nerissa, we can't afford it," Scott said quietly. "Where would we get the money?"

Nerissa clenched her teeth. Her happy family vision disintegrated like someone stomping over a lovingly built sandcastle.

"Nerissa?"

"It was just an idea."

"Not only can't we afford it, it won't be very practical. Besides when we're in our new home at Surfboard Point it will be just like on holiday. There's nothing at Aqua Bay that we won't be able to do at Surfboard Point."

Nerissa fought back tears and ran a hand through her hair where it caught in one of her curls. *That wasn't true.* She needed to hang onto her connection with Aqua Bay. Scott didn't understand or feel the same way.

"I tell you what," Scott said. "When we win Lotto I'll buy you as many cottages as you want."

Her idea had been impulsive and impractical and would never come to fruition. "I'll hold you to that promise."

"I'd better go. My dinner's just about ready. I'll text you tomorrow. Love you."

"Love you. Bye." Nerissa stared at the flyer. Yes, just an impractical silly dream. And with that she crumpled up the flyer into a ball.

Chapter 7

Nerissa swivelled back in forth in the chair in Peter's office as they planned her light duties for the week.

"I want to get out on the boat," she said, as she crossed her arms and looked out over the sparkling brilliant blue of Aqua Bay.

"You get those stitches out and the all clear from the doctor before you take on too much. Remember, you've had a concussion," Peter insisted. He two-fingered tapped away on the keyboard. "By the way, I've had lots of great comments about your debating skills on Saturday night."

"It was a team effort."

Laughter rang out from the foyer as excited tourists prepared to board *Seabird*.

"Don't go brushing it off so casually, girl. It took a lot of courage to do what you did."

"I just hope that we've managed to get the community thinking about what this could mean for them."

"Rachel said you've been doing a lot of research."

"Only because she's given me so much information. What do you think we should do now?"

"Well, I'm certainly not letting any American come here and ruin our lives," Peter said gruffly. "I'm happy to give you any support you need."

"Maybe I could spend the afternoon reviewing all the information Rachel has given me."

Peter agreed.

She locked herself away in one of the back offices. Before long papers were strewn over the table. She trawled through a number of websites to get a better understanding of the issues involved and before long her note pad was full of doodles and notes.

At the end of the day she updated Peter.

"There's an excellent case for Aqua Bay to become an eco-town and be given United Nations Biosphere status. And if we could obtain marine reserve status, this could be one way for drilling to be banned."

"Whoa! Slow down, Nerissa. This is big stuff."

"I know! I know! But we can do this. Though it's going to take a lot of work." She paced up and down. "I'm going to send out an invitation for a meeting on Thursday for those interested in discussing these options further."

Peter gave her the thumbs up. She raced outside to *Seabird* where Katey was just finishing her duties.

"Hey, Katey. I'm organising a meeting tomorrow night to talk about Aqua Bay and the oil drilling. Can I put you down as a 'yes'?"

Katey wiped a mop over the deck sloshing water over the side of the boat. "Enrolments for the accounting papers close this Friday and Scott thinks it's not too late for me to start the first semester."

"But this is important. This is about Aqua Bay, Dolphin Eco-tours and how oil drilling could affect us and the whole community."

"Yeah, I know, but I really want to give this accounting thing a good shot."

"You haven't enrolled yet. You could still give us a hand tomorrow night even if it's just moral support."

"Sorry, Nerissa."

Nerissa's shoulders slumped. "OK, if you change your mind we'd love your opinion." She turned away and walked back to the reception area. Katey obviously didn't see this as a priority. There was a time when Katey would've been right behind her. Supporting her without question. She'd just have to rely on whomever turned up tomorrow night.

And in the end, ten people showed up at Nerissa's cottage including Sam, Peter, Mavis and Angie.

"Guys, we wanted to see what we could do to work on making our views clear to everyone that deep sea oil drilling isn't going to be acceptable here," Nerissa began.

Heads nodding encouraged her to continue and before long the discussion was flowing, Nerissa tapping away on her iPad capturing the ideas.

"So let's recap," Nerissa said, as the ideas began to trail off. "Things we can do – write to the newspapers, raise the issue with Greenpeace, make up banners and get stickers painted. Put pressure on David Douglas too. I like Sam's idea about getting a petition going to prevent oil drilling in the Aqua Bay area."

"What about a protest march?" Angie asked.

"Another good idea," Nerissa acknowledged.

"And as Taxxoil is in town I think we should get them to front up," Angie said.

"Rachel's spoken to the guy who seems to be the spokesperson for Taxxoil. Jackson somebody-or-other," Mavis said. "Maybe we could get her to arrange something."

"What about you Nerissa? He being your hero and all." Sam mocked her good-naturedly.

And there Jackson was again. In just over two weeks, this man was strutting round in her head and just wouldn't leave. He refused to be shut out, the long black hair, the cheeky eyes and the full mouth that had whispered against her cheek. "Nerissa?"

She cleared her throat and the cocky Jackson disappeared. "I haven't had much to do with him really. Besides Rachel's probably got better coercive skills than me."

"Rachel can be a little too enthusiastic," Mavis added.

"OK. Well, leave it with me then," Nerissa said.

After the group came up with a name for their venture – Operation Protect – they called it a night. Each of them had a small task to do and Nerissa promised to arrange a meeting in a few weeks' time to discuss progress.

Back at the cottage her senses were buzzing and her head spun with ideas. Her phone rang.

"You still up?" Scott asked. His voice was strained and tired.

"Just on my way to bed," Nerissa said, flicking off the hall lights.

"How was your day?"

"Good. I get my stitches out tomorrow and I think I'll be able to go out on the boat on Friday. Some of us got together tonight to look at things we can do to stop this oil drilling."

She could just make out the soft sounds of the late night TV news through the phone. "Scott?"

"Yes, sorry."

"The main issue is the lack of consultation by the government when they put the petroleum block offers up for tender. What about you? You sound stressed."

"We've been frantic. Securing the DNP contract has caused some major re-allocation of work amongst staff. I've been debriefing while I transfer my workload, which is one of the reasons I'm ringing. I'm not going to be able to get up this weekend, sorry. There's simply too much to do."

Nerissa opened the curtains in the bedroom. The night was clear and calm. In the distance a light glowed faintly from the cottage down the road. The cottage where Jackson was staying. *So he's up late too. What was he doing? Was he working, looking over maps of the best possible places to drill?*

"I thought that was why you started work early this week." She sat down on the bed and lowered her head.

"It was, but one of the senior accountants has gone off sick and won't be back for a couple of weeks. The pressure is on. I'm sorry," he said again.

"Don't worry about it," Nerissa assured him. "It's only one weekend."

"I'm probably going to be at least another hour here so I'd better go," Scott said hurriedly.

"Don't work too hard," Nerissa replied.

"Good luck with your stitches. I'll ring you later."

"OK. Love you."

"Love you."

Nerissa sighed. When work got heavy for both of them she'd give up all that she had to be with Scott. Even if that meant the inevitable move to the city.

But ever since her attack, she craved Scott's touch. Him being with her made her feel safe.

She'd keep busy and chase the nagging thoughts away by focusing on the drilling plans.

***

A glint of steel.

Hands pulling at her, smothering her.

A knife at her neck.

Bright lights, then suffocating darkness.

She sat up in fright with a half-stifled scream still in her throat, bathed in sweat.

A nightmare. Until now she'd slept well after her attack. Was this a delayed reaction?

Her breathing was quick and rapid. She gulped big breaths to calm herself and reached for the glass of water she kept on the bedside stand.

She threw off her cotton PJs and used the top to wipe her forehead and chest. Shivering, she crawled back under the duvet.

Her hands stroked the other side of the bed, so cold compared to the heat on her side. She missed Scott so much, it hurt. Why wasn't he here? She pulled the pillow towards her cuddling into it. If she hugged it hard enough maybe it would turn into Scott. He would make it better. Silent tears fell finally drying when the first light of dawn peeked up over the horizon.

***

Friday and her stitches came out.

"Your hand is healing well. You can resume full work duties," her doctor said.

After leaving the doctor's she headed towards the police station, a tiny building further down the esplanade.

She pushed open the door. A man and woman were in the waiting room. The woman was bobbing a crying baby on her lap and the shrill screeching and whining stood the hairs on her

108

neck on end. Could she do this? Was she really doing this? Maybe she should've talked to a counsellor first.

"Can I help you?" asked the policeman behind the desk.

Nerissa opened her mouth, but nothing came out. Her throat was as dry as the desert.

A radio squawked in the background.

She swallowed hard. "Is Senior Constable Valerie Appleton here?"

"I think so. I'll just check." He wandered down the corridor.

Nerissa looked round. She'd never been in the Aqua Bay Police Station before. The place was tidy and there was a faint odour of disinfectant. She studied the noticeboard which was covered with posters on everything from domestic violence and remembering to lock your car over the summer holidays, to a request of information on a missing person.

"Nerissa?" She jumped then turned back round.

"Valerie. Can we talk?"

"Come on through." Valerie pushed the button on the door and let Nerissa in. "We can pop into this interview room."

Nerissa followed Valerie into the room, which was sparsely furnished with only a desk and two chairs. "How have you been?" She pointed Nerissa to a chair.

"I've just had my stitches out and I've been given the all clear to go back to work."

"Marvellous. So you're here about the attack?"

Nerissa nodded and fought to take a breath. Why was this so hard to do? She was taking a stand, fighting for herself and then fighting for Aqua Bay. And she didn't need her mother's permission or opinion. "I want to press charges." And there - it was out and having said it, a weight lifted from her shoulders.

"It's the right decision, Nerissa," said Valerie, who outlined the process and helped her fill out the necessary forms.

Once the documentation was complete, Valerie escorted her back out to the reception area. The family, along with the screaming baby, had gone.

"We've also put out posters of your attacker and we have the border being monitored in case he's an international trying to get out of the country quickly. Don't worry, Nerissa. He'll surface eventually and when he does we'll get him."

Nerissa thanked Valerie and lifted her chin as she walked down the street. She threw some coins into the hat of a teenage busker doing a good cover of "Sitting on the Dock of the Bay".

Her attacker was still out there somewhere, but she'd made a decision for herself, by herself. He wouldn't get away with his cowardly act.

She walked past the Blue Penguin Café filled with tourists buying rolls, cakes, muffins and drinks. She sniffed the air. Blueberry, today's muffin of the day.

Stopping outside the next block of shops, she picked up an empty, sticky can and placed it in the rubbish bin.

It was time for her to implement the next part of her plan. She dialled Peter's number. "How are bookings looking on Sunday?"

"Hang on. I'll have a look. Sunday afternoon bookings are light. I might transfer them to the morning."

"Perfect. I need to ask you a favour. No questions."

"Is it to do with Operation Protect?"

"Yes."

"Then you have my full support."

"Can we take *Seabird* out on Sunday afternoon?"

"That should be all right."

"Thanks Peter. I'm on my way back to work. I'll see you soon."

Nerissa walked up the stairs of the Taxxoil offices and was greeted by the unmistakable huskiness of Jackson's voice.

He had his back to her and he was on the phone. "Yeah... no... going OK... Just examining the maps for the seismic surveying location... yeah... we should be able to get that to you within the next week."

Nerissa cleared her throat.

Jackson swung round on his chair and raised his eyebrows. "Yep... we're on track... Once the *Perspeculor* arrives we'll be good to go... It looks promising... The locals? Frosty." He kept his eye on Nerissa. "They'll come around once they see how this can work for them."

Nerissa frowned. How presumptuous! But she refused to let Jackson push her buttons. She bit her lip, determined not to react.

"OK... yep... see you in the next few weeks. Should be able to do the rest by email. Yep... yep... bye.

"Well, curly. I knew my natural charisma would be too hard to resist," Jackson teased. "I thought you and I were off limits."

He eased up from his chair. How could a man as tall as him move so gracefully? It set her senses buzzing and her stomach in a twist.

"I'd like to take you out on *Seabird* on Sunday afternoon." She moved a little closer.

"So pushing me overboard will solve your problems?"

She smiled. She loved this guy's sense of humour. "I thought while you're here you won't get much of a chance to get out on the sea just for leisure's sake. I'd like to show you round the area." Here would be a fun challenge he wouldn't be able to resist.

Jackson stared at her so intently that she had to look away. "OK. You're on."

"Can you meet me at Dolphin Eco-tours down by the wharf about 1ish?"

"Anything I need to bring?

"You wouldn't happen to have a wetsuit would you?"

"Despite you thinking I have no idea what to do with my time off, I heard this place is great for diving. I brought my wetsuit with me. Are we going diving?"

"Better than that, but you'll have to wait until Sunday."

"I'm intrigued. I still think you're planning to kill me off."

"You'll have to take that risk," she jibed.

"How about a drink on Saturday night? I'm a lonely boy far away from home."

This man did not know when to give up. "Don't push it," she said. "Besides haven't you jacked up another date with Tanya?"

He screwed up his face. "Not really my type."

What sort of woman was his type?

The phone rang. "Better take this. See you Sunday."

Nerissa nodded. Warmth radiated through her chest.

The first part of her plan was set.

Chapter 8

"So what's the plan?" Katey asked.

"You'll see." Nerissa stood behind the reception desk. She watched Peter bring *Seabird* in against the wharf as the clock's hands crept closer to 1 pm. The engine chugged in time to the clicking clock.

Her hands tingled in anticipation and her stomach weaved in to knots.

"Are you waiting for someone?" Katey persisted, following Nerissa's gaze which had shifted to the footpath.

"Yes."

Jackson, head and shoulders above the people milling round, glided quietly down the footpath like a wild cat stalking his prey, his black hair gently wavering over his shoulders with the breeze.

"That man is a walking sex god."

"Katey!" But she was right. He was someone who people stopped and stared at, pulled in by his charisma.

"What are you up to?" Katey's eyes narrowed.

"We're going out on the boat."

"What?"

"I'll explain later."

"Afternoon ladies," Jackson said.

"Hi," said Katey, all doe eyes. "I'm Katey."

"Pleased to meet you," Jackson said. "You're staring."

Katey blushed a furious red. "I'll leave you two."

"Come on out to *Seabird*," Nerissa said, taking a sports bag off the counter. "Ready for an adventure?"

"Always ready for an adventure."

They walked towards the nine-metre, custom built, 20 seater powerboat. The round windows offered 360 degree, open views from inside, while the deck seating was designed to catch the sunshine.

"Come on board," Nerissa said. "Peter, I'm here. I want you to meet someone."

Peter, who had been on the other side of the boat, made his way over.

"Peter, this is Jackson."

The two men shook hands.

"Do I know you?" Peter asked. "You look familiar."

"You might have seen me around town," Jackson said coyly.

"Yeah. I do know you. You're that Taxxoil guy," Peter said gruffly, pointing his finger at Jackson. He looked at Nerissa. "What's this about?"

"You promised you'd support me–."

"You didn't tell me about him-."

"I knew you'd react like this, that's why."

115

"Is it any wonder? We shouldn't have anything to do with this guy."

"I'm sorry," Jackson said. "Maybe I should high-tail it."

"No, no," Nerissa exclaimed, placing her hand on Jackson's arm. "Peter, you said you wouldn't ask questions."

"This is different, Nerissa."

"Please. Trust me."

"I think she's going to kill me, sir."

Peter's eyes swung from Jackson to Nerissa.

"I don't know what you're up to girl, but it better be worth it."

Nerissa threw her arms round Peter's neck. "Thank you."

"There's bathrooms aft. Why don't you put your wetsuit on?" Nerissa suggested.

"The wardrobe of death," Jackson muttered.

Nerissa untied the big, scratchy ropes, and jumped back on board. Before long, Peter had them past the 10 knot sign and at cruising speed.

She leant over the side of *Seabird*. The ocean hugged her. She closed her eyes and took in an enormous breath of crisp salt air. If she could bottle a scent and wear it forever it would be this one. She had so missed being out on the water, free. The sea seemed to make life simple. Tiny waves with little peaks and troughs rose and fell. The sun shimmered on the water reflecting the opaqueness and then the sudden darkness of the constantly changing sea-blue – reflecting every shade of blue, turquoise, azure, teal and aqua.

Out in the distance a few commercial fishing boats and smaller recreational craft bobbed on the water. A seagull cruised alongside, drifting lazily on a down draught.

Nerissa stripped off her tracksuit pants and top revealing her wetsuit.

"How's it looking today?" Nerissa asked Peter.

"Good. Over there. I think I see some movement."

"Excellent."

Jackson exited the bathrooms. The skin-tight black wetsuit emphasised his long muscular lines.

"How would you like to swim with the dolphins?" Nerissa asked.

Jackson's grin widened. "Better than being eaten by sharks."

"Ever done this before?"

"Nope."

"OK. A couple of things about dolphin etiquette. The dolphins may not want to swim with us so we take our lead from them. They dictate the level of interaction. Try not to splash too much and we swim with, not at the dolphins. Stay by me and just relax."

Jackson nodded. They put on their masks, snorkels and fins.

"Nerissa, it needs to be now!" Peter yelled out.

"OK. Timing's critical. Ready?" Nerissa asked.

"Yep."

Nerissa and Jackson stepped off the board into the water and were at once surrounded by a pod of about 20 dolphins calling out a high-pitched "eeee" who were in the mood to play.

The dolphins twisted and turned.

She found herself between two dolphins and swam with long, strong strokes careful to stay parallel to them so she didn't change their speed or course.

Jackson mimicked her movements, spiralling gently beneath the waves. The dolphins plunged and soared round them.

Nerissa kicked lightly toward one dolphin that swayed up and down in the water. The beautiful creatures seemed to be in no hurry; weaving, gracefully, amongst the water revealing their powerful strength. She kicked up to the top of the water behind five dolphins and as one, the dolphins and she glided back under again. Glancing down, the pod continued on and passed lazily underneath her.

She broke the surface. Jackson's head and shoulders bobbed above the water as two dolphins swam round him. One dolphin skimmed the top of the water, the other beneath it in a complete mirror image. They darted quickly round Jackson, weaving up and down. Turning this way and that, their noses occasionally breaking the surface, teasing him. She smiled. The dolphins were dancing with him.

Nerissa descended under the water again. More dolphins cruised over her, waving their tails. One broke ranks and darted playfully round Nerissa exposing its stomach. She rolled onto her back exposing her stomach too. Peace and tranquillity washed over her. If only she could stay like this forever, at one with the dolphins. They were having so much fun playing. But she could sense now that they were ready to move on and she rose back up to the surface. She had to wave three times at Jackson to get him to head back to the boat.

Reaching the bottom of the stairs, she pulled herself up dripping water over the deck.

Peter had placed two towels on the seats just inside the cabin doors.

She grabbed one and threw the other to Jackson.

Jackson unzipped the back of his wetsuit and pulled it half-way down. His tanned skin glistened in the sun and highlighted his six-pack. This was one seriously hot, rugged bod. Tattoos of fire and a rocky landscape dominated one side of his chest. In the middle of his stomach was a large zipper-like scar. It was an I've-experienced-life body that told a story.

Katey was right. Jackson looked like a sex god. This was a man who was proud of his physique. He stood tall, legs spread wide and with his chin thrust out. He definitely wasn't shy, that was for sure. She couldn't help comparing him to Scott. While Scott also had a great tanned and muscular body, it was on a smaller scale. It was scarless and tattoo free.

119

The brashness in his eyes were sending her a message. She tucked a curl that had come loose back into her hairclip. Her body burned with desire despite the swim. Could another dip in the ocean put out the fire?

A discreet cough sounded from inside the cabin, breaking the spell.

"I've made some hot drinks," Peter said, handing them both a mug.

"Good idea," Nerissa replied.

Jackson sipped his coffee.

"What did you think?" Nerissa asked.

"Magic."

That one simple word summed it up perfectly. She nodded in understanding.

"Nerissa," Peter said. "Look."

Nerissa and Jackson hurried over to the port side. A pod of dolphins swam beside the boat.

"Oh wow," Jackson exclaimed.

They were putting on a good show; somersaulting, side slapping, back flipping. The gem-shaped water dew-drops they created glittered in the sun. Their carefree spirit captivated her. She glanced across at Jackson. The expression on his face was one of sheer joy making some of the tense lines on his face disappear. His loud laugh rippled through the air as the dolphins skimmed back and forth matching the speed of the boat. Then as suddenly as they had arrived they-changed course and moved away.

"That was pretty cool."

"No one ever forgets something like this," she replied.

They made their way back inside picking up their coffee cups.

"Tell me more about the dolphins," Jackson said.

"The ones you've just seen are bottlenose dolphins, which we get here all year round and the tourists love them. We also have the world's rarest and smallest dolphin, Hector's dolphin."

"Have you seen them?"

"Sure, but only a couple of times a year. They're so small compared to the bottlenose dolphins. We photo ID the dolphins so we can track, identify and study them. Some people tag them, but photo IDing them is less invasive. We catalogue the dolphins too so we can monitor distribution and movement patterns."

Jackson nodded.

Now it was time to make her point. "If seismic surveying takes place here, it could create noise pollution that can distress the marine life."

She waited for a reaction, but Jackson's face held still, devoid of any expression.

Nerissa continued on. "Whales are more likely to be affected than dolphins due to their low vocalisation frequencies. The stronger and higher frequency sonar pulses used by navy ships are believed to have caused whales to strand or suffer decompression sickness if they surface too quickly. And a whale beached in the North Island last year when seismic surveying was being undertaken. Other problems can include social upheaval, stress, and permanent hearing loss that affect their ability to hunt prey, and the reduction in the number of calves being born. There is nothing in place to protect these creatures. Your seismic surveying could have a real effect on their environment." Nerissa's voice caught in her throat.

Being out on the boat and so close to the dolphins today brought the love and passion she held for these animals to the surface. She must protect them. She must make Jackson see what irretrievable damage Taxxoil could do that would destroy it all. Did he understand?

His face was blank. She had been ready for him to put up an argument in his usual cocky manner giving her the opportunity to argue her point, but his lack of response threw her. Maybe if she didn't say any more and left him to process what she had said it would make a bigger impact than having an all-out war of words.

"Come outside again," Nerissa said. "I'll show you some more wildlife."

Parallel to the coastline she pointed out the seals that sunbathed on the rocks their lazy eyes followed the passing boat.

"We see albatrosses out here," Nerissa said. "There's a shearwater." She pointed to a medium sized brown and white bird, silently soaring high above them. "Aqua Bay is also the place little blue penguins like to live and breed. These penguins are one of the world's smallest and are incredibly good divers."

"Hey, what's that?" Jackson nodded at a large piece of driftwood that had washed up on shore.

A shag, entangled in fishing line that had caught on the driftwood, struggled to free itself.

"Peter, can you stop the boat?" Nerissa yelled out. "We've a shag in trouble."

Peter looked out the window and immediately noticed the bird's plight.

"What're you going to do?" Jackson asked.

"Save it, of course," Nerissa said.

She tied a towel round her waist, strapped a knife to her calf and dived off the side of the boat. With long strokes and a powerful kick she swam the short distance to shore. Her feet touched the pebbly bottom and she emerged onto the beach.

Splashing water from behind her caught her attention. She turned round as Jackson walked out of the sea.

"Thought you might need a hand."

This wasn't a sit-back kind of guy.

"Let's take a closer look," Nerissa said. She walked slowly and deliberately towards the bird.

The shag had spied bait left on the fishing line and in an attempt to eat it had become entangled. The more it had struggled the more it had got caught up in the never-ending opaque thread.

"I'll grab the bird," Nerissa said.

The shag flapped its wings, entangling it further.

She waited a few moments and then snatched at the bird, struggling to control its incessant flapping. She tucked the wings close to the shag's body and draped the towel over its head holding it securely.

"He hasn't swallowed the hook-"

"See if you can cut the lines," she instructed Jackson. "But don't get too close. They have a good bite."

"Darn, I knew you were going to feed me to some animal," Jackson said through gritted teeth. He reached down to extract the knife from Nerissa's calf. There was a horrible, tangled mess of fishing line everywhere. He worked quickly cutting the line from where it had wrapped itself round various parts of the driftwood.

Nerissa and the shag struggled against each other. The shag was strong and determined, but her will was stronger and she held fast.

"OK. That's it," Jackson said, untwining and winding the last thread away from Nerissa and the shag.

She turned the bird away from her face and removed the towel.

The shag, initially confused, looked round to find its bearings. Satisfied it knew where it was, it flapped its wings, this time unhindered.

Nerissa shaded her eyes against the sun as she watched the shag gain height, and then flap strongly out over the sea.

Picking up the remnants of the fishing line, Jackson wound it round his hand then passed it to Nerissa.

She thoroughly checked round the driftwood to make sure they had all the stray line. "I wish people were more careful when they're fishing."

"Does it happen often?"

"More than I want to think about. Although the shag was stressed it hadn't exhausted itself physically so it was lucky we came along when we did." She shoved the offending fishing line safely into her knife sheath.

They waded out into the sea. Jackson was a powerful swimmer and could've easily overtaken her, but stuck close to her side.

Back on the boat Peter handed them more towels. "The shag's landed on some rocks close to land." He put his binoculars down.

They dried themselves and changed back into their clothes.

As *Seabird* chugged into the harbour they sat in silence watching the Aqua Bay township come closer into view.

Nerissa stretched lazily drawing strength from the comfort of the sea. This was what completed her.

"I'll let you guys off here," said Peter, pulling up alongside the wharf. "I need to refuel the boat."

Nerissa and Jackson gathered their gear, disembarked and walked up the path towards the office.

She didn't want the day to end and spending a long evening alone didn't enthral her. "Would you like to come over for dinner tonight?" The words escaped and tumbled over each other.

"Why, that's a mighty fine idea," Jackson said.

"I haven't had a chance to thank you properly yet for being my hero and all that," Nerissa fumbled. "About 7?"

"Shall I bring anything?"

"No. No. Just turn up."

"OK. 7 then," Jackson said, as they parted ways in the car park.

She sat in the car with the window down, a mixture of tiredness and satisfaction crept over her. She breathed in the briny air mixed with diesel from a fishing boat that was just docking. The fishermen yelled out to a couple of kids to get away from the bollards. Shutting her eyes, she lifted her head to the warmth of the afternoon sun. Her plan had been a success.

She would so miss Aqua Bay when she left at the end of summer. She'd lost count of the number of times she'd swam with the dolphins and every time the feelings she experienced left her complete. Nothing in the city would ever come close to it. She wanted to be with Scott, but Aqua Bay pulled her in even more.

She sighed. She would do all she could while she was here to stop this crazy plan of seismic surveying.

The tail end of the Rover glowed red as it left the car park. A spark of energy flicked through her with the sweet anticipation of seeing Jackson again tonight.

Chapter 9

"Hey, anyone home?" the husky voice yelled.

"In here," Nerissa sang out from the kitchen as she tossed the salad. She watched Jackson pass through the French doors. His black jeans emphasised his long legs and his black T-shirt hugged his chest.

"I've brought — what do you locals call it? — a few Steinies?" Jackson said, referring to the New Zealand made beer, Steinlager.

Nerissa laughed. "It hasn't taken you long to pick up on the lingo."

"I'm trying to fit in."

"You'll need to work a bit harder on that." Nerissa passed him a bottle opener. He popped the cap off, the gas escaping with a hiss.

"Are you hungry?" She sipped her wine.

"Famished. I'm sure the sea air has molecules in it that increases hunger."

"Dinner's ready. Come on over." Nerissa carried the salad and a plate of steaming boiled potatoes to the table and placed them next to the bread and a selection of cold meats.

"Dig in," she invited.

Jackson helped himself to the food, piling it on his plate. "You're not eating much." He eyed her plate. "No meat?"

"I'm a vegetarian," she explained.

"Have you always been a vegetarian?"

"Pretty much."

"Is it because you don't like meat or is it an ethical thing?"

"The thought of eating an animal makes me cringe. How can people eat lambs?"

"Do you eat fish?"

"No."

"You're surrounded by an abundance of sea food yet you won't eat it?"

"There are some fish species that face the threat of being overfished in Aqua Bay."

"I hope you didn't buy the meat just for me."

Nerissa nodded.

"What will you do with it after tonight? I won't be able to eat all of this."

"You can take it with you. Put it in your lunch for tomorrow."

"You don't happen to have any salsa do you?"

"Ah, no. What do you need salsa for?"

"I'm a Texan. Us Texans have salsa on everything. Never mind. This is a good salad," Jackson said, in between mouthfuls.

"All the vegies have been grown in my garden – the lettuce, radishes, carrots, tomatoes, watercress, and sprouts.

The eggs are from the chicken coop out the back. Do you have trouble sleeping?"

Jackson raised an eyebrow. "No – should I?"

"The white part of the lettuce contains an ingredient which helps us to sleep."

"Well, I'll be darned."

They continued to chat and eat. Jackson cracked open another beer and Nerissa topped up her wine glass. Brad Paisley and Carrie Underwood's *Remind Me* played in the background.

"It's such a lovely night," Nerissa said. "Let's sit outside. I didn't do dessert, but there's still some chocolates left over from the box you gave me."

"You've been very restrained," Jackson said, eyeing the three-quarters filled box.

"I've been nibbling away."

The trees swayed back and forth stirred by the salt air as it drifted off the sea. The wind chimes clattered idly.

They plonked down on the bean bags.

"The mint chocolate ones are all gone," he said.

"Mmm. I ate those." She grinned. "Try this one." She pointed to the love heart shaped one. "This is my favourite."

"And you're letting me have it?"

"The things we do." Her knee bumped up against his.

They sat for a bit, munching on the chocolates and humming to the music. The space between them seemed to sizzle with something alive, something dangerous that simmered away on the surface. She stole a glance his way. Why did he fill her with so many conflicting emotions, make her breath uneasy? Anticipate that he could play havoc with her future?

"I noticed the guitar inside. Do you play?" he asked.

"I'm not sure 'play' is the right word. I'm trying to remember the last time I touched the guitar other than to move it out of the way while I vacuumed. I've always had a dream of being able to play, but I haven't put in the time. I prefer to paint."

"May I?"

"Sure. Go ahead."

Jackson picked up the guitar from inside and began strumming some chords. Not only was the guy a sex god. He had the whole rock god thing going on.

"You grew up in the country?" Nerissa asked.

"Yep. Thirty miles out from a town called Clearfield, right on the edge of the desert. Dry and barren, but the one thing I loved most about it was digging in the dirt. There wasn't much to do and we were miles away from the nearest neighbour so as a kid I'd spend hours and hours rooting out rock and then analysing it with my geology kit. I knew then that there was only one thing I wanted to be when I grew up, a geologist."

He stopped strumming the guitar, propping it up against the side of the house. "I had this absolute passion about rocks. And, yeah, I had pet rocks, my favourite rocks. Kids at school even called me Fred, after Fred Flintstone. Now my mates call me Flinty."

Nerissa grinned. He kind of suited Fred Flintstone.

The wine flooded inside her head. Now was the time to ask the question that she'd been so curious about. She leaned toward him. "You have a large scar on your stomach."

Jackson's mouth lost its merriment and his face hardened. A cold and distant look appeared in his eyes. "I was shot."

"Shot?" Wild, romantic visions of a southern bar brawl where Jackson was defending some woman's honour jumped round in her head.

"My old man shot me."

Her hand flew up to her mouth as she gasped. His father had shot him? Her dinner turned in her stomach.

Jackson was lost, faraway in another time.

"I'm sorry," she whispered.

He took a long swig at his beer. "Don't be. It was bound to happen eventually. I could never please my car-wreck-son-of-a-bitch father. Old Man Joe they called him."

And little by little Jackson told his story.

He'd remembered a happy family in the beginning. His mother, Isabella, young and beautiful, with the long black hair marking her Spanish heritage, one she'd passed to her two sons – Jackson and his younger brother, Antoni, a weak and sickly child who was a disappointment to his macho father. But even living in the prosperous oil and gold territory, Old Man Joe was laid off when the gold prices took a slide and profit margins were squeezed. His reputation as a hard worker preceded him, but he was more renowned for his fiery temper. Anything would set him off and coupled with an increased thirst for booze, the job offers dwindled. If he got a job he was let go within months, the misfortunate company explaining there was "a lack of team fit". Apathy and boredom became Old Man Joe's best friend.

Isabella slaved away as a community health worker, but the money brought in was barely enough to pay the bills. And when letters from the bank arrived as the mortgage defaulted, things got worse.

"I would spend hours after school exploring the desert and digging up rocks. The further away from the house the safer I felt."

Old Man Joe, wallowing in his self-pity and misery, took his fists to his oldest son. "You good for nothing excuse. Hands always filthy playing with those stupid rocks of yours. Why don't you make yourself more useful? Get a job after school. Help out round the house. You thick bastard," he'd yell.

If Old Man Joe had taken one bit of interest in his son's high school education with A plus grades in math, science, chemistry and physics, he would have known his son was a bright boy.

"All hell broke loose one evening. I can't even remember what it was that had set him into a fuming rage," Jackson continued. "But before I knew it, Old Man Joe was laying into Antoni."

Antoni had been off school for a week with glandular fever. The illness had wrenched the energy from the already underweight teenage boy. He could barely get out of bed.

"If it's not enough to have a dense son, but I have to have a sick one as well," Old Man Joe fumed. "Get out of bed, you lazy son of a bitch." He grabbed Antoni by his shoulder and wrenched him away from the bed. Antoni immediately dropped to the floor, legs weak from lack of food and exercise.

"Joe, just leave him," Isabella pleaded from the doorway. "He's not well."

"He's never well. Get up!" Old Man Joe demanded, kicking Antoni in the legs.

Jackson, already nudging 6 foot at seventeen, stood beside his mother and glared at his father.

"Leave him be," Jackson's voice was low. He had always been too afraid to stand up to his father, passively accepting the physical and mental abuse. But now something broke inside him as he watched his old man abuse Antoni.

Old Man Joe cocked his head not believing what he'd heard. "What did you say?"

"Leave him be," Jackson replied, staring down his father.

Isabella, tense, knowing that the situation could escalate out of control placed a hand on Jackson's chest. "Go to your room. I can handle this."

"Don't tell me what to do in my own house," Old Man Joe warned, as he moved closer to Jackson.

"Then act like the man of the house instead of the low-down snake-in-the-grass you've become." He could stand the odd punch from the old man, but his temper boiled when the focus turned to his mom or Antoni.

Old Man Joe's eyes blazed, and in a flash, a fist landed on the side of Jackson's head. Stars flew as he stumbled back into the hall.

"Joe! Joe! Stop!" Isabella yelled, using her body to block Joe advancing towards Jackson.

"Get out of my way woman," he shouted, pushing Isabella to the side. She lost her balance and fell, knocking her head on the chest of drawers.

She yelped in pain.

It was enough to see blood trail down his mom's face to ignite a fierce hatred in Jackson. He ploughed into Joe and beat the shit out of him in a rage of fury. But Joe returned every blow and as the two fought through the hall and into the lounge, overturning furniture and smashing ornaments they moved closer and closer to the shotgun leaning against the wall by the front door. Old Man Joe grabbed the gun and pointed it at Jackson.

"You wouldn't dare," Jackson yelled. As soon as the words left his mouth he knew he'd said the wrong thing. Old Man Joe's eyes, his bourbon-reddened face, the hard line of his mouth dripped with hate. Hatred for a life he loathed, for what he'd become, for the nothing that he stood for.

Jackson backed away slowly down the hall feeling the sides of the walls with his hands. He didn't know where to look – to stare his maniac old man in the eye or stare straight at the shotgun barrel.

All that Jackson remembered next was a loud explosion and something ripping into his stomach. He placed his hand over the warm stickiness and lifted his head in time to see Old Man Joe walk out the front door without so much as a glance behind him.

Nerissa's heart stood in shock. "God, what happened next?"

Jackson looked at Nerissa and drained the last of his beer.

"Mom got me to the hospital. I was there for two weeks not only recovering from the shotgun wound but a nasty infection that had set in. I almost died."

In the first 24 hours after the shooting, his life hanging in the balance, Isabella held a vigil at the bedside of her eldest son, with Antoni in pieces beside her. She held Jackson's hand through a haze of painkillers. He barely made out the words as she begged for forgiveness. But Old Man Joe, through some of his cronies, lay threats against Jackson. A police guard was placed outside his door freaking Isabella out who fled, with a terrified Antoni at her side.

"I never saw mom or my brother again. Two months later the police tracked Old Man Joe to a bar in New Mexico where he was arrested for attempted murder and shoved into prison."

"Is he still there?" Nerissa asked.

"No idea. And I don't care if I never see or hear from him again," Jackson said brusquely.

"What about your mum and Antoni?"

"I don't know what happened to them."

"You mean you don't know where they are?"

"Nope." Jagged shards of hurt riddled his voice.

"Have you tried to?"

"Yep. But after a while everything led to dead ends and as far as I know neither mom or Antoni have tried to contact me. So I figured that they didn't want to be found and I was just a reminder of a past they'd rather forget and I quit looking."

"But surely with Facebook-"

"As I said, I quit looking," Jackson interrupted harshly, indicating that part of his life was now behind closed doors.

Nerissa studied Jackson closely. The deep lines on his forehead and face weren't just from the weather. They reflected bad, sad memories of pain, worry and heartache. Even the tiny grey hairs sneaking through his hairline that she hadn't noticed before were a testament to an uneasy life. She shivered at a sudden drop in temperature. "Let's move inside."

Nerissa sat on the couch and Jackson slumped opposite her. He opened his third bottle, helped himself to another chocolate and picked up where he left off.

"After I was discharged from the hospital I never went back home. There was nothing there for me anymore.

"I hitched a ride to Odessa and lived on the streets for a while. The dream of becoming a geologist seemed so out of reach, but a chance run in with an aid worker at the soup kitchen helped me to fast track my last year in high school. The following year I started working towards a geology degree at The University of Texas. Four years later I graduated and spent a fair amount of time gaining experience in oil fields and mines."

Was it the beer or a happier time in Jackson's life that brought back his jovial spirit?

"You must have worked in some interesting places," Nerissa said.

"Yeah." Jackson's mouth broke into in an ear-to-ear grin. "Kazakhstan; quick exit from Krakatoa as it started to erupt...-"

"Oh."

"Prudhoe Bay Oil Field, Alaska; Greenland; Ethiopia. Chased by bandits there."

Nerissa laughed.

"South-East Asia, Arctic Ocean, Devil's Ankle in Australia – got bitten by a snake and was helicoptered to the hospital."

"Ouch!"

"Patagonia. Fracked in North Dakota." Jackson held her gaze.

Nerissa upended the last of her wine, placed the glass on the floor and tucked her legs under her. "I'm not rising to the bait. I'll just let that pass." She waved her hand. Now was not the time to get into a conflict with Jackson. "Sounds like tough and dangerous work."

"Yep. Amongst the snakes and eruptions there's been earthquakes, flash floods, falling stalactites, quicksand, avalanches, sunstroke in West Africa. Not complaining about the money though. Somehow completed my master's degree in marine geology along the way."

"It must be tough on relationships." Nerissa licked a few stray wine drops from her lips.

"Unbelievingly so." He twisted a stray strand of wool on the throw on the back of the chair.

"No Mrs Darnell then?" Nerissa stroked her thigh. Why was she asking this and why did she sense that something more was about to be revealed?

"Nope. The longest relationship I had lasted three years. But it was too hard for Petra. I don't blame her. I was away for long periods of time and it was difficult to try and pick up where we'd left off. Difficult for Ben too."

"Ben?"

"My son."

And there it was.

139

"He's seven."

"Do you have a photo?" Nerissa asked.

"Yeah." Jackson pulled his phone out. "It's not very recent." He handed his phone to Nerissa. A beaming cute black-haired boy, the splitting image of his father, holding a teddy bear stared back at her.

"He's adorable. Does he poke round in the dirt like his dad?" Nerissa handed the phone back to Jackson.

"To tell you the truth I haven't seen him since I took that photo, over two years ago."

"You haven't seen Ben for two years?" she exclaimed.

"You say it like it's a crime."

"Sorry, I can't understand how that can be."

"You sound like Petra." An edge of hostility crept into Jackson's voice. "It's fairly simple. My job takes me the world over and I haven't had time to play happy family."

"Has Petra made it difficult for you to see Ben?"

"Not at all but —"

Nerissa jumped as her cell phone buzzed. A brief glance told her Scott was calling. She put out her hand to answer it, but let it continue to ring.

"I'd better hit the road," Jackson said, standing up abruptly.

She didn't want the evening to end. She was curious to know more about the strained relationship with Ben — and Petra.

"Thanks for the dinner and the company," Jackson said.

"My pleasure. Do you want to borrow the guitar?"

"Would you mind?"

"Go ahead. It's just gathering dust."

"That's mighty kind of you."

They walked together to the front door.

"Twice in one week, walking home from your house. The neighbours will be talking," Jackson said.

"That's one good thing about living on this road - the neighbours are few and far between."

"I had a great time today," Jackson said. "I can see how much the sea and the dolphins mean to you and I know what you were doing."

"Pardon?" Nerissa said.

"Showing me the dolphins and what damage drilling could do."

A rush surged over her face. How naïve could she be? He had seen right through her plan. "Well, it worked didn't it?"

"Keep your friends close and your enemies closer. Would that be about right?"

"In a way. I thought if I could show you what we have here in Aqua Bay you'd be able to stop the drilling," Nerissa said, staring at the ground.

"I'm not the enemy here. I can't change what I've been asked to do. It's my job."

"Do you ever stop to think how all your digging round under the sea has the potential to destroy so much?" Nerissa's voice rose and she looked directly at Jackson.

"You see it as all bad." Jackson nodded towards her Ford Anglia. "Is that your car?"

"Yes. What's that got to do with anything?"

"Think about it."

Nerissa shook her head. Where was he going with this?

"What does it need to make it work?"

"Petrol."

"And where does that come from?"

Oh God. It had never crossed her mind. The petrol she put in her car probably came from an ocean oil rig. "Point taken," she said, crossing her arms.

Jackson looked down at her. "So before you try and suggest what I can do, how about thinking about whether what you're doing is hypocritical?"

If she could just melt into the ground about now. He was right, but there was a lack of emotion in his voice. He wasn't speaking to her scornfully or derisively. He was opening her mind up. Encouraging her to ensure that her actions, her words, her way of living were all consistent.

"Rather than directing your anger and energy at me, stand up to the big guns. I know you have the courage to do that."

"And what about you?"

142

"I'm always going to be digging in the dirt. I'll always be a geologist. Nothing will change that. I guess we'll just have to agree to disagree."

"Do you think we can still do what we do and be friends?" She frowned.

"I think that it will take an effort on both parts, but let's focus on what we have in common."

"Like chocolate."

"And the sea."

"Yes."

"And the guitar."

"Hmm. I'd have to hear you play first."

Nerissa punched him playfully on the arm. "I'd have to hear *you* play first."

Jackson swung the guitar across his chest. "Night, ma'am."

"Night, Jackson."

And for the second time in a week she watched the tall Texan with the cocky, cavalier attitude walk home.

She checked her phone. Three missed calls from Scott. It was too late to ring now. She'd catch up with him tomorrow.

Chapter 10

Nerissa dipped her toes in, testing the water. A little on the chilly side but once she got started she'd be good.

The pool was virtually empty. At this time of the day, 8 am, it was just the hard core, serious swimmers. Two lifeguards were chatting down one end. A little girl squealed when her mother splashed her with a pool noodle.

She sank further into the water until she was completely immersed and then back up to the top.

After her attack and being unable to get out on the boat, she'd gotten out of the habit of taking an early morning swim and she missed the water flowing over her, round her, and her own time to think.

She glided forward and with long strokes of her arms and powerful leg kicks she completed the first lap of the pool. She let her mind wander. Every time her arm came up to stroke through the water her mind spun from imagined scene to imagined scene.

The picture of a frightened, but brave teenage boy standing up to a gutless father, the misery and confusion of being abandoned by his mother and a runaway living on the streets. He was lucky to have escaped with his life, setting a pattern for his many future escapades. The ability to pick himself up and follow his passion showed strength of character. Jackson had lived, and what had she done? Where was her mark on the world? She kicked and stroked harder, cutting through the water like a shark. Could it lie in Aqua Bay? Was she the catalyst that would get people thinking about protecting the environment? Not only for everyone here now, but for those that came after. Like her children. Could that be her legacy? Something that people would remember her for?

***

Operation Protect had its second meeting on Tuesday night at Nerissa's. She placed a plate of lemon and poppy seed muffins on the table.

Sam grabbed one and munched. "These are seriously good."

"Sorry, I didn't home make them."

Sam smiled and patted his stomach. He didn't seem to mind.

A quick round the table revealed that:

Sam had written to the editor of the Aqua Bay Brief to generate discussion plus had drafted up templates that community members could use to write to the government.

Angie was in the process of raising the issue with Greenpeace.

Peter was talking to the local printers to get some banners and stickers printed.

"What about you, Nerissa?" Mavis asked.

"I've discovered that not only did the government not consult with the community, they were required to by law."

"Holy heck," exclaimed Sam.

"Here, I'll read you the part from the Petroleum Drilling Act: 'Government must consult with Maori, authorities and the community on health and safety issues, environmental risk, protection of areas of local, historical and cultural importance, and to be able to prove any economic advantages have a clear, direct local influence.'"

"You mean that the government has broken its own law?"

"Yes."

Everyone looked at each other as the significance of this information sank in.

"You know, this is serious," said Peter. "Here we have Taxxoil on our doorstep ready to start surveying in the next few weeks and they could be doing it illegally."

"Can we stop them?" Sam asked.

"This is a path definitely worth pursuing," Angie said, "but I think we need to get some legal advice."

"That's something we haven't discussed yet." Peter twiddled his pen round his fingers. "Where are we going to get the money to fund our activities?"

"I think local businesses would be happy to donate money for the stickers and banners, but lawyers' fees are a different matter," Angie replied.

"Let's have a think about that. We might be able to get some legal advice pro bono." Nerissa tapped a note into her iPad.

"Maybe the easiest thing to get underway initially is a petition. Regardless of what the government should've done we need to show we're against any drilling," Mavis offered. "How about you and Peter work on that?"

"Sure. I'm also thinking that what we're going to do is a great step in the right direction, but I feel we could be doing more," Nerissa said.

"What do you have in mind, girl?" Peter asked.

"Well, from the stuff I've been reading I just keep getting a sense that we should investigate things like trying to get Aqua Bay eco-town status and turning the area into a marine reserve."

"You've mentioned this before; that's big stuff."

"I know, I know," Nerissa replied, as she leant forward. "If we could get that status, it would assure Aqua Bay would never be drilled."

"That could take years."

"We have to start somewhere at some time, why not now?"

"It seems we've got two things going on here," Angie said, counting them off on her perfectly painted nails. "The immediate things that we need to do to prevent Taxxoil from getting too far down the track, and the big picture stuff. Nerissa, you seem to be quite passionate about the latter. Why don't you concentrate on that side and the rest of us will look at what can be done now?"

The others nodded in agreement.

"Yes, thanks," Nerissa replied. This was perfect. It would give her the chance to tackle the real, meaty stuff.

As the meeting broke up and Nerissa walked her friends out to their cars, Peter said," I still don't know what you were trying to do bringing that no-good guy out on the boat on Sunday."

"His name's Jackson. I was just trying to show him what we have here in Aqua Bay and what impact drilling could have. It wasn't a social thing," Nerissa said. Had Peter got the wrong impression?

"Do you think it worked?"

"I don't know." Nerissa sighed. "He certainly enjoyed going out, but to tell you the truth I think he's heard it all before."

"I hope most people can see what you were trying to do, but I have to be careful. I can't be seen associating with Jackson what's-his-name out on the boat and be against Taxxoil at the same time. I might be seen as a hypocrite."

"I understand," Nerissa said.

"Good girl. See you tomorrow."

She looked up at the pitch-black sky. Stars twinkled and gleamed, glowing like a million pebbles on the beach.

Scott rang. "What have you been doing?

"I'm just leaving a meeting about Taxxoil. We've discovered the government has slipped up big time – they haven't consulted with the community. We're going to bail them up on that."

Dolphins and the sea-blue of Aqua Bay flashed through her mind. "We need to get legal advice. That's going to cost, which is our biggest worry at the moment."

"I'm sure there'll be a local firm that wouldn't mind getting involved for a minimal fee. What did you get up to over the weekend? I tried to call you a number of times on Sunday night."

Yes, the missed calls. She pulled her cardigan round her. "Not much."

"You took Jackson out on the boat," Scott said, his voice rising.

"How do you know?" She gripped the phone tight.

"I was talking to Katey."

"You were talking to Katey. What about?"

"She wanted some help on her first accounting paper. It's been a while since she's done some study and she's struggling."

"I'm sure she appreciates it," Nerissa said. "That's one of the things I love about you – you're always helping people."

"Yeah, that's me. A good regular helpful guy. So what were you doing taking Jackson out?"

149

"I was trying to give him a hands-on experience at being up close with dolphins so he could see just what Taxxoil could end up destroying."

"Be careful, babe. I'm not sure I trust him," Scott warned, then changed the subject. "It's lonely at the flat without you."

"It's lonely at the cottage without you. Are you coming up this weekend?"

"No, I can't. I'm sorry babe."

"Oh, Scott. That will be two weekends in a row." Her heart withered.

"I know, but I'm making headway, so next weekend's looking good." Scott paused. "Or maybe you could down here?"

"That will be difficult for me. I've got a lot going on too. I've decided to sell Maisie and I've put it up for auction on the web. The bidding closes Saturday. Plus Angie's put up a For Sale sign so I need to start looking for another place to live. And this stuff with Taxxoil is taking time – "

"Wait a minute. You're selling Maisie? You love that car."

"I know, but if I can get a good price for it the money will be good. We're not going to need two cars when I move to the city," Nerissa said.

"I'd prefer if you'd have another think about it, but I'd better go. Take it easy," Scott said. "I'll call you Sunday night. Love you.'

"Love you too."

***

Nerissa and Katey were catching up over lunch the next day before Katey went out on the afternoon tour.

"How's the study going?" Nerissa asked.

Katey laughed. "Stressful. There's just so much to learn and my first assignment is due in a couple of weeks. I seem to be doing nothing but working and studying. Everything's crazy-busy."

"We haven't had time to catch up much over the last few weeks. You should come over for dinner one night."

"Hmm," Katey said, biting into her sandwich. "Great idea."

"Scott helping?" Nerissa bit into her salad brushed a crumb away.

"Yeah. He's been great. He just listens to my rants and raves."

"He does have a knack for calming people," Nerissa said. "He's the kind of guy you want round when you're under pressure. He never raises his voice."

"So spill," Katey said. "What was this thing about with Jackson on Sunday?"

Nerissa explained her reasoning.

Katey scowled. "Unless others round here know what is behind your thinking you'll give them the wrong idea."

"What do you mean?" Was Katey referring to the gossip that was bound to accompany her being seen with Jackson?

"People will think you're siding with Taxxoil."

"That's not true. Although Peter kind of made the same suggestion. And I don't know why they would think that. People know my stand on drilling."

"I just think you're sending people the wrong message, that's all. Anyway, what are my chances of you hooking me up with Jackson?"

"I don't think that's a good idea. He doesn't strike me as a one-woman-man. You saw him with Tanya." She twisted the lid of her drink bottle back and forward.

"Well, she's only good for a one-night stand."

"He did casually mention you though."

"He did?" Katey's eyes widened. "Mmm. A summer fling with a Texan. Tempting, but I'm not sure how long I'm going to be here. There are better opportunities for me in the city. And once I get my accounting degree I'll be earning more money."

"And your summer flings don't have happy endings," Nerissa reminded Katey. "You tend to start things with transients who are just passing through and they leave you heartbroken. Why keep putting yourself through that?"

"Why can't you let me have some fun?" Katey snapped the lid shut on her lunch container.

"I just hate seeing you get hurt." *And I'd have to be there, as always, to pick up the pieces.* How many times had Katey ended up at her front door sobbing as the latest summer romance left to continue his travels elsewhere? She'd be down and swearing off men until the next lonely heart arrived in town.

"You're jealous because you can't have Jackson." Katey's pointy chin lifted slightly.

Nerissa gasped. Here was the nasty streak she'd seen occasionally in Katey. Heat rose in her cheeks and she turned her head away. "I don't want him. I'm with Scott. What an awful thing to say?"

"Yes, sorry. I shouldn't have said that," Katey apologised. "But can you put in a good word for me?"

"What makes you think I'll be seeing Jackson again anyway?"

"Really? It's a small town. You're bound to run into each other again. Besides you're going to hook us up."

Nerissa raised her hands in defeat. "OK. OK. I'll sound him out. But don't say I didn't warn you."

"Hey, give it a chance."

"Katey!" yelled Peter from the front office. "Come and help me prep the boat."

"We must do that meal," Katey said. She wiped her mouth and hurried out the door.

"Let me know when it suits." *And she must talk to Katey about the wedding.*

***

Jackson was waiting beside Maisie when she finished work.

Her pulse quickened. "This is a surprise. How did you know what time I finished?"

"I didn't. I took a guess." He leant back against her car.

"You might have been waiting a while."

"I decided to take my chances." The *couldn't care less Jackson* was back.

"I'm not sure you should be near Maisie given your past driving record," she teased.

"Enough of that." His eyes danced in merriment. "Who's Maisie?"

"The car."

"Maisie?"

"She's named after the 80-year-old I bought her off."

"Well, Maisie needs petrol for it to work, remember?"

"Yes, I know," Nerissa said. "I've been thinking about that. You're right. My values need to be aligned. I've put Maisie up for sale on the web."

Jackson raised his eyebrows. "How will you get round?"

"Bike. Walk. The exercise will be good."

"This must be a collector's item." Jackson studied the paintwork and peered through the windows. "It's been looked after pretty good."

"Did you want to see me about something?"

"Do you think your friend Katey would be interested in going out?"

So the attraction was mutual. "I don't know. She's busy at the moment," Nerissa said. She didn't want Katey to get involved in a short-term relationship, but was that her real motive? "Tanya not doing it for you then?"

"Nothing like variety."

"You're hopeless." She swatted at a fly. "Why don't you ask Katey yourself instead of getting me to do your dirty work?"

"Your buttons are so easy to push."

"Can you please move out the way so I can get into my car?" Nerissa jiggled her keys.

"On one condition."

"What?"

"Come out with me on Sunday."

"What? Why?"

"Does there have to be a reason?"

"Yes."

"Why?" he shot back.

"I don't know."

"How about throwing caution to the wind and see what happens?"

"I don't feel like throwing caution to the wind. I was attacked recently, remember?"

"Yes. Darn. That wasn't the right way to go about it."

"Go about what?"

"Why are we talking in circles?"

"You're being vague."

"OK," Jackson said. "You invited me out last Sunday and you had a hidden motive."

"Yes, so?"

"I went along with it. Now I'm asking the same of you."

"Where are we going?"

"Not telling. You'll have to wait until Sunday."

"How will I know what to wear?"

"I'll tell you later. So you're coming?"

Nerissa hesitated. "Jackson, I don't think..."

"Do you trust me?"

Nerissa looked Jackson directly in the eye. His mood had changed from playful to serious in an instant. He held her gaze until she had to look away.

"Yes," she said quietly.

"Then that's all you need to know." He tipped his Stetson. "I'll call you later in the week."

"You don't have my number."

"Peter gave it to me."

"Well, he shouldn't have."

"Hang up when I call then."

"You're really frustrating, you know that," she called out to him.

"Yep," he said, spinning round and walking backwards up the hill. "I wouldn't be an American otherwise."

Nerissa laughed. What was Jackson up to?

***

156

After work on Saturday Nerissa pored over documents and searched through websites which described the process to obtain eco-town and marine reserve status.

Exhaustion hit her as the shadows grew longer from the late afternoon sun. There was so much information, facts, data, and figures to sort out.

It was not only what could be done in the future, but planning how Taxxoil could be stopped now.

A text came through from Angie.

Just talked to a lawyer. He thinks we've got a good legal case against the government. He's looking into it ☺

Good news. Nerissa texted back.

She rubbed her eyes. Papers lay sprawled across the table and more were on the floor. Her untouched copy of *Modern Bride* sat on a corner of the table. She moved it to the magazine pile in the lounge. She picked the papers up off the floor and placed them on the table. She'd tidy them up later, for tomorrow her work would continue…

Chapter 11

Nerissa's cell phone buzzed pulling her out of a restless sleep. She shielded her eyes from the bright sun hitting the drapes. Her hands fumbled round on the dresser until she located her phone.

Jackson: *Will pick you up at 2.00. Wear trousers and something you won't mind getting dirty.*

Her head thumped. Maybe she should cancel. She had been looking forward to today, but she wasn't feeling up to it now. She typed in that she'd take a rain check, but stopped mid text. What had Jackson planned? She sat up and put her feet tentatively on the floor. If she got up slowly and moved round maybe her head would stop pounding.

She took a Panadol, spent the morning tidying up the cottage and then took a peek at the bidding on Maisie, which was up to $1,000, $200 past her asking price. There was a bidding war going on for her 'baby'.

Finding the key to the backyard shed and after moving all sorts of stuff out of the way, she located her bike at the back. She wheeled it outside where the stark daylight emphasised its muddy and cobwebbed state. The chain was hanging lifelessly off its sprocket. The bike had seen better days, but with some work she was sure she would be able to use it again. Scott would no doubt be able to get it back into working order.

"Is that how you'll be getting round now?"

Nerissa jumped.

"Oops, sorry," Jackson said.

"Don't sneak up on me!" Nerissa snapped.

"Hey, you OK? You don't look OK."

"Thanks," she muttered.

"No, no. That's not what I meant."

"Let's just start again." Nerissa sighed. "Hello."

"Hi, ma'am." He tilted his Stetson.

"You don't need to call me ma'am." She stared at her bike. "It needs some TLC."

"Yeah. Sure does." Jackson knelt down inspecting the chain.

"I'll get Scott to look at it when he's up next."

"I'd be happy to fix it for you." He squinted up at her.

"That would be great," Nerissa said. It would be quicker for Jackson to do it.

"Are you ready?"

"Sure. I'll just get my things and lock up."

They jumped in the Rover and Jackson drove through the township and headed north. It didn't take long to get anywhere in Aqua Bay and soon Jackson was pulling up outside a farmstead. A white sign announcing Aqua Bay Stables welcomed them.

They got out of the Rover and walked over toward a guy who was inside a ring leading a horse round.

"Jackson, right?"

"Yep."

"We've got two horses saddled for you over in the stables. Jaguar is the black gelding; Auryn is the chestnut mare. They're all yours."

"Great."

"What are we doing?" Nerissa asked. She bit her lip.

"We're going horseback riding." Jackson grinned.

"I haven't been on a horse in years."

"Me neither. We kept horses back in Clearfield and I rode them all the time before Old Man Joe had to sell them." Jackson stroked Jaguar's side. "You ready?"

"Sure." Auryn nuzzled Nerissa's hand. Adrenaline flowed through her blood and her stomach quivered.

"I can't remember how to mount a horse." She laughed. She really didn't want to embarrass herself.

"Here let me help." Jackson moved round to her side. "Hang onto the reins." He turned the stirrup towards Nerissa. "Put your foot into the stirrup... that's right... hold onto the saddle horn." A moment later she was sitting in the saddle.

She'd taken horse-riding lessons as a child. Wasn't she supposed to squeeze her calves against the horse to signal it to walk?

Auryn responded at once and followed behind Jackson and Jaguar.

"There's a path here that takes us through the forest that goes for about five kilometres. Apparently the views of Aqua Bay are stunning from the lookout point."

It was an easy walk for the horses, even though the path twisted and turned. The coolness provided by the trees and massive ferns was a welcome shelter from the heat of the day and a lightness spread over her. She relaxed and swayed with the horse's movements.

Jackson was a natural on Jaguar as he clutched the reins with one hand. With his Stetson perched on his head he looked the ultimate cowboy.

The clopping of the horses' hooves accentuated the eerie silence.

"Jackson, stop," Nerissa called out.

He turned round. "What's wrong?"

She put her fingers to her lips and looked up at the trees trying to locate the tui, the distinctive blue bird with its white crest.

"There," she whispered, pointing out the bird.

Jackson craned his neck to get a better look. "Pretty cool," he whispered back.

The tui looked down at them inquisitively, happy in its warbling birdsong. Suddenly it lost interest in the onlookers and flew off deep into the forest.

They continued on. Nerissa relaxed as she got used to the gentle rocking motion of the horse.

Before long the forest thinned out onto an exposed ridge. They had reached the lookout point.

"Do you want a hand getting off?" Jackson asked.

"No. I'm fine. It always seems easier getting off than getting on," she said, as she dismounted.

Jackson took the reins of both horses and tied them to the fence. A chain extended across the path and a sign, 'Danger – Do Not Enter' dangled from it. He stepped over the chain and walked towards the edge of the cliff.

Nerissa remained behind the chain.

"Are you coming?" Jackson asked.

"It says 'Danger – Do Not Enter'." Nerissa pointed to the faded sign.

"It'll be fine."

"Why are there rules that don't apply to you?"

"Don't be so dramatic," Jackson said. "Come on. I'll catch you if you go hurtling over the edge."

She hesitated.

"Come on. I know you can do it," he teased.

Overly cautious she stepped over the chain and followed Jackson up the rise.

"I can't believe all the time I've been living in Aqua Bay I had no idea this lookout was here. Probably because technically the look-out is closed."

"I'd say it's been forgotten about." He pointed at the cliff face. "Looks like there was a slip here at some stage given the amount of debris that's lying over the path."

"How did you find out about this place?" Nerissa sat down on a weathered bench.

"I asked round. I was looking for something outdoorsy to do and when someone suggested there was this horse riding place up here I thought it would be the perfect thing to do."

"And you decided I should join you because...?

"You shared the dolphins with me, although there was a hidden motive," Jackson joked. "I'd thought that it would only be fair to return the favour – from a land-based animal viewpoint."

"Do *you* have a hidden motive?" Nerissa asked, as they settled into their usual banter.

"How did you come to live in Aqua Bay?" Jackson asked, ignoring her question.

"My folks brought us here for family holidays every summer for as long as I can remember. Summers that would go on forever. I loved it. Day after day of brilliant sunshine and life that revolved round the sea. Fresh mouth-watering crayfish and paua to eat. I was a conservation volunteer for the baby seals, which involved giving talks to the tourists and just keeping an eye on the seals. We'd haul up stacks of seaweed for Harold the hermit, who lives up the valley. Help him make this foul-smelling, disgusting brew which he used to fertilise his mint. It obviously worked. He has the biggest bunches of mint I've ever seen." She looked out over the sparkling sea in the distance and the township, nestled round the natural harbour. "It was during those years that my interest in the sea, marine life and the environment led me to uni and a career in eco-tourism, much to my mother's disgust."

"Oh," Jackson said, taking off his sunglasses.

"My older sisters all chose traditional and established career paths – nursing, teaching. They got married and had children, strictly in that order. I don't fit my mother's idea of the way things should be done. I've somehow disappointed her by choosing a less recognised career plus she thinks I'll give it all up when I get married."

"And will you?"

"There's an expectation that I move to the city at the end of the summer and work in, I don't know, some other area."

"I take it that's not what you want," Jackson prompted.

"I have tried really hard to concentrate on the good points about city life, but I just think that the real me lies here." She brushed away dirt from the seat.

"And what about Scott?"

"He keeps pressuring me to set a wedding date and I keep delaying."

"Have you talked about it?"

"No." Nerissa bowed her head. "I love Scott to bits. I want to marry him and have children, but I... I don't know how to

164

describe it. Aqua Bay is in my heart. It's my passion and I feel now with all that's happening with you guys that I'm on some kind of crusade. There's just so much to do. We've set up a group to investigate things that we can do." Should she tell Jackson they were looking at getting an injunction? No, early days yet. She rushed on. "I just see so much potential here. We can be an eco-town and apply for marine reserve status, but it could take years and a lot of hard work and I feel exhausted just reading through all the research papers and websites, and -" She stood up abruptly.

"Hey," Jackson interrupted. "Slow down. Rome wasn't built in a day."

Nerissa rubbed the back of her neck. "Do you think of Ben much?"

Jackson twisted uncomfortably on the seat. "Yeah, yeah. I do. Years and years of living out of a backpack is exciting, but dangerous places start to lose their appeal. Long hours, shift and weekend work even when I was in Clearfield prevented me from forming a permanent relationship with Petra and Ben. But in the last two years the work has become more office based with less field work. It's more about planning programmes for exploration sites, preparing reports and analysing data than hands-on stuff." He bent down and scooped up a handful of dirt letting it trickle slowly between his fingers. The wind shifted and turned the grey dirt into dust and it disappeared. "I've tried to live a life of having both a career and a family and have failed miserably at the family part. Somehow the gloss of travel and even work isn't as shiny as it used to be. I'm not sure Ben would even remember me."

Nerissa suspected that Jackson was hiding the real reason why he had not made an effort to keep in touch with his son. "He was only five when you saw him last."

"Kids have short memories."

"Kids remember their fathers."

"Some for the wrong reasons."

It was then that Nerissa understood what was concerning Jackson. "You're afraid you're going to make the same mistakes as your father."

"I don't want to shoot Ben."

"I can't see how that that would ever happen."

"You haven't seen me when I get mad. I have a temper." The seriousness in his eyes was all too real.

Could Jackson's happy-go-lucky persona quickly change to anger? But surely, he wouldn't shoot anyone?

"I can imagine how what's happened in your past could colour your relationship with Ben. But what about a young boy on the other side of the world who wonders if his father has forgotten him, wonders when, if ever, he will see him again? Do you want Ben to grow up not knowing who his father was, is?"

Jackson turned away. "You know there is something that we might be able to help you with."

There he was changing the subject again when it got way too close for him to handle. She wouldn't push it. "What do you mean?"

"Have you heard of Environmental Protection Values?"

She shook her head.

"Taxxoil started an initiative last year for all of our ship surveys using the EPV. New Zealand has no legislation protecting marine life and this is something that could be the basis other oil companies follow. It's possible that I could get you on board the *Perspeculor* as an observer so you can see how the EPVs are adhered to."

"Really?" Nerissa exclaimed. *I could concentrate more if my headache would go away.*

"Possibly. I can't promise anything."

"That would be amazing if you could." The concept of EPV and being able to observe effects of surveying on dolphins would be an amazing opportunity. She envisaged that the information she might gain would be unbelievably helpful.

"I'll have a word with Mac, the boss-guy, tomorrow. See if I can twist his arm," Jackson said. "We should get back."

They walked over to where the horses were tied.

"Would you like me to help you get back on, curly?"

"I'll be fine. And please don't call me curly or ma'am. I prefer Nerissa."

The devil-smile again. "Sure," he replied. He winked at her.

167

Was Jackson just being friendly or was her flirting with her? Whatever, he looked so damned attractive while doing it.

Nerissa mounted Aryun and they were off again, the forest quickly enveloping them. Just as she was relaxing, the horse tripped over an overgrown tree root and losing her balance she slid sideways off the saddle. With a loud thud, she landed on the ground. She couldn't breathe. Her lungs screamed out for air as she struggled against a vice like grip in her chest.

"Nerissa," Jackson said. He dismounted his horse quickly and ran over to her.

She moaned.

"Here. You've winded yourself." He loosened the top two buttons on her blouse.

Nerissa struggled to sit up.

"Put your head between your knees. It'll help you breathe."

Within a couple of moments her stomach muscles relaxed and she was able to take deeper breaths.

"OK?"

She nodded.

"Did you hurt anything?"

"No," she said. Her breathing steadied. "Only my pride."

"Well, no-one else was around to see so, your secret's safe with me."

She touched her head. The spinning earlier had now turned into a full blown thunderstorm raging in her head. "I can't believe how accident prone I seem to be round you. This is embarrassing."

"I kind of do that to the ladies," he teased. "They just fall head-over-heels for me."

She laughed and then winced as the claps of thunder in her head screamed back at her. "I get so frustrated sometimes." She put her hands up to her face. "I don't know how I'm ever going to be able to do everything and please everybody. There's just too much to do."

"Who do you need to please?"

"My mother, Scott, the Aqua Bay community. It's all too becoming too much and too hard."

"The only person you have to please is yourself," Jackson said, rubbing her back gently. "You set your own path and you stick to it. It's that simple."

Nerissa looked at him through her tears. It couldn't be that simple. Things never were.

"One step at a time. Don't think you have to try and achieve it all in one day. You'll run yourself into the ground. OK?"

She gulped. "Yeah. It just seems overwhelming at times."

"Come on." Jackson stood up and stretched out his hand to her.

As he pulled her up his arms went round her waist drawing her close. His eyes locked onto hers and some force prevented her from looking away. She was mesmerised. Silent questions lay hidden in his dark chocolate eyes. Her hands came up and she placed them on his chest. She had to back away, now, but her heart told her otherwise. He stirred her up inside. Everything swirled and a tension of unspoken feelings flickered in the air between them. She could feel his breath, warm and close to her face, his arms muscular and strong round her. In the silence her feelings were too vast and too deep to ignore. There was no denying she had an affinity with him but then the same old conflicting sense that he would never hurt her, but could hurt all that she loved resurfaced. She stepped back. How much time had passed she had no idea. Was it just a moment or a lifetime?

Jackson turned away quickly. "Let me help you get back on."

"No. I'm fine," she said sharply. Could she trust herself if he touched her again?

Jackson checked Aryun to make sure she wasn't injured. "She's OK. Here." He held out the reins to her.

She stood frozen to the spot. Suddenly the horse looked too big and large and what if she fell off again? She shook her head. "I can't."

"Yeah, you can."

"No I can't."

"Yes, you can." Jackson's voice was low and firm.

"I'm not arguing with you."

"Then don't, so get back on."

"I hate you," Nerissa said.

"No you don't. Get back on the horse."

She stared at him, her temper simmering. Was this the pattern that would always be between them? Moments that went from complete understanding to poles apart. "I can't."

"If you don't get back on now you'll never get back on."

Nerissa heaved a sigh. She scowled at him, but he was right. Face the fear and face it now. And she didn't want to lose face in front of Jackson. With her shoulders back and fresh determination, she cautiously approached Aryun and remounted as if she did it every day. "What are you waiting for cowboy?"

"I don't suppose you want to race back?" Jackson asked.

"Ah no. I've had enough excitement for one day, thank you."

"OK, ma'am," he said, tilting his Stetson.

"Stop calling me ma'am," she said to his back.

His annoying chuckle was his reply. A chuckle that hid the mask of a man who was struggling with his identity. But then wasn't she struggling with her own?

Chapter 12

The next meeting of Operation Protect was on Monday night at Angie's office. She introduced the lawyer, Christopher Rye, from Rye and Astor.

Nerissa stood up and shook Chris's hand. She'd seen him round town. His ginger buzz cut and neat ginger beard standing out. Everyone shuffled into their seats and Chris began explaining the process involved in filing a lawsuit against the government. She wrote down some notes, some big words, some even bigger words. She'd had little dealings with lawyers in the past and she placed them in two groups – those who spoke in plain English without all the legal jargon and those who didn't. Chris fell in the latter category.

Sam tried to summarise what Chris had been saying. "So you think we've a very good case, but it's not going to help us immediately."

"No it won't, but what we can do is file the lawsuit first and then immediately take out a temporary injunction which would prevent Taxxoil from doing any seismic surveying when they're here. I understood the *Perspeculor* is due to arrive in the next few weeks. Of course there is a cost involved to this and while we'd be happy to look at a reduction in fees your best option is probably to get the ORD, the Ocean Resources

Department, to fast track the consultation process. That way you and everyone can avoid a sticky and lengthy court process."

"Getting the consultation process underway could take time and I doubt whether that could be done satisfactorily before the *Perspeculor* arrives," said Mavis.

Chris adjusted his tie. "If we wrote to the ORD that should be enough for them to take some prompt action. I wouldn't go as far as threatening them with legal action, but I'm sure they'll get the message."

"This sounds like a good place to start," Sam agreed.

"How about I draft up a letter and send it to Angie to look over first?" Chris suggested, snapping shut the clips on his briefcase.

Everyone agreed and after Angie had shown Chris out Sam updated everyone on the petition.

"We have over 600 signatures so far and I thought once we get to 1,000 that would be a good number to take to the government."

Peter then showed the mock-up of the stickers and banners and with a few minor changes they were approved for printing.

"OK, what next?" Angie asked. "How about you, Nerissa?'

"I'm still ploughing through all the documents required for eco-town and marine reserve status, but Jackson mentioned something about Environmental Protection Values or EPV, which is a Taxxoil initiative. He's hoping he might be able to get me on the *Perspeculor* as an observer."

"Well, it might be a wasted trip for the ship. We want to stop it from doing anything in our waters, remember?" Peter said gruffly.

Nerissa frowned. If their preventative actions were successful the *Perspeculor* wouldn't get anywhere near Aqua Bay. But she had to find out what the ship was capable of doing out at sea. It was a double-edged sword. "I think we should get Taxxoil to answer some of our questions. Why don't we get a community meeting organised?"

"That would be good. Taxxoil needs to receive a loud and clear message that we're not lying down without a fight and we're not going to make it easy for them," Angie said.

Because time was both working for and against them it was agreed that Nerissa set up a meeting within the next week. More discussion took place round arranging a protest march and Nerissa added this to her never-ending 'things to do' list.

She drove home in Maisie, the windows wound down. The licorice-smell of wild fennel that grew in the valley lingered in the dusk air. The slight roar of the ocean comforted her.

She pulled up outside the cottage. The Taxxoil Rover was parked outside and Jackson was sitting on the front doorstep, unannounced - again.

"Howdy," he said, tipping his Stetson.

Why did that tiny gesture make her heart thump louder?

"Howdy," she said back. "Come to borrow a cup of sugar?"

"Nope. I've brought my magic tool kit." His eyes blinked lazily, lingering on her lips a moment too long.

Nerissa glanced down at a big metal box. "I don't have anything that's broken."

"Your bike needs fixing."

"Oh, yes. The bike."

"Did you want to do it now?"

"Sure." Did he detect the wavering in her voice?

Jackson unravelled his long legs drawing himself to his feet so that he was standing right beside her. His presence washed over her like a crashing wave. His arm brushed lightly against her swamping her in a heat that shimmered across her body. She breathed him in. He so thrilled and confused her all at once. Resisting the urge to flee, she dug her toes into the ground.

"Well, I'll unlock the garage and it's all yours. Have you eaten?"

"Uh-huh." A big burp escaped from his lips.

"Charming."

"Sorry ma'am. I think I ate too much meat for dinner." He clutched his stomach.

"Have you thought about going vegetarian?"

"And be all free-love hippy?"

"Vegetarians are not free-loving hippies." She pushed the garage door open. "There are lots of people who are vegetarians."

"Your buttons are so easy to push."

"Stop it." She smiled up at him. "And, honestly, will you stop calling me ma'am. It makes me feel old." She wheeled her bike out. "I'm just going to get something to eat."

Her phone buzzed. It was Scott.

"Hi," she said, turning away from Jackson.

"Hi. What are you doing?"

"I've just got home from an Operation Protect meeting." She walked inside to the kitchen.

"How's it going?"

"Lots of work to do, but we're looking at our options."

"I've got some good news there," Scott said. "Maindonald Jones Crowley want to contribute to legal costs."

"Really? That's terrific. Did they mention how much?"

"About $10,000 initially."

"Scott, that's so generous." There he was again – forever helping. Was this his way of apologising to her for supporting the other team? Letting her know he really was on her side? Something about the gesture didn't seem quite right, but what exactly, she couldn't put her finger on it.

She glanced out the lounge window. Jackson was hunched over the bike fiddling with the chain. Maybe he could do with a beer. She grabbed a Steinlager out of the fridge, zapped off the top and strolled outside. She handed Jackson the bottle. Shivers crested down her spine when he winked at her. He dropped a spoke wrench on the concrete and she jumped.

"Sorry," he mouthed.

"What was that?" Scott asked.

"Just Jackson dropping a wrench."

"Jackson? What's he doing?"

"He's fixing my bike."

"I could have done that for you."

"Well, he offered. Besides, I need the bike now. The auction on Maisie has closed off."

"How much did you get for her?"

"12,000."

"12,000! I wish you'd talked to me first about setting the reserve. You could have got more for her than that. She's a collectible."

Maybe she could have, but she didn't have to consult with Scott on this. "Oh well. I'm happy with that. And you can check the bike over in the weekend to make sure it's OK." Her stomach grumbled. "Scott?"

"Ummm."

An inner instinct hinted at what Scott was going to say next. "You're not coming up this weekend are you?"

"No, I'm sorry."

"Yeah. I know. Work's busy." She lowered her voice. Jackson cocked an eyebrow.

"This will be the longest time we've been apart."

"I'm sorry," Scott said again. "Why don't you come down?"

It was like ground hog day. Didn't they almost have the same conversation a week ago?

"No. Scott I can't," she said tiredly. Another lonely weekend in an empty bed brought her to tears.

"I'll make it up to you. I promise," Scott said.

There was no response.

"Nerissa?"

"Yeah, sure. I'd better go. I need something to eat."

"OK. I'll ring you later in the week. Love you."

Nerissa rang off.

Jackson dribbled oil on the chain and slowly turned the pedals. "Trouble in paradise?"

"It's rude to eavesdrop!"

"Well, you could've talked somewhere else."

She ignored his comment. "Did it need much work?"

"A few tweaks here and there. A bit of oil and she's almost new." He wiped his hands on an old cloth and burped loudly. "Oh." He clutched his stomach.

"You OK?"

"I don't think that beer was a good idea."

Nerissa looked at the empty bottle. "You didn't need to drink it so fast."

He belched again and grimaced. "I might finish this off tomorrow. I'm feeling a bit off colour. The gunshot to the stomach interferes with my digestion sometimes."

Nerissa studied his face. He did look peaky. "OK. Sorry you're not feeling well."

"I'm sure I'll be fine by morning." He packed up his tool kit and they walked together out to the Rover.

"Thanks for fixing the bike," she said.

He threw the toolkit into the back of the Rover. "I'll call tomorrow," he called out, as he got into the Rover and pulled away.

A massive toolkit was what she needed to fix the threat that was descending on Aqua Bay and the disquiet roving inside of her.

Chapter 13

Nerissa opened the doors of the Aqua Bay Brief offices and was blasted with the hum of journalists and reporters talking frantically on the phone and typing away. Rachel wasn't at her workstation.

She gave the advertising copy of the community meeting to the receptionist and walked up the stairs to the Taxxoil offices.

Two men were there but there was no sign of Jackson.

"You must be Nerissa," said Mac, with a distinct Australian accent.

"Yeah. How did you know?"

"Flinty's mentioned you a few times." Mac pulled a high visual vest off a coat hook.

"This is Brodie."

"Hi ya." Brodie looked up briefly from his lap top and waved a hand in her direction.

"Jackson round?" she asked.

"No. He's feeling poorly. He called in sick."

"More like a hangover." Brodie chuckled. "Can I help you with something?"

"We're having a community meeting on Thursday night and we'd like Taxxoil to come and answer some of our questions." Nerissa handed him a flyer.

"Yeah, sure. We were wondering how long it was going to be before we'd be summoned." Mac studied the flyer.

"Will you let Jackson know?"

"Sure thing. He's our official spokesperson so he'll be the one who deals with this."

"Thanks," Nerissa replied, as she exited the room.

Her feet were automatically taking her through the route she'd taken so many times before.

The entrance to the alleyway loomed large. She stopped dead in her tracks, swallowing down the white-hot panic. Even at this distance the dampness coming from inside almost made her gag. She gripped her bag tighter.

Her attacker was still out there, but he wouldn't be here again. Yet could some other low-life be waiting to pounce on her, make her weak, suck the courage from her? It wasn't worth the risk. She turned away, not prepared to take the risk. She'd walk the long way round.

Reaching the van, she jumped in, locked the doors and texted Jackson.

Nerissa: You're not well?

A response came back immediately.

Jackson: No.

Nerissa: Sorry about that.

Jackson: I have a stomach bug.

Nerissa: Can I get you anything?

Jackson: A new stomach.

Nerissa: LOL!

She smiled and threw her phone in her bag.

***

Nerissa had invited Katey for dinner that night and once they'd finished their meal they cleaned the kitchen bench in preparation for one of their favourite activities – baking cupcakes.

Sipping on their wine, they placed the ingredients on the bench.

"When was the last time we did this?" Nerissa asked.

"Before life got too busy." Katey jiggled the flour around in the sifter.

"This whole thing with Taxxoil is consuming a lot of time."

"Speaking of which, did you put in a good word for me with Jackson?"

"I don't think that's an option anymore," Nerissa said vaguely.

"Oh?" Katey questioned, cutting up the butter.

"I don't think he's dating material."

"How do you know? Did he tell you he didn't want to get together?"

"Not exactly, but I met two of his mates today – Mac and Brodie. You might have a better chance with them."

"You've been spending some time with Jackson, haven't you?" Her voice rose.

"We went horseback riding on Sunday."

"Really?"

"Yeah. His idea." Nerissa opened the box of paper cups and placed them on the oven tray.

Katey stopped mixing the batter. "Is there something going on between you and Jackson?"

"Heavens no," Nerissa replied, as she turned away. "Jackson and I are poles apart particularly round the drilling, seismic surveying and Aqua Bay. We have different values."

"Not to mention that you're a happily engaged woman," Katey said.

"Yes, that too." Why hadn't she mentioned anything about Scott instead of focusing on Jackson?

"I've known you a long time. I can tell when you're bluffing. You like Jackson, don't you? Spill!" She pointed the spoon at her.

Nerissa tilted her head back as she tipped the last of her wine down her throat. "OK, OK. I must admit I do find him attractive."

"I knew it!" Katey exclaimed. "And I should be mad at you. You have been putting roadblocks between Jackson and me, but I do get your point. He smells like trouble." She poured the mixture into the paper cups and placed them on the tray then into the hot oven. "Tell me more, girlfriend. We need to have a heart-to-heart."

Nerissa poured them both more wine and they sat at the dining table. "Despite our obvious differences there's something about Jackson that's so not Scott."

"Scott's every woman's ideal of the perfect man. He's kind and generous and he supports you so much," Katey said.

Nerissa looked at Katey curiously. "You seem to think so."

"A woman would give anything to have what you and Scott have. You can always rely on him, that's for sure. "

Nerissa laughed. "True. He's very predictable." Way too predictable. Was this boring her? Scott and Jackson were different in so many ways. She and Scott had an easy relationship, but it was far from exciting. "Jackson just gives me a thrill. I get an adrenaline rush any time I'm anywhere near him."

"Who wouldn't? That eye candy is enough to make your heart pound and then some. He's a chick magnet." Katey rested her head on her hand. "There's something about him though. I think he's hiding something; he comes across as kind of broken."

"Yeah, he's had a tough life. Broken and trodden on a few hearts too."

Katey's eyes narrowed. "I hope you're not thinking you can change him. I know you Nerissa Taylor."

"Hmm. I'm working on it. But we both have strong values. We each believe that what we're doing is right. Besides, he won't admit he has responsibilities."

"To the environment?"

"To his son."

Katey slapped her hands on the table. "I knew it. He's the ultimate bad boy."

"See I told you he wouldn't be worth getting involved with. He'd just love and leave you."

"Thanks, girlfriend. I'm not ready to be a step-mum."

"And you don't want his ex-harassing you either." Nerissa waved a finger at Katey. "Messy, exes. Despite that, I don't know. Jackson has this confidence about him and an indifference that drives me nuts. You should hear the stories he tells, the places he's lived, the adventures he's had. It makes my life seem boring and monotonous."

Katey jumped up as the timer on the stove bleeped. "You're talking as if your life is over already." She grabbed the oven cloth and pulled the hot tray out of the oven. "You're going to have lots of adventures and that'll include Scott and that cute little family you'll have."

Maybe this emptiness that kept pinging away at her was because she hadn't seen Scott for over three weeks.

"Jackson abides by no rules. He marches to the beat of his own drum." Jackson had freedom and she envied his ability to tell the world, "I'll do it the way I want to do it". Maybe that was her problem. She lived by other people's rules – bending to please others, conforming to their expectations. Worrying about whether what she was doing would meet the approval of others. What would her mother think of Jackson? A directed, purposely intentioned comment and you would be left with no doubt of her disapproval.

"Besides," Katey's voice pulled her back. "All this stuff you're doing to stop this drilling is no easy task. I think you're going to have a fight on your hands there."

Nerissa sniffed. Warm cinnamon mixed with cocoa had her mouth watering. "Hey, they look good, and smell amazing."

"If I don't say so myself. I'd love to hang round for the icing part, but I better get moving. I'm only half-way through my first assignment due Monday."

"Oh, come on. We've got heaps more to talk about. We've only just started and you're already studying too hard."

"Well, as it doesn't look like I'm going to acquire myself a sugar daddy any time soon, I'll have to get my accounting degree and sleep my way to the top."

Nerissa threw a towel at her. "You're not sore at me for steering you away from Jackson?"

"Nah, of course not. Like you say, he's intriguing, but too much hard work. I just don't have the time for that right now." Katey picked up her handbag and phone off the table. "Now I expect these cupcakes will be perfectly iced for us to eat at morning tea tomorrow."

"Sure thing. Hey, and thanks for coming over. I've missed our girly talks."

Katey gave her a quick hug. "One last thing about Jackson."

"Yes?"

"It's OK to look, but don't touch."

"No harm in admiring from a distance," Nerissa agreed.

After Katey left, Nerissa checked to see if the cupcakes had cooled down sufficiently then whipped up the icing sugar and butter. Her favourite themed cupcakes were dolphins so she added some blue food colouring to the icing, piped the icing on the cupcakes and placed a dolphin in the centre of each one.

She licked the sweet icing off the spatula and stepped back to admire her work.

If Jackson was still sick maybe he might need cheering up. She carefully placed four cupcakes into a big container and set off down the road to his cottage.

She walked up the path. The garden could do with a good tidy up as she surveyed the over-grown weeds, and roses that needed deadheading.

Knocking on the door she waited only moments before it was opened.

"Hello," she said.

"Well, what a surprise," Jackson said. "You're a sight for sore eyes and a guts ache."

Nerissa clutched the cupcake container closer. "I just thought I'd drop by and see how you're doing."

"I've been throwing up most of the day."

Nerissa screwed up her nose. "Thanks for sharing."

He looked worse than he did on Sunday; his hair was unruly and he hadn't shaved for a couple of days. He was wearing the same clothes today that he had worn on Sunday – his usual black jeans and black T-shirt.

"Um, do you want to come in? I might be contagious though," he warned.

"I really only popped over to see how you were and I brought these." Nerissa held out the container.

Jackson peeled off the lid and laughed. "You're a dolphin fanatic! I'm sure you're trying to brainwash me."

"I think a constant reminder to you of what I'm trying to protect wouldn't go astray."

"I get the point. Could I save them for later? Food's not sitting too well with me at the moment. The idea of blue icing is already making me feel green. Come in." He opened the door wider and she stepped into the lounge.

It was sparsely furnished. A couch, some lounge chairs and a dining room table barely filled the biggest room in the house. Her guitar leant up against the wall beside the TV. The table had maps strewn all over it. Dirty plates and glasses were piled high on the kitchen bench.

"Sorry," Jackson said. "If I knew you were coming over I'd have done the dishes."

"My place isn't much better. I've still got baking and dinner dishes to wash."

"Wine?"

"Sure," she said.

She looked over the lounge again. A pink, sparkly scarf peeked out from a pile of clean, but unfolded clothes. She'd seen the scarf somewhere before, but where? Oh, yes. This was the scarf Tanya was wearing the night Jackson had bumped into her at The Crab and Apple. Jealousy in all its green glory swept over her. So Tanya had been here and she knew it wouldn't have been for a cup of tea.

She picked up the scarf dangling it from one finger as though it was diseased. It was time to get one up. "I didn't think pink was your colour."

Jackson looked up from pouring wine, his face reddening. "Gee, I wondered where that had got to."

He resumed pouring her wine, handed her the glass, snatched the scarf and threw it in the rubbish bin.

"Don't you return articles of clothing to your ladies who leave them behind?" Nerissa smirked, and took a sip of wine.

"I'd hardly call Tanya a lady!"

Nerissa spluttered, drops of wine escaping from her mouth. "So true. But you've obviously discovered that yourself."

"What did you want to see me about at work?" Jackson asked.

"We're having a community meeting on Thursday night and I was delivering a personal invitation for Taxxoil to attend."

"That's not much warning."

"Well, we've got to keep things moving. Your ship will be here soon."

"OK. Nothing I'm sure we haven't handled before."

"Don't underestimate us. We are a rarked up community."

"A what?"

"Rarked up – it means we're angry."

"Still getting used to your vocab here. You have some funny sayings."

"As do you Americans."

"Say what? Funny sayings. Name one."

But before she had a chance to reply Jackson was running down the hall to the bathroom.

Poor thing.

He reappeared five minutes later clutching his stomach and looking very pale. "I think I'm dying." He collapsed on the couch.

Nerissa laughed. "That's what all men say when they're ill. Time to harden up."

"Oh." He groaned and wiped his forehead.

She filled up a glass of cold water.

"Here," she said gently. "You need to keep your fluids up."

He took a few swallows.

She spied a blanket on one of the chairs and threw it over him. His eyes were closed and the wrinkles and lines on his face twitched. His weathered lips were colourless and there was a tiny scar at the corner. His eyelashes, long and black, and completely wasted on a man, contrasted against his pale skin.

Caught in a spell, she slowly stretched her hand out to touch his face. He muttered something and his eyes opened. She snatched her hand away.

He stared at her.

"Perhaps you should see the doctor," Nerissa said, taking a step back.

"I'll wait until the morning," he croaked.

Well, while I'm here I'll make myself useful. She washed and dried the dishes, put the dolphin cupcakes in the fridge and folded up his clothes. When she had finished she tiptoed over to the couch.

The steady rise and fall of his chest indicated he was sleeping, which was good.

As much as it was a blessing to have the man quiet, he needed to be well enough to address the community meeting. Even if she had to spoon feed him medicine, take him to the doctor's or nurse him 24-hours a day. The meeting was too important for Taxxoil's key player not to be there.

Chapter 14

Nerissa spent the rest of the week organising the community meeting – the hall was booked, refreshments ordered, and invitations sent out to everyone using every method possible.

On Thursday morning Katey phoned in sick. "I think I've got that bug that's been going round," she said, when Nerissa answered the phone.

"Stay in bed until you get better," Nerissa advised.

She grabbed the day's tour stats off the printer. A bus pulled up outside and a group of babbling tourists got off. She would have to cover Katey's shift, but she didn't mind. She relished the opportunity to do two stints on the boat. Both outings resulted in a great display of performing dolphins. The delight on the tourists' faces was priceless.

The last tour was late getting back leaving her scurrying to change into a pair of jeans and sweatshirt. She hadn't even had time today to check to see how Jackson was doing or if he'd even be there.

She arrived at the hall at 6.30 pm to check to see that everything was in order. She went round opening up all the windows to let in the sea breeze. By 6.50 all the seats were taken and it was standing room only. She looked at her watch. Still no sign of the Taxxoil guys. Had they changed their mind at the last minute? Nerissa was just about to ring Jackson when he, Mac and Brodie sauntered in.

"This is cutting it a bit fine," Nerissa said to Jackson.

"And a good day to you ma'am," Jackson said, removing his Stetson. "We said we'd be here and here we are."

"I'll show you where you can set up." Nerissa studied Jackson. He looked pale; his face was thinner and his movements slower. That wise-cracking smile hadn't surfaced. He'd made an effort to tidy himself up. He was clean shaven and his usual hands-on work clothes were replaced by a white shirt with a Taxxoil logo on it and black trousers. He scrubbed up pretty good, although half his shirt was untucked.

Together the three men set about unzipping briefcases, powering up the lap top and connecting it to the datashow equipment.

An older Maori woman, a *kuia*, leaning on an intricately carved walking stick, limped up to the front of the hall. "I need to sit up here, dearie, so I can hear," she explained.

Every available seat in the front row was taken.

"Here ma'am. Let me help," Jackson said. He negotiated with some teenagers a couple of rows back until they reluctantly relinquished a chair. He manoeuvred the chair over the tops of people's heads and set it down in the only remaining space. "There you go, ma'am."

"Thank you young man. I'm not sure I trust you Americans, but your manners are impeccable."

Nerissa smiled. Typical Jackson style. Turning on the charm to score brownie points. She strode up the stairs to the stage. The last time she'd stood here she'd been incredibly nervous. But not tonight. She waved to Angie and Mavis.

"Ladies and gentlemen. We'll get started," Nerissa said, speaking into the microphone. Her voice reverberated loudly throughout the hall. "The purpose of tonight's meeting is to get Taxxoil to answer our questions round deep sea oil drilling." She introduced Jackson, Mac and Brodie and explained their roles. "I'll just hand them over."

"Thank you for inviting us to this meeting," Jackson said, speaking into the lapel mic. "I thought I'd start off by explaining what we'll be doing when the *Perspeculor* arrives." He referred to the PowerPoint slide up on the screen. "We'll be undertaking a process called seismic surveying. We do these surveys to help us understand the geological make-up of the area and help us ascertain whether the area is suitable to extract hydrocarbons."

Jackson ran through five more slides outlining the process involved. Without using industry jargon, he explained the process in lay-man's terms. It was a smart presentation, given with professionalism and expertise.

But, by about the eighth slide, audience side conversations and shuffling feet indicated that he was taking too long to get to the point.

"How about you start answering some of the questions that we have?" A large woman in the second row yelled out.

"Yeah. Let's cut through the crap and get to what's really important," a male voice boomed.

"Hear, hear."

Jackson looked at Nerissa. If his face was pale before, it was even paler now.

"That's a good idea," Nerissa said, speaking out to the audience.

"I don't mind getting the ball rolling."

She spotted Peter in the third row back. "Peter, what's your question?"

"As you know, I run a successful dolphin eco-tour business. My concern is about the risks to marine mammals."

"Yes, Peter. A good question," Jackson acknowledged. "Taxxoil has had a lot of experience working in areas where dolphins and whales serve as revenue for the community. There are a number of international guidelines we adhere to. We would welcome discussion as to how best we can protect the marine mammals in Aqua Bay."

"If oil drilling happens, how will any oil spill risk be managed?" the large woman asked.

Mac answered this one. "We want to focus on prevention first. We have an exemplary safety record and we have extensive oil spill risk management and response plans and we are more than happy to provide copies."

"How many jobs will be created if this all goes ahead?" someone yelled out from down the back.

"It's too early to put a figure on this. We won't have any idea until we know whether there are any commercially viable packets to be drilled," Brodie said.

The questions continued ranging from Taxxoil's analysis of the Gulf oil spill, whether jack-up rigs would be used in case of a blow-out, where oil profits would go and whether Taxxoil would take liability if there was an oil spill.

Jackson answered the majority of the questions. He was heckled a few times, but he maintained control without coming across as too cocky.

Nerissa glanced at her watch. The meeting had been in swing for just over an hour. The questions started to dwindle and it was a good time to wind things up.

"We have time for one more question," Nerissa said.

Sam had his hand up. "I've heard a lawsuit is going to be taken out against the government for failing to consult with Aqua Bay. What would your response be if an injunction prevented Taxxoil from doing any seismic surveying?"

Way to go Sam. This would throw Jackson.

Jackson's head flinched back slightly. "Um... ah.... I've not heard about this." He scratched his cheek and looked over towards Nerissa with narrowed eyes.

She'd let him squirm a bit longer.

Mac and Brodie whispered to each other.

Expectant eyes drilled into Jackson.

"Maybe I can help here," said Nerissa. "As a member of Operation Protect I can say that we're looking at some legal options to prevent the seismic surveying from taking place."

The audience started to clap and there were a few whistles.

"But," she continued, holding up her hand. "This is an unlikely option given the cost and timeframe involved. There is a big process to go through and we will keep you updated as things progress. And, I'm sure, Taxxoil will be kept up to date as well." She turned and smiled sweetly at Jackson.

Nerissa wrapped up the meeting letting everyone know that there would be a regular column in the Aqua Bay Brief with updates.

She hung round for a while as people stopped to ask some additional questions and say hello. Her eyes scanned the hall looking for Jackson, but it looked like he, Mac and Brodie had made a quick exit.

It was still light outside as she unlocked her bike from the stand in the car park. She cycled round the cars and just as she passed the Taxxoil Rover the door swung open. She swerved to the right narrowly avoiding colliding with the door.

Jackson stepped out of the Rover.

"For the love of... You're a menace in that vehicle," Nerissa fumed.

"Well, you certainly need your wits about you round here." He propped his elbows behind him as he leaned up against the vehicle.

"What do you mean by that?"

"Some pre-warning about this legal action would've been appreciated. I feel like I've been blindsided."

"It's early days. It's just a possible option we're looking at," Nerissa said, dismissively.

"I thought we would be able to work more closely on this," Jackson said.

"I have to do whatever I need to do to ensure we are getting a fair deal. I didn't think I was required to report to you on everything."

"I don't expect that. A little heads-up would've been good."

"You can read about what we're doing in the paper."

"You want to play dirty?"

"It's not playing dirty. I just don't feel I have to tell you everything that's going on."

"Nerissa, this is serious. If we're stopped from doing our work here it could mean delays for us that could drag on and compromise the whole project. Costs would escalate. Plus, we might not get paid."

"Is that all you care about? Getting paid? I thought you oil companies were rolling in dough. All you think about is yourself."

"I'm just asking you to reconsider this legal stuff. It could cause a lot of complications all round."

"It's supposed to be about complications and delays. You don't get it, do you? We don't want you here."

"Is it Taxxoil you don't want here or is it me? What are you really scared of?"

Nerissa jerked her head to the side. This conversation was getting out of hand, way too personal and cutting close to the bone.

"I'm late," she muttered.

"Late for what? There's no one waiting at the cottage for you."

God, he could be so infuriating – and mean.

He climbed back into the Rover and banged the door shut. "By the way, blue dolphin cupcakes make an interesting breakfast." He grinned at her.

"I hope you spew up the whole lot."

Jackson threw back his head and bellowed. "So easy to push those buttons." He switched on the engine, pumped the accelerator to a roaring crescendo and took off, gravel firing out behind him.

Turning her head, she coughed away the dry dust as the Rover thundered out onto the open road. She had intended to ask him how he was, but he blew hot and cold. She could never be sure when he was playing the fool or being serious and he always caught her off guard.

She pedalled back to her cottage. Her empty cottage, as Jackson couldn't resist pointing out. Damn him!

Chapter 15

Katey was still sick on Friday so Nerissa worked a double stint again. As everyone disembarked from *Seabird*, the weather swung round to the south. Squally clouds let go buckets of rain and the wind whipped up churning waves.

She ran up to the office.

"You can't bike home in this," Mavis said. "Take the van home. Peter can pick it up tomorrow."

"Thanks, Mavis."

That evening she fixed herself a quinoa and veggie salad. She topped up her wine glass and smiled at Katey's comment: *You can't drink by yourself.* Well, actually you can. *I have no problems drinking a glass or two without anyone's help.*

Looking round the lounge, she surveyed the usual mess that seemed to accumulate by the end of the week. *Scott would be wanting me to tidy up.* Well, Scott wasn't here so she'd leave it another day.

She wandered over to her half-completed painting. Maybe she could spend a couple of hours painting. The light was still good enough, despite the grey evening. But it seemed too much of an effort to get all the paints out.

She sipped her wine and flicked through a magazine when there was a knock at the door.

"Hello, Nerissa?"

"Hey, Rachel," Nerissa said as she opened the door. "Come in."

"You by yourself?"

"Hmm. Scott wasn't able to come up this weekend and Katey's got that flu bug so I'm all by myself."

"And drinking all alone," Rachel said, pointing to Nerissa's half-filled wine glass.

"What is it about not being able to drink alone?"

"I don't know. It kind of paints a vision of a lonely person with no friends," Rachel said, juggling a pile of papers.

"I have friends." *But maybe I am lonely.* "How about you help me drink the wine?"

"Love to, but I'm on my way to a birthday party. I stopped off to show you something you'd definitely be interested in." Rachel pulled a set of papers out of the pile handing a page to Nerissa. "Have a look at this."

It was an email from Jackson to a William.

To: w.smith@taxxoil.com

From: j.darnell@taxxoil.com

Subject Observer on Perspeculor

Hey William

Have a blonde chick causing us a few problems.

I kind of made some noises about getting her on the Perspeculor as an observer as part of our commitment to EPV.

Do you think we could make this happen? It would be to our advantage and could be enough to pacify her without us having to make too many promises.

I need her off my back!

Kind regards

Flinty

Nerissa's blood boiled as she scanned the email a second time. Blonde chick… pacify her… get her off my back…"Where did you get this?"

"Umm… Not revealing my source," Rachel said, coyly.

"Please don't tell me someone hacked into Jackson's email?"

"The less you know the better," Rachel said. "But it's probably best you don't show anyone. It's for your eyes only. Do with it what you want to. I have to say though there is talk round the town."

"What do you mean?"

"People know how hard you're working to help us keep Taxxoil away from here, but tongues talk and gossip starts up. Whether it's true or not. People have noticed the amount of time you're spending with Jackson."

"It's been helpful to talk to Jackson. I'm trying to get him on our side."

"Just be careful is all I'm saying. His true intentions could be different to what you're seeing."

Nerissa bit her lip. Where did the real Jackson start and end? "Thanks Rachel. I appreciate what you've done. But please don't go and hack into people's emails."

"Who said anything about hacking?" she said evasively.

"OK. I'll stop there."

"Have another glass of wine," Rachel said, as she made her way towards the front door.

Nerissa took a big gulp of wine, almost choking as she re-read the email again. Jackson had some explaining to do.

By now the last of the daylight had faded and in amongst the swaying trees and drizzly rain, the light in Jackson's cottage twinkled. What was he doing home this early on a Friday night?

She grabbed the keys to the van and the email and drove the short distance to his cottage.

The slight drizzle was just enough to be a nuisance. She pulled her cardigan over her head for protection, running down the path and banging on the front door.

The door opened. Jackson didn't seem at all surprised to see her as he leant against the door frame with a Steinlager in his hand.

"Hello neighbour," he drawled.

"This isn't a social call." Nerissa pushed past him.

"What's wrong?"

"You think this is all a game, don't you?" She threw the email at him.

His reflexes were good enough to snatch it with one hand. He put the Steinlager down on the table.

She watched him in silence, her heart pounding.

"Where did you get this?" His eyes clouded over.

"It doesn't matter. What matters is how trivial you make all of this, me. I'm just 'a blonde chick'? Why couldn't you have at least called me by my name?"

"You're taking this too personally."

"See, there you go trivialising it again. And pacifying me? Were you really genuine about getting me on the *Perspeculor* or was it just to shut me up?"

Jackson's face reddened and his fists clenched.

"I thought so. I know that we believe in and stand for different things, but I thought we had at least some kind of understanding. To try and keep it professional."

"I *am* trying to get you on the *Perspeculor*."

"I don't believe you. Is this some kind of revenge because I didn't tell you about the possible legal action?" she yelled.

"No... No..."

"You're just trying to humour me."

Jackson stepped towards her. "I'm not the enemy here. You're lashing out at me. But it's not me you should be directing your anger at. You're angry at whatever it is that could destroy your paradise whether it is Aqua Bay or your personal life."

"My personal life is of no concern of yours," she shot back.

"And your personal life is not all that hot either."

205

Jackson flinched. "I'm sorry. You're right. That email was insensitive."

"Just stay away from me. I mean it this time." She turned away from him, but he grabbed her arm.

"Nerissa, stop." He pulled her against him. His arms went round her waist, his rough stubble scratched against her face and his mouth was on hers, hot and hungry.

She pushed her hands against him, resisting the desire to either slap him or hold him. He took the decision away from her as one strong arm clasped her tighter and the other dug into the back of her neck, lost in her curls.

His mouth travelled down her neck and she moaned as she arched her head back. He broke away. His black-as-oil eyes stared deep into hers.

Jackson pulled her T-shirt over her head.

As soon as her arms were free, her hands fumbled on his top shirt button. The button refused to go back out the hole. Frantically, she yanked the shirt apart buttons popping everywhere.

She surrendered, pressed up against Jackson's chest, and melted into the exquisiteness of skin-on-skin. His rough lips pressed on hers and she responded with urgency. She breathed him in; the raw earthiness, mixed faintly with dry sweat, cologne and beer.

His greedy mouth was busy again along her neck, then down further. He pushed the front of her lacy bra aside with his tongue and encircled his wet mouth over an erect nipple. She kissed him with abandonment and moaned louder.

"Oh hell," he whispered.

A voice inside of Nerissa's head yelled *stop, stop, stop, no, no, no* but the excited pounding of her heart was too intense to ignore. He lifted her off her feet, she wrapped her legs round his hips and he carried her down the hall flinging her on to the bed.

Mouth was on fiery mouth again. He undid the belt on her jeans and unzipped her jeans.

One hand traced the top of her panties, inside, then down further into her wet folds.

"Oh," she gasped, grabbing his butt and pulling him closer.

His other hand lowered his zipper, releasing him. With one thrust he plunged into her. Nerissa cried out in a combination of pain and pleasure that she'd never felt before. Everything that she'd fought hard to contain – frustration, fascination and curiosity – collided all at once. He moved slow at first, then faster, until their bodies rocked furiously to one rhythm. She arched her back, brought him to the brink and he exploded into her. Her muscles clenched round him and she shuddered as a glorious wave passed through her.

"Ah, Nerissa," he whispered. He kissed the top of her forehead and then gently rolled off her.

They lay side by side, panting.

Nerissa stared up at the ceiling. This was a different type of sex than she had ever experienced before – hard and fast, wild and furious and she liked it. But her euphoria suddenly turned into a nightmare, slamming into her.

The enormity of what had happened hit her. She put her hands over her face. "Oh no. What've I done? What've I done?"

She stood up in a panic, pulling up her jeans. "I've got to get out of here."

"Wait." Jackson's hand grasped her arm.

"Don't touch me," Nerissa said, wrenching away.

She stumbled down the hall looking for her T-shirt.

"Nerissa, wait, please."

She flung her T-shirt over her, located her keys and phone and ran out to the van. Tears coursed down her cheeks and blinded her vision. Jackson was on the porch, yelling. Throwing the van into gear she swung out onto the road, scraping the side of the van against the Rover. She gulped, but kept driving. Wiping her tears away, she pulled into her driveway, clipping the fence. There was a splintering sound as wood met metal. Nerissa braked hard jerking the van to a stop.

She ran inside and bolted the door. She paced up and down, back and forward her head whirling. *What have I done? What have I done?* The question went, over and over and over in her head. She banged the heel of her hand against her forehead and let out an anguished, "Argh!"

Hurling herself onto the couch she cried and cried and cried against her shaking hands.

Katey. She scrolled through her contacts. F, G, H, I, J – Jackson. A new surge of tears erupted. K – Katey. The cell dialled the number.

Katey picked up on the second ring.

"Katey. Can you come over please?"

"Sure, Nerissa. What's wrong? Are you OK?"

"No. No. Katey, please come now."

"I'm on my way."

***

"Tell me what's wrong?" Katey said, sitting down beside Nerissa, and hugging her shoulders.

Nerissa took a couple of deep breaths and blew her nose in a tissue.

"I went over to Jackson's. He and I... We... Umm... did it."

"Oh my God!" Katey exclaimed. "Did he hurt you?"

"No, no. It was nothing like that. We both knew what we were doing," Nerissa said. "I... we... it just happened. I went over there to confront him about an e-mail. I was so angry. We touched. He pounced on me. In one crazy uncontrolled moment, I couldn't stop myself. It was all over in a few minutes. I still had most of my clothes on." She hung her head and wiped her eyes.

"What happened then?"

"I was beside myself. I couldn't believe what I'd done. I left in such a hurry. I was crying and I dinged his Rover and then my fence. Shit, Katey. What am I going to do?' she asked in desperation.

"First," Katey said. "I'm getting you a Milo. Then we'll think about it some more."

"I don't want to think about it. I wish I could just erase the last half hour of my life. Make it all go away."

Katey put on the jug on and made the Milos. Nerissa sipped her hot drink.

"Better?" Katey asked.

"I'm sorry I dragged you out here. You're probably still sick."

"I'm feeling much better. To tell the truth, I probably could've come to work today but hey, it's Friday."

Nerissa's mouth turned up in a half-smile. That was a typical Katey action. Work was just the means to an end. She had no vested interest in the eco-tour business. Work was secondary to late sleep-ins and scoring the next man.

"What am I going to do about Scott?"

"Do you love him?"

"Yes, of course I do. I would never intentionally hurt him. This was something that just happened, that should never have happened. Oh, God. Should I tell him?"

"I would think very carefully before doing that," Katey said.

"But then I'd be lying."

"Well, no. you wouldn't be lying. You just wouldn't be telling him everything. They're two different things."

"I don't think I could bear carrying round this guilt," Nerissa said.

"OK. What do you think would happen if you told him?"

"He'd be devastated."

"Do you think he'd break up with you?"

Nerissa shivered. Would he? She had no idea. She shook her head. No, Scott wouldn't.

"What if you didn't tell him?"

Nerissa was silent. Could she live with her dishonesty? "I don't know if I could do that."

"Look, who's gonna know? I know, you know and Jackson knows and he's only here for a short while and then he'll be winging his way back to the good ole US of A. Problem gone. You'll just have to swear him to secrecy, and stay away from him."

Was it that simple? Katey wouldn't say anything, but what about Jackson? She'd have to talk to him. No, that wouldn't do. She didn't want to talk to him. She'd send him a text. Yes, that would be the best thing. "Perhaps you're right. It wasn't like we planned for it to happen. I'll just put it behind me and forget about it.'

"Yeah. Best idea."

"Thanks Katey. You're a great friend."

"No probs. I'd better go. I kind of made some loose arrangements to meet up with the new bar guy at The Crab and Apple."

"Yeah, sure. Be safe," Nerissa said.

Katey laughed and gave Nerissa a quick hug. "You too."

Chapter 16

His scent was still on her. She scrubbed and scrubbed until her skin was raw. Her tears mingled with the fire-hot water, which beat over her. She washed the lather of soap away. If it was only that easy to wash away her guilt. She stared at the water as it spiralled round the drain. If it were any bigger and faster maybe it could pull her down as well.

She turned the tap off, wrapped a towel round her and stood on the bathmat watching the misty steam beads twirl and whirl round her. She rubbed her red skin dry.

A loud thump came from somewhere inside the house. She froze.

Silence.

Nothing.

She hung the towel on the back of the door and flung her dressing gown on.

There was a bang against the outside of the bathroom wall. The bedroom was on the other side. A drawer opened and shut. God, there was somebody inside the house. Her legs shook. She grasped one leg to steady it. Did she forget to lock the front door? Was it Jackson? How did he get in? Was she being burgled? Did her attacker know where she lived? Steam floated in the air round her head. Sweat broke out on her face and she brushed the beads from her lip. Keys crashed to the floor. A male voice swore.

She took a deep breath and opened the bathroom door a fraction. The wardrobe door squeaked shut. She looked desperately round the hall for something that could serve as a weapon.

The man was still in the bedroom.

She peered round the door.

"Scott!" What are you doing here?"

"Surprise!"

A mixture of relief and shame enveloped her. She walked over and slumped onto the bed.

"Work's returned to a more steady pattern so I thought I'd come up for the weekend and surprise you." He rolled up his shirt sleeves, loosened his tie and sat down on the bed beside her. "What are you doing having a shower at this time of night?"

"I was.. um.. painting. I got paint over my arms, and it's been a hot day." She scratched her neck.

"Hmm. You smell nice." He kissed her head.

"I'm sorry," she said. Tears crept down her face. "I'm so sorry."

"Hey, babe. What's wrong?" Scott rubbed the small of her back.

"I've been so lonely. I've just missed you so much. Hold me."

"Aw, babe. It's me who should be apologising. Work has taken over. We shouldn't be apart for so long like this. I've missed you like crazy too." He wrapped his arms round her and kissed her gently on the mouth.

They fell back on the bed. Nerissa's dressing gown fell open exposing her nakedness. She quivered as the roughness of Scott's trousers against her skin rekindled an image of another half-dressed scene.

Scott's eager lips travelled down over her breasts, her stomach and back up to her face. She whimpered as his fingers glided over her mouth. She flicked her tongue over his little finger, sucking it. Scott, the gentle, oh-so-considerate lover, taking care of her needs, taking his time to make sure she was ready. But it was too predictable and not enough for her any more. She had always let him take the lead and that had been enough for her. But another part of her had now been awakened. It was her turn to take control.

They were locked in a sumptuous kiss. Nerissa reached down between Scott's legs.

"Whoa! Nerissa, careful. Slow down," Scott yelped.

"Scott, please, hurry. I need you inside me – now."

Nerissa's hand guided him to the tip of her and he easily slid in. They rocked together slowly at first then their movements gathered force and speed.

"Faster," she groaned.

Scott upped the tempo. He emptied himself into her and she cried out, her body spasming. She laid her teeth into his shoulder.

"Ouch! Shit! Nerissa, what're you doing?" Scott pulled away.

"Sorry." What had come over her? She was like an untamed animal. She needed to make love to him, needed him, and wanted him, not only because she missed him, but to erase the memory of what had happened. Was it only a couple of hours ago?

Scott rubbed his hand over the grooves made by Nerissa's teeth.

Her hand ran lazily across her moist stomach. The tension now released made her drowsy.

"That's the best homecoming present a guy could ask for." He kissed her cheek.

Nerissa threw a leg over his. "Who said it had to be just one present?" Her need for him stirred in her again and her hands wandered south.

Scott gently halted her hands. "Hey, I need some recovery time. Plus a shower." He hopped off the bed. "I'll be back soon."

Nerissa watched as he walked past her and into the bathroom. She let out a long sigh. Emptiness swamped over her with a strange calmness, leaving her unfilled.

She buried her head in her pillow, willing her mind to banish Jackson. Muffled sounds of water in the shower next door and now a steady rain on the roof provoked her into an unsettled drowsiness.

***

Scott lay awake in the darkness, sleep elusive.

Maybe the long hours of working, trying to fit in time training for the next run, and his dash up to Aqua Bay to be with Nerissa were preventing him from relaxing properly.

He turned on his side, his mind wandering to his twenty–first birthday seven years ago, a day he would never forget.

Lou and Sharon, proud parents, had thrown him the typical twenty-first birthday party. His uni mates, relatives, his girlfriend, and a-couple of old school friends completed the small gathering.

The speech Lou had made left him no doubt that he was expected to join his father in the family's accounting business when he'd complete his accounting degree. He was a natural with figures. He'd topped all his grades in high school in maths, accounting, and economics. Seven years ago he could think of nothing else but joining his father in the business as a junior, where he would work his way up in the firm, becoming a partner and eventually owning the business when his father retired. It was the Maindonald family tradition. Lou had inherited the business following in the footsteps of his father, who had built it to be one of the oldest and most respected in the city. Lou was even thinking about expanding the business to other parts of New Zealand.

217

No one had held a gun to his head, it was the course of an only child. After years of trying unsuccessfully for another child, Lou and Sharon put their disappointment behind them and threw all their attention and energy into Scott. He was the apple of their eye, their darling.

As the years ticked by, Scott slowly gained the accounting experience required. He met the love of his life, proposed to Nerissa and with the nest egg they had together had chosen a spot of land to build their dream home and one day start a family. His own son or daughter to eventually join him in the business. His life would be complete. He would be satisfied.

But why was it that in the last six months he had struggled with the extra pressures of work, his father's plans to expand the business and take on exciting, but demanding, new clients. And there was Nerissa. Her attack had frightened him beyond belief. He hated being so far away from her. Although this was something they had discussed and agreed to, she seemed to be resisting moving to the city. She was slipping away from him. He couldn't put his finger on when this had started to happen, but a persistent alarm bell had been ringing, desperately in his mind. And desperate thoughts had required desperate action.

Nerissa stirred beside him. Her blonde hair, a mass of uncontrolled tangles fanned out over the pillow.

She murmured. What was she saying? She tossed her head from side to side, her breathing erratic. "No, no," she cried.

She muttered something. Did she just say 'Jackson'? Confused he moved closer, straining to hear.

She whimpered, but the words were now gibberish.

"Shhh," he said gently, caressing her forehead. "Shhh."

Her breathing steadied, her head stopped moving and there was silence.

Unease threaded his mind. *Come back to me, Nerissa.*

Work would settle down and with the summer ending and Nerissa joining him in the city, life would be stable and certain once again.

Why would he believe otherwise?

Chapter 17

Nerissa slipped out of bed and made breakfast.

She prepared a tray and carried it into the bedroom setting it down on the dresser.

Scott was dozing. She pulled the curtains, letting the sun stream in. The rain from the night before had left droplets of water covering the garden and as she opened a window she breathed in the gorgeous dampness, mixed with the summer's scents.

"Good morning. I've made you breakfast," Nerissa said. She kissed him on the lips.

"That's my job to bring you breakfast in bed," he said. He rubbed his eyes and pushed himself up into a sitting position.

"I just wanted to show you how much I appreciated you coming up here. I missed you."

"I couldn't stand being away from you any longer," he said, taking a bite from the toast and taking a long swig of OJ. "Geez, I'm hungry."

"I've got a surprise for you. " She sat down on the bed and passed him a piece of paper. "Here."

Scott stared at the date: 14 June 2018. "Is this the day the world ends?' he asked.

"Nooo."

"Something to do with dolphins?"

"Nooo."

"We win lotto?"

"Nooo."

"OK. I give up. The suspense is killing me."

"This is the date you and I will get married." She smiled.

"You've picked a date?'

"Yes. As long as you're OK with it. I think we shouldn't delay any longer."

"Nerissa, I'm so pleased," he said, reaching out for her hand. "I feel like we've been in limbo."

"Me too."

Scott squinted at the date again. "This is only five months away. It doesn't give us much time to organise it."

"It's been done before in a lot shorter time."

"Why don't we move it out further?"

"No, no," she snapped.

Scott's eyes widened. "It was just a suggestion. I know I've been pushing for a date but we don't have to do it this fast. I don't want to see you getting stressed after what you've been through."

Nerissa sighed. She shouldn't have spoken so sharply. She entwined her fingers in his. "I'm sorry. I just really, really want to get married."

"That makes me a very happy man to hear you say that."

Nerissa leaned forward to kiss Scott. His hands enveloped the curve of her back pulling her to him. His mouth covered her face with light, feathery kisses that became more demanding.

"Make love to me," she whispered.

"You're insatiable, but I couldn't think of a better way to start the day," Scott said, as he moved on top of her.

***

Nerissa spent the morning in the garden pulling out weeds, deheading flowers, turning over the compost and gathering the eggs from the chicken coop. Her small herb patch was doing well. The oregano had burst out into white and pink flowers sending the bees into overdrive.

Scott checked over her bike and cycled up and down the drive to test it. "What happened here?" He bent down to pull a broken fence pail into place.

"I hit the fence last night in the van," Nerissa said. She yanked a weed out of the dirt.

"I thought you stayed home and painted last night."

She swallowed hard and turned round inspecting the damage on the van. "I did. After I went for a few drinks with Katey." Katey would back up her story.

"Oh," he said, tilting his head to the side.

"Something wrong?" She turned back round to face him.

"No. No. I'll just get a hammer and knock a few nails in. I think that'll be enough. Be a bit more careful, babe."

Nerissa watched him as he headed back to the garage. Could Scott tell something wasn't quite right? She gulped. She'd have to be more careful.

Later on, they prepared dinner together.

Nerissa whipped up the eggs, milk and flour for the veggie frittata she was making. "Can you get the cheese for me?"

Scott pulled open the fridge door. "Since when've you started drinking beer?"

"I haven't. They're Jackson's." *Best to be straight here.*

"Jackson's?"

"Yes. I invited him round for dinner last weekend." *Keep it light, keep it light.* " Why, are you jealous?" She came up behind him and wrapped her arms round his hips.

"No, of course not. It's just that you seem to be spending a fair amount of time with him lately."

She dragged her hands through her hair. "How else am I supposed to spend my time every weekend when you're not here?"

"There's Katey."

"Katey's turned into a very studious student. She's quite serious about these accounting papers she's doing."

"That's a good thing for her."

Keep the topic away from Jackson. "I know. It's good for her to have something worthwhile to work towards."

She chopped up the veggies and kept her head down. Scott nattered on about how committed Katey was to her studies.

They ate dinner on the back porch. The hens pecked round the garden, their squawking almost drowned out by the roaring of the sea at high tide.

When they had finished Scott presented her with a piece of paper. "Here."

She scanned it and straightened up in her chair. It was a bank confirmation of $10,000 from Maindonald's to Operation Protect.

"Remember I said we'd help cover the legal costs?"

"Scott, I don't know what to say. I didn't think it would actually happen. This is so generous." She leant over to kiss him on the cheek. This was such a sweet and typical Scott thing. A painful lump formed at the back of her throat. And she still couldn't hold eye contact with him for any longer than a second.

She cleared her throat. "Thank you. This will be really helpful. You're a star."

"I hope it helps. We do support what you're doing even if there's no clear outcome yet."

"Hopefully we can get further ahead this week with the consultation issue at least. How will we able to repay you?"

"I don't know about the 'we', but I know what you can do."

"Mmm, what's that?" She smiled at him.

"Feel like an early night?"

"You bet."

***

"I'm glad I came up for the weekend." Scott kissed her on the top of her head.

"Me too." She focused on the bonnet of the car.

"I'll see you soon." He gave her a final squeeze, placed his bag in the boot then drove down the road back to the city.

Nerissa stumbled inside and collapsed in a heap on the couch. The tension within her since Scott had arrived at the cottage had been unbearable. It was all she could do to keep it together. She clutched a cushion to her chest. The guilt was tearing her apart.

How could she have let a moment of weakness almost destroy everything? She was such a hypocrite. So busy convincing everyone else about right from wrong. She couldn't even follow her own 'rules'.

Scott arriving when he had on Friday night had been a close call. If she had been an hour later...

How had she been able to keep herself under control all weekend when all she had wanted to do was cry? And confess. It had been on the tip of her tongue so many times just to blurt it all out to Scott, but something always stopped her. She had lied about where she'd been on Friday night. Had Scott suspected? Lying meant covering up, making up other lies and eventually it could come undone.

225

She twisted a corner of the cushion. Maybe Katey's advice was the best. Let sleeping dogs lie. Scott must never know. She didn't want to hurt him and all confessing would do would release her guilt.

And Jackson? She would stay as far away from him as possible. She would not let him destroy Aqua Bay or jeopardise her relationship with Scott. Ever. She had a new goal now. A wedding to organise.

Her cell buzzed.

Jackson: Are you OK?

Now he wants to check on me? He had probably seen Scott's car outside the cottage over the weekend. At least he'd had the foresight to wait until he'd gone.

She deleted the message without replying.

Chapter 18

Monday morning

Nerissa confessed to Peter she'd dinged the van, which didn't go down too well. "We've just had it fixed after the last ding," he mumbled.

To escape his gruffs and mumblings, she drove into town to the Blue Penguin Café to do everyone's 'real coffee' orders.

"Hi, Nerissa," Yvette, the barista, said. "The usual?"

"Thanks." She placed her refillable cup on the counter. Yvette banged out the used coffee grounds.

She flicked through the latest edition of the Aqua Bay Brief as people were coming and going with their drink orders.

Off to the side she spied Mac and Brodie ploughing into one of the Blue Penguin Café's specialities, the Great Kiwi breakfast – eggs, bacon, tomatoes, hash browns and baked beans.

Her ears pricked up as she caught snippets of their conversation in between the coffee machine frothing.

"...*Perspeculor*'s arriving Friday..."

"...not sure ETA..."

"...can start the seismic surveying..."

"...finally, can get out in the field..."

"…good for Jackson. He was like a tightly wound up spring yesterday."

She leaned closer. *What was that about Jackson?*

"…some foul mood…"

"…woman trouble…"

"…more likely women trouble…"

"…stay out of his way…"

Never mind about Jackson. The *Perspeculor* would soon be here to seismic survey, but not if she could help it!

"Here, Nerissa," Yvette yelled out.

Back at work as they drank their coffees, Nerissa relayed the news to Peter, Mavis and Katey.

"I don't think we can do anything to stop this if they're that close to arriving," Mavis said.

"It would be a perfect time to do a protest march. And remember we still can get Chris to push the lack of consultation thing."

"Thursday doesn't give us much time."

"It won't be that hard. I know we can organise it by then."

"Go ahead, Nerissa," Peter said. "Take as much work time as needed in between tours to do it."

After an invigorating morning tour where the dolphins put on a good show, Nerissa posted the march details on Operation Protect's Facebook page. *Don't let deep sea oil drilling destroy Aqua Bay. Take a stand against Taxxoil.* Response came in fast; over 400 people said they'd be there.

Sam had taken charge of getting a group organised to design and make banners and signs.

"The difficult thing about this is that we don't know exactly what time the Perspeculor's arriving," Nerissa said, at a hastily arranged Operation Protect meeting that night. Temptation to text Jackson to see if she could get an inside word was strong, but she stood fast on her promise to stay away from him.

"Rachel," Angie said.

The same way the e-mail that "had fallen off the back of truck" had been obtained?

Nerissa bit her lip. She wanted everything to be done above board, but if it was a way of getting the information they needed…"I'll leave you to contact Rachel."

Tuesday

Nerissa received a phone call from Rachel. "Inside information says the *Perspeculor* has been located out at sea and has an ETA of 3.00 pm Friday."

"Thanks Rachel. Can I ask where did you get your information?"

"Hey, I'm a journalist. I could tell you, but then I'd have to kill you."

Now she had enough information to arrange the logistics of the march to coincide with the arrival of the ship.

Friday 2.30 pm

Nerissa peeled off her work clothes and pulled on an old pair of shorts and a bikini top.

Cars tooting and the excited chatter of people wafted through the open windows of the public toilets down on the water front.

Placing a large plastic container on the cold steel bench, she opened the top, releasing the sweetness of a ready-made mixture of corn oil, starch and cocoa powder. Perfect! She gave the mixture a quick stir.

She poured a thin layer of molasses across her chest, arms and legs. Dipping her hands into the corn starch she wiped the sticky mixture over the molasses.

Women coming in and out of the toilets gave her a combination of strange and slightly amused looks. Teenage girls pointed and giggled.

She ignored them as she stared at herself in the mirror. It wasn't enough. There needed to be more. Up-ending the tub of molasses over her hair, she watched it trickle down her face and form dark lumps on her head. She rubbed it into her hair, creating a sticky tangled mess.

Now that looked more like it. She closed her eyes. This would be what it felt like to be a dolphin, seal or bird covered in black oil weighed down by a thick glutinous slick. Oil that had leaked from a deep sea oil rig.

A fiery light in her eyes burned with determination. She would make damn sure nobody would hurt her beloved animals. They didn't have a voice so, she would be their voice.

She pulled her shoulders back and breathed in deeply.

She had a point to prove and nothing was going to stop her.

2.45 pm

Women with strollers, men of all ages, and a large contingent of students had gathered at the bottom of Craypot Road. There were special interest groups – hunting and fishing, diving, the SPCA, fishers, representatives from businesses: - people who probably didn't have an opinion either way, but came out to see what all the fuss was about, the surf lifesaving club and 'greenies' with their dreadlocks and peace T-shirts.

Nerissa threaded her way through the swelling crowd, ignoring their stares.

At the front Peter, Mavis, Katey, Angie and Sam stood with a huge black banner with white letters, 'No drill, no spill'.

"Nerissa!" Sam exclaimed. "My God. What have you done?"

"Way to go!" Katey said.

"This is taking it a bit far, girl," said Peter, eyeing her up and down.

"I don't care. Let's do this," Nerissa said. The noise from the crowd beat in time to the adrenalin pounding through her veins.

Sam checked his cell. "Our timing is perfect. The Perspeculor is in the harbour and just about to dock."

She looked behind her. The banners and posters were held aloft in the air: *Say no to deep sea oil drilling*, *'We'll die* (with photos of dolphins and whales) and *You're not welcome, Taxxoil* (with the Xs emphasised as skulls and crossbones).

"Here take this," Sam said, pushing a loudhailer into her hand.

"What? Why me?" Nerissa protested.

"You look the part. You're our 'Save our community' poster girl. Come on, Nerissa. We need a leader. You're it."

If there was ever a time to step up and show she really meant it, demonstrate her powerful conviction, this was it.

"OK. Let's get this show on the road." She licked her sticky lips as the fake oil started to melt in the hot sun.

They needed a chant. *What? What? What?* She raised the loudhailer to her mouth and turned to the crowd.

"What do we want? No drill. Do we ever want it?"

"No!" yelled back the crowd.

"Say no to drilling," she yelled out.

"No drilling."

"What do we want?"

"No drilling."

The excited crowd moved forward jostling their banners and chanting.

Nerissa looked up Craypot Road. The *Perspeculor* was docking.

The drilling equipment was clearly visible and it made her blood boil. Now this was a reality. This was really happening.

The gated entrance to the wharf prevented access to anyone who was not there on business. A security guard stood at the gates. Next to the wharf access was a picnic area where the crowd assembled. Nerissa walked up to the top of the stairs overlooking the crowd.

"Thanks everyone for coming today and supporting what we want to tell Taxxoil – we don't want them here," her voice boomed out. "We have a very clear message for Taxxoil and the government. Leave us alone. Let's not put our environment, the food we get from the sea, the beaches we play on and the money we make from the sea, at unacceptable risk. We will be forcing the government to consult with us before the *Perspeculor* goes anywhere. The government does not have a mandate to drill for oil and we will never agree to it."

The crowd roared, bouncing their banners.

"Be strong in your support. Sign our petition. And we'll make Taxxoil go away. Thank you."

The crowd clapped as she walked down the stairs and joined the rest of Operation Protect members.

A television crew had been filming the march. Perfect. This would give them wider coverage at a national level. An opportunity for more people to hear them and join them in opposition.

Rachel introduced Nerissa to Howard, the TV reporter.

"Let's go over here," Howard said. "That way we can get a shot of the crowd with the Perspeculor in the background."

Nerissa swatted at a bee that was attracted by the sticky mixture. The bee settled on her, its legs and wings becoming entrapped. Before she could flick it off, it stung her. She winced.

"Ouch!" she exclaimed.

"You're a walking bee magnet," Howard said.

"Yeah. The things we do."

"OK. Just tell us a bit about what you're hoping to achieve here today."

"We'll do whatever it takes to send Taxxoil home. We don't want a Gulf oil spill here. Oil spill modelling reports show that a blow-out on an oil rig could have irreversible consequences. It would wipe out Aqua Bay. We want to be the first country in the world to ban deep sea oil drilling."

"Thanks Nerissa. Look at the news tonight. We hope to get this item up as one of the lead stories."

Rachel cast her eyes up and down Nerissa and laughed. "You look a mess!"

"It was a great idea at the time, but a shower would be good and I need to look at this bee sting. I'll shower off in the public toilets."

But as she made her way through the dispersing crowd towards the toilet block, the Taxxoil Rover was driving slowly down Craypot Road towards the wharf.

She glanced over towards the television crew who were taking last minute shots of the crowd. This was her chance to make an even bigger statement. She ran over towards the guarded gate and sat down right in the middle of the driveway preventing the Rover from entering.

"Hey, you can't do that," shouted the security guard.

Nerissa ignored him. She sat cross-legged, her back tall, and stared straight at the advancing vehicle.

Howard yelled out to the cameraman. "Make sure you get this."

Some of the remaining crowd picking up on a brewing situation renewed their interest and started drifting towards Nerissa, the Rover and the security guard.

A man with long dreadlocks sat down beside her. Two high school girls sat on her other side. Soon about 10 people had joined the small group.

"Come on guys. You can't sit there. You're blocking the entrance," the security guard repeated.

The small sit-down group, taking Nerissa's lead, remained silent staring at the Rover which had now come to a complete stop 5 metres in front of them.

Jackson, Brodie and Mac stepped out of the Rover.

The security guard said something into his radio then addressed the group. "Come on guys. You'll have to move," his authoritative voice boomed out.

Both schoolgirls relented. This was not a game. They stood up, waved to the camera and walked off.

Nerissa stared straight ahead refusing to look at Jackson.

A police car with its lights flashing pulled up behind the Rover and Valerie and Win stepped out.

"OK guys. Show's over," Valerie said. "You'll need to get up."

Five people quibbled a bit and then reluctantly left. That left Nerissa and the dread-locked man.

She folded her arms tighter, refusing to budge. She stared up at the *Perspeculor*. The ship seemed much bigger from a sitting position. Black menacing smoke bellowed from its funnel.

Valerie, with her hands or her hips said, "You can't sit here. You're blocking traffic and a public walkway. Be sensible now. That's a warning."

The dreadlocked man turned to Nerissa. "I think we should give it up."

"I'm staying. You go."

He didn't put up much of a fight and sauntered off.

Valerie had wandered over to speak to Jackson.

Nerissa watched the two in conversation. What were they up to?

Brodie, Mac and Valerie hung back as Jackson walked over.

"This is taking it a bit far," Jackson said.

Nerissa refused to look at him keeping her eyes fixed on the Rover.

"We get your point," he tried again.

The camera crew was still filming.

Jackson sat down in front of her. "Come on, Nerissa. Don't be a dang-fool."

She locked eyes with Jackson. His gaze seemed to bore straight into her, right into her soul. His mere presence threw her off. He was so damned attractive, but she wouldn't waver. She was just as determined as he was and she glared back at him.

"Is this a standoff?" he asked.

"You could call it that."

He chuckled. "I might have guessed. You're one determined lady."

"You know, I was just about to get up. But you laughing changed my mind. You've probably had to deal with those protests every place you've gone to. I don't know and I don't care how these protests turned out, but I do know one thing. Laughing in my face is the worst thing you could do. You've just forced me to take this further."

"I haven't forced you to do anything. We get your point. You have a choice. Make the right choice now."

She shook her head.

"Nerissa, they're going to arrest you if you don't move," he pleaded.

"You're bluffing."

"No. I'm not. Valerie asked me to come and talk to you. To get you to move off the driveway."

"I'm not going."

"Think carefully. You don't want to jeopardise all your hard work."

Nerissa's eyes darted over towards the camera crew who were still filming. This would be a perfect opportunity to up the coverage. She shook her head again.

"Man, you're stubborn. OK then." Jackson rose to his feet and walked back to Valerie.

Nerissa watched again as a further conversation took place. Jackson was doing a lot of nodding.

Valerie and Win walked back over to Nerissa.

"Nerissa, I'm going to have to ask you one final time to remove yourself from this driveway," Valerie said.

Nerissa sat.

Five seconds passed.

"OK. You're under arrest for blocking a public walkway."

Holy crap! He hadn't been bluffing!

Valerie removed her handcuffs from her belt. "Stand up."

It was over. She'd hedged her bets and lost. She rose slowly to her feet and put her hands behind her back, the cold steel snapping against her wrists. She was informed of her rights including the right to a lawyer.

"Um," Win said, eyeing Nerissa up and down. "You're going to make a mess all over the car seat."

"Sorry about that," Nerissa mumbled. Fake oil dribbled down her legs.

Valerie escorted her to the police car, the camera crew following as she got into the back seat. She watched as the security guard unlocked the gate and the Rover drove through.

At the police station she was 'processed'. She gave her name, address, date of birth, occupation and she was photographed. She had never had the need for a lawyer in Aqua Bay and the only person she could think of was Chris.

"Well, I can't say I've had to represent someone covered in molasses before," he said when he saw her.

She ignored his comment. "Now what?"

"I'll have a chat with Senior Constable Appleton and see what we're going to do. Frankly I think they've gone a bit overboard."

The door to the interview room opened and Valerie called Chris out.

She sat alone, the consequences of her actions dawned on her. If someone had told her this morning that by the end of the day she would be arrested she would've laughed. Should she be proud or ashamed? She had just done what needed to be done.

She looked herself over; she was unbearably sticky and smelly. She wiped her hands over her hair, now knotted in a tangled mess. The bee sting throbbed.

The door opened and Chris reappeared.

"Right. After talking to Valerie and her supervisor they've deemed your individual protest to be a minor incident. Charges won't be laid against you so you're free to go."

Nerissa blew out her cheeks. Thank goodness! She didn't relish the complications of an arrest and subsequent court case.

"But you've been issued with a warning. Any further incidents and you won't be so lucky next time."

"Thanks, Chris. I promise I'll behave. You know, this is all for the dolphins."

"Well, be sure to tell them that when you see them next. By the way, there's someone been waiting for you outside for a while."

Someone must've rung Scott and he was here to take her home.

After she signed some papers and walked into the reception area, it wasn't Scott waiting for her, but Jackson.

Chapter 19

"I figured you'd need a way of getting home," Jackson said, lounging in a reception chair.

She looked around the empty foyer. "Why aren't some of the others here? They can take me home."

"I don't think they know what's happened. But that's about to change."

"Why?"

"Seems like the march is going to be right up there on the news tonight."

She beamed. To make national TV was more than she could've hoped for.

"So do you want a ride?"

She didn't want to be anywhere near him, but the practicalities of getting home were an issue. She hesitated for just a moment. "OK."

He stood up and held out two towels. "Try and get as much oil off you as you can."

She took the towels and rubbed her arms and legs of the remaining goop which was starting to harden.

Jackson leaned up against the wall grinning at her. "My, you are a sight."

"Oh, hush!" The more she rubbed, the worse it got as the fluff from the towels stuck to the goop. She clenched her teeth. How much more embarrassing could this get?

"Just wrap the towels round you. It will be enough," Jackson said.

She settled into the Rover keeping her body on the towels. She gazed out the side window as Jackson pulled out from behind the police station and drove towards Craypot Road. Night had enveloped the bay and the surf crashed onto the beach.

Thank goodness the car had tinted windows. What would people think if they saw them – the anti-oil drilling crusader with the oil explorer?

She shuffled in her seat. Jackson's bare arms were close enough for her to touch, begging her to take notice. Those strong arms had already embraced her, held her.

She bit her tongue. *Don't say anything! Don't engage.* The quicker they got home the better.

Jackson pulled up outside her cottage.

"Thanks for the lift," Nerissa said.

Jackson turned to her, all serious eyes. "Are we going to talk about what happened?"

"I sat in a public driveway and was arrested."

"No, not that. About what happened between us."

"No, I don't want to talk about it. I just want to forget it."

"You can't deny there's something between us. I know you feel it too."

"Leave it!"

He reached out for her arm.

"Stay away from me. Just leave me alone why don't you?" she snapped.

"Nerissa, we really need to-."

"No we don't. I wish I'd never met you."

She couldn't stay in the Rover any longer. She flung open the door and ran up the path. The Rover pulled away sharply, the screeching tyres reverberating in her ears.

She got to the front door, but where was her bag? *No.* She'd left her bag with the cottage keys and phone back at work. She rubbed her forehead. How was it possible she was able to organise a protest march, but not the practicalities of getting back into her cottage afterwards?

She wheeled round with her hands on her hips.

There was only one option available. She'd have to go to Jackson's and use his phone. His was the nearest cottage.

She set off down the road, her feet squelching in her molasses-filled shoes.

Striding up Jackson's path, she banged on his door which opened immediately.

"Back so soon," he said, cocking his head to the side.

"I… um… I've got a small problem," she mumbled, hanging her head.

"Yes?"

"My bag with my keys and phone are back at work. Everyone will be gone by now. I'm locked out of my cottage."

"You could break a window," Jackson suggested.

"Seriously?"

"Mmm. What a predicament. What to do? What to do?" Jackson tapped the door frame.

"You're enjoying this, aren't you?"

He chuckled. "You obviously need to fix yourself up. I'm guessing you're hungry and I'm dying to see what the news has picked up."

"What are you suggesting?"

"The obvious. Have a shower here. I'll fix you something to eat and then we'll figure out how to get you into your cottage."

Nerissa looked at him. "You're kidding me!"

"Come up with a better plan then."

She could walk back into town, but her feet ached, her body was sticky and yes, she was hungry.

"Listen," he said, putting his hands up. "I promise I'll keep at least five metres away from you at all times. I'll even sit outside here on the porch while you take a shower."

How could she even be in the same room as Jackson? Was it Jackson she didn't trust or herself? She sighed. "That won't be necessary."

"Come on in" he said, opening the door wider. "Still wished you'd never met me?"

"Don't push it," she said, itching her arm.

"Ouch! That looks sore."

"A bee stung me."

"Not surprising. You do smell good enough to eat."

Her cheeks burned like red-hot fire. Was there no end to this guy's taunting?

Jackson pulled some towels out of the linen cupboard. "You'll probably need some clean clothes. Here's an old pair of shorts and a T-shirt. Shower's second door on the left." He pointed down the hall. "I'll fix something to eat."

Nerissa closed the bathroom door – and made doubly sure she locked it.

***

It had taken a good scrubbing and a truck-load of shampoo to come up sparkling clean. The shorts and T-shirt were way too big, completely swamping her. They were clean, but Jackson's scent still lingered, setting off a fire inside her.

She emerged from the bathroom with a towel wrapped round her hair.

"I remembered you're a vegetarian and so I've whipped up an American staple for you – mac and cheese," Jackson said, eyeing her up and down. "Much better."

"That concoction was a devil to get out of my hair. Anything I can help with?"

"Just finishing a salad. You can toss it if you like. Sorry, it won't be as nice as yours with all your home-grown stuff."

"I'm sure it'll be just fine."

Jackson pulled a dish out of the oven and served up the mac and cheese. He carried both plates over to the table and then grabbed a Steiny out of the fridge.

She sniffed the air. Mac and cheese, comfort food.

"There's some wine here." Jackson scooped a large spoonful of salsa on top of his plate.

"I didn't think you would drink wine." She manoeuvred the spoons round the bowl.

"I don't. It's for other people who visit." He poured her a glass.

"What other people?" She swallowed some wine, the golden liquid hitting the back of her throat just where she needed it.

He avoided answering the question as he switched on the TV, just in time to hear the newsreader say, "and one arrest at an anti-oil exploration protest march."

Nerissa's heart thumped and her eyes were glued to the screen. Details of the first items were about a missing boatie, a hunting accident and a politician's lover's jealous wrath, and then...

"We all want New Zealand on the map and our actions can be significant enough for others to take notice. An American film crew posted this item an hour ago."

The picture shifted to a blonde woman news anchor. "Leading up to the fourth anniversary of the Gulf oil spill, a tiny seaside community on the other side of the world is taking a stand against Taxxoil, the world's biggest oil exploration company."

The view shifted to a shot of the protest march on Craypot Road and a snippet of Nerissa's speech.

"The march was peaceful, but police were called when Nerissa Taylor, the organiser of the protest, was arrested for blocking a public driveway preventing Taxxoil representatives from rendezvousing with their ship, the *Perspeculor*."

The picture switched to a shot of Valerie handcuffing Nerissa and leading her to the police car.

"When Taxxoil was asked to comment about the protest and damage their seismic surveying equipment might cause, Jackson Darnell had this to say."

"We're used to people protesting; it's their right. But that won't stop us from undertaking our intensive programme, which begins next week. Our techniques are safe and won't hurt the marine mammals. Aqua Bay needs to focus on the positive aspects that oil drilling can bring to the community."

Nerissa humphed.

Next, comments were taken from a number of protesters.

"We need to get our message out there." A picture of Sam came up on the screen. "We have a weapon to do that and that is our voices. Many voices or just one voice – Nerissa – the guardian angel of Aqua Bay."

"And now to other news stories of the day..."

"They could have mentioned that the charges were dropped," Nerissa said.

"Guardian Angel of Aqua Bay, nice," commented Jackson.

It did have a certain ring to it.

"How can you make a comment about safe techniques when you know that's not true?" Nerissa asked, turning the heat up on Jackson.

Jackson piled some mac and cheese onto his fork and shoved it in his mouth. He didn't respond until his mouth was empty. "There's something you and I need to discuss."

"I told you. I'm not talking about it." Nerissa banged her knife down on her plate.

"Don't get your knickers in a twist. I heard you loud and clear that you don't want to talk about... us. You want to keep this professional. Fine. Just listen to what I have to say. The email that you saw about you coming out onto the *Perspeculor* as an observer, you've been given approval," Jackson finished.

"Really?"

"Really. Although I hope that won't change after today. I didn't want you to take your protest too far as I knew it might jeopardise your chances of being allowed on the ship."

"Why didn't you tell me?"

"You wouldn't listen to me."

A quivering started in her stomach. "Do you think I've blown it?"

"Hard to say. I'll be better able to assess the situation on Monday."

"Thank you. I really appreciate it." She chased a macaroni spiral round her plate with a fork.

"So, all going to plan, it could be as early as Tuesday or Wednesday and we'll have you out at sea."

"Wow."

"Nerissa, promise me though you'll keep an open mind about what we're going to be doing."

"I'll try. It's hard to keep the emotion separate from reality sometimes."

"Yeah. I know." He stared at her long and hard. "Let's take a look at that bee sting."

He wandered off down the hall and came back with a first aid kit which he opened pulling out bandages, antiseptic ointment and Panadol. He looked closely at the bee sting. His breath was so close to her it made the hairs stand up on her arm. He gently turned her arm from side to side.

Nerissa's stomach clenched in a knot.

"I'll need to take the stinger out." Jackson walked into the kitchen, took something from out of a drawer, ran it under the tap and then was back. "OK." He drew a knife up to the sting.

Nerissa jumped up so fast she knocked over the chair. "Shit! What are you doing?" The all too familiar image of a knife being pointed at her flashed in front of her. Her blood spiked like jagged points of ice.

Jackson looked at the knife and the pain on Nerissa's face instantly connecting the two. "God, I'm sorry. I didn't think." He rubbed his forehead. "Sorry."

"It's OK," Nerissa said, picking up the chair and sitting back down. "I have a panic attack round knives, particularly when I'm not expecting it."

"That was really insensitive of me." Concern etched over his face.

"I'll turn my head the other way so I can't see the knife."

"I could use something else."

"No. No. Let's get it over with."

"OK. Hold still."

Nerissa turned her head away as Jackson scraped the knife across the sting. She focused on her guitar that was leaning up against the wall.

"It's all out. I'll just clean it again." He bathed the area in soap and cold water, patted it dry and applied an antiseptic ointment. "Do you think you need a Panadol?"

"It's a little tender, but Panadol and wine is probably not a good mix."

"Good point. I think you've done enough damage for one day."

Nerissa laughed. "Mmm. I think you're right there. How's the guitar playing going?"

"Yeah, I strum - badly – every night."

They spent the next couple of hours sitting on the front porch drinking, and talking about everything and nothing. Jackson had the guitar on his lap and strummed a Keith Urban song. They both sang and laughed when they forgot the words or Jackson hit a bum note. She gradually relaxed; it was just like the previous time they'd shared a meal and each other's company. They kept a respectable distance from each other and Jackson stuck to his word about not bringing up 'that' subject.

Nerissa stifled a yawn. "What time is it?"

"Almost midnight."

"I'd better see about getting back home," she said half-heartedly. The cottage would be dark and empty and she would be alone.

"Who do you want to call?"

"Katey."

"Here's my phone," he said, handing it to her.

She gazed at it as she brought up the key pad.

"Um," she said, after thirty seconds.

"What's wrong?"

"I can't remember her number." She laughed. "All my contacts are on auto-dial."

"The joys of modern communication."

"Now what?"

They sat in silence.

"I could just go to Katey's, but I've a feeling she might not be alone," Nerissa pondered.

"You could stay here the night," Jackson offered, with a poker face. "On the couch."

Was he genuinely trying to help her or was he insane? She didn't need, or want, temptation laid out in front of her. Could she trust him? He'd behaved like a perfect gentleman all evening.

"While you're thinking about it, I'll get a pillow and blanket," Jackson said, stepping inside then down the hall.

God. Would it be OK? Where else was she going to go at this time of night?

"Here," Jackson said, handing her the blanket and pillow.

She stood up. "Thanks."

"You're welcome," Jackson replied. He locked the front door, pulled the curtains and turned off the lounge light.

Nerissa watched him as he sauntered back down the hall.

He stopped at his bedroom door and turned round. "Night. Night."

The light caught the softness in his brown eyes.

"Night. Night."

"And don't go dreaming up crazy schemes like blowing up our ship."

Nerissa smothered a smile. "Can't promise anything."

"I wouldn't expect anything less."

Nerissa lay down on the couch and pulled the blanket over her. What a day. She had achieved what she had wanted to – *and* more. She'd scored a visit on the *Perspeculor*.

She drifted off to sleep with Jackson's blanket rubbing on her skin and his scent filling her nose.

Chapter 20

In an apartment somewhere in New Mexico, a woman sat on the edge of the couch riveted to the TV, tears streaming down her face.

She clutched her hands together so hard the fingernails bit into her palms.

"Jackson, Jackson, Jackson," she cried, over and over.

She picked up her phone and dialled the Taxxoil head office.

Chapter 21

She woke up with a start. Where was she?

A cottage, but not her's. Jackson's cottage. That's right. Yesterday's events ran through her mind like a movie.

The sun was streaming through the kitchen window and she figured it was about 9 am.

She threw the blanket off her and stood up, stretching, relishing in the quietness.

Was Jackson awake? Should she go check? She was keen to get to work to collect her things.

She quietly opened the back door. Her bikini top and shorts from yesterday were hanging on the line. She walked down the steps drinking in the sun and raising her head to catch the morning breeze.

Returning back inside she changed into her clothes. Noises came from the bathroom. Jackson was up.

"How'd you sleep?" Jackson asked, strolling into the lounge dressed in his standard black T-shirt and shorts.

"Very good. And how did you sleep?"

"Like a log. In my own bed."

Nerissa scowled. He wouldn't let this thing go.

They quickly ate breakfast and Jackson drove her back to work.

"Perhaps you can drop me off just round the corner. I'll walk the rest of the way."

Jackson glanced at her. "Why? Are you embarrassed to be seen with me?"

"Keep your eyes on the road!" She still didn't trust his driving. "I just think it's better that people don't see us together."

"Ahh, so we're back to that again. I thought you were over caring what other people think of you? It's not like we spent the night together, well, not in that way."

"I don't want people to talk."

"Oh, you don't have to worry about that. They already are. But only you and I know the truth."

Nerissa stared straight ahead. The truth. The secret she had to keep.

"Anyway, too late. We're here," Jackson said, as he pulled up outside Dolphin Eco-tours.

One of the staff was hosing down the slipway.

Nerissa barely opened the car door before Jackson put on the handbrake. She banged the car door shut and leant through the window.

"Thank you – for saving me."

"Always happy to help," Jackson said, tilting his Stetson. "I'm sure we'll be bumping into each other again no doubt."

"I suspect so." She turned back round not waiting for a response and walked into the reception area.

"What are you doing here?" Katey said. "Did you forget it's Saturday? Was that Jackson who dropped you off?"

"So many questions," Nerissa said, walking out back to the lockers, Katey following her.

"I left my phone and keys here yesterday and after I finished at the police station I was kind of stranded. Jackson picked me up."

"Where did you stay last night?"

"Jackson's."

"After he jumped you?" Katey asked, incredulously.

"Hush! Keep your voice down," Nerissa warned. "It was all above board and adult like. I had nowhere else to go. Nothing happened."

"You didn't think to call me?"

"I couldn't remember your number and it was late. Besides, I got the impression you were probably entertaining."

"Yeah. I was a bit tied up – literally." She giggled.

"Katey!"

"Anyway, you're a star. TV and everything."

"We got some really good coverage."

Mavis poked her head round the door. "Nerissa, I thought I heard your voice. Everyone's been talking about you."

"So I hear. We did all right yesterday."

"I'm glad you're here now. Peter and I would like to have a word with you both," Mavis said.

Nerissa and Katey looked at each other. Something serious was going on.

"Let's go into the meeting room," Mavis said.

Nerissa and Katey climbed the stairs.

Peter was making coffee. He'd opened the windows. Waves gently slapped against the rocks below.

"The Guardian of Aqua Bay," Peter said, slapping Nerissa on the back. "We knew you'd do us proud."

"Thanks Peter. World-wide exposure is not too shabby."

They sat down at the wooden table.

"We wanted to tell you the news first before you heard it from someone else," Mavis said.

"We've put the business up for sale," Peter said.

"What?" Nerissa and Katey said in unison. Shocked glances passed between them.

"Why?" Nerissa asked. The reflection from the sun on the window hit her full in the face.

"Mavis and I have been thinking about retirement for some time now. We know that both of you will be leaving at the end of summer and that makes the timing workable."

The hairs on her arms pricked upwards and a flicker of pain travelled across her bee sting. Leaving? No, she did not want to be leaving.

"There is another reason," Peter continued. "With all this Taxxoil business, it's going to make it harder to keep the business going."

"But we're making headway," Nerissa protested. "Surely after the exposure we received yesterday that will only strengthen our case. We will win this thing. We just need time. And we're only just beginning."

"That's the thing. Mavis and I don't feel like we have time."

"Is someone dying?" Katey asked.

"No, of course not. If we were younger and more energetic we'd go up against Taxxoil. We would stay on."

"Don't you think we will win?" Nerissa asked, her voice quiet and small.

"It's a big task. Taxxoil has the resources to get what they want. We're just small fry to them." Peter sighed. "I think we're fighting a battle we're going to lose."

Nerissa slumped in her seat. She couldn't tell what Katey was thinking. It wasn't such a big deal for her and she'd made up her mind that the best chance-for her was in the city.

"I know this is a shock," Mavis said.

"I just thought that you guys believed we could make a difference," Nerissa said. She struggled to hold back the tears.

"We do," Peter said. "But we don't want it to be our fight."

The elation from yesterday melted away. She was about to lose not only the cottage, but her place of work, places she belonged.

"We're putting the business on the market on Monday. We think we'll get some good interest even from overseas buyers and maybe there won't be any buyers until after you girls have gone. Then you won't have to worry," Peter said.

"We appreciate you giving us a heads up." Nerissa sniffed. "Will you still stay in Aqua Bay?"

"We haven't decided yet. We've had a long-talked about dream of touring New Zealand in a campervan," Mavis said.

Peter shook his head. "Do you think we can stand being together in such a confined area day in, day out?"

"We work well together here," Mavis said, looking at her husband affectionately.

Peter took his wife's hand. "We do at that."

Katey looked at her watch. "We'd better get moving if we're to get the 10 am tour out on time."

"Do you want to come out on the boat with us?" Mavis asked, placing a comforting hand on Nerissa's shoulder.

"No thanks. I've got some calls to make," Nerissa said, and then she was left alone.

Peter and Mavis's unexpected news had thrown her a curveball. Her heart and soul were invested in the business and it wasn't even her business.

Her phone showed five missed calls from Scott and a message from her mother.

She listened to the message. "Nerissa. Your father and I have just seen the news." A sigh. "Being arrested. People will be talking about us all over the place. It's not a good look." Another sigh. "Why can't you be more like your sisters? You don't see them protesting half-naked for some hippy cause. I don't know." Another deeper, louder sigh. "The sooner you move to the city the better. At least we can keep an eye on you and suggest some more suitable activities. Anyway, can you give us a call? Your father wants to talk to you too."

Typical. All about her and what the neighbours would think. Nerissa deleted the message.

Her phone rang. It was Scott.

"Where've you been? I've been calling since 6 last night."

"I'm sorry. I left my phone in the locker at work and I had no way of getting it until this morning."

"You were arrested."

She caught the disapproval in his tone – just like her mother.

"Yes, I was. But it's all been sorted. They let me off. It really was an overreaction by the police." Why didn't he say something about the great media coverage the protest march had received?

"Well, that's a relief."

"Relief for whom?"

"For all of us."

"What do you mean?"

"Your mother has been ringing me. She's none too pleased."

"You should hear the message she left. Pretty predictable."

Nerissa filled Scott in on her mother's reaction.

"She does have a point," Scott replied.

Nerissa gritted her teeth. "I thought you might've come up for the march."

"I couldn't just drop everything. My work is important."

And her work wasn't?

"Anyway," Scott continued. "It looks like it's all worked out OK. Good news. I can come up next Friday. How's the wedding arrangements going?"

Wedding arrangements? When had she had time to think about the wedding?

"Katey and I are looking at venues." She grimaced. The lies she were telling Scott were mounting.

"That's great. We can settle on one next weekend. And I have a few ideas where we can go for our honeymoon."

Honeymoon. The thing after a wedding. By then she would be living in the city.

"Nerissa?"

"Yes, yes. Sounds grand. I'd better go. I've got a busy Saturday ahead."

"Me too. I'll see you Friday, and you should ring your mother. Love you."

"Love you."

Her cell rang. It was her mother.

She sighed. She really couldn't go on ignoring her mother forever. She answered the call.

"Nerissa, I've been trying to get hold of you."

"I've had stuff going on."

"Yes, I know. Did you get my message?"

"Mmm. What did you want?"

"Please don't use that tone. I don't want to see my daughter half-naked on the TV."

"I wasn't half-naked. Do you know what we've achieved? Global exposure of a really important issue. This means something to me and everyone else in Aqua Bay. Why can't you see that this is something that needs saving? Why on earth would you and dad take us to Aqua Bay for holidays year after year and yet not want to give something back?" Her voice rose.

"Dear, there's no need to shout at me. I just wish what you're doing wasn't so... visible."

"Like having a safe job like Erin and Danielle? Like not brushing off something that happened to me so people wouldn't talk about it so you wouldn't be embarrassed."

"Nerissa, don't talk to me like this-"

"Mother, I'm not seeking your permission. You can either support me or not. But I'm continuing with my work in Aqua Bay." She bit her lip and struggled to fight back tears. "That's the way it is."

There was silence at the other end and then, "Oh, well. I guess every family has a black sheep."

Is that what she was? The Taylor family's black sheep? It would take more than a day to convince her mother that her journey was just as worthy as her sisters'. And it was going to take more than a day to achieve all the other things she wanted to do. But she'd just keep chipping away. If her mother never placed any value on what she was doing then that wouldn't stop her. "Is dad there? He wanted to talk to me too."

"He's gone out. I have to go as I have visitors this afternoon. I have a cake in the oven due to come out."

She left her mother to keep up her neighbourly appearances.

The tears that she'd brushed away formed again and ran down her cheeks.

Why did she even try to make an effort with her mother? And why was she getting so upset about it? It seemed that the people closest to her didn't really care about what she was trying to achieve.

And now there was another challenge. Dolphin Eco-tours was up for sale and Peter and Mavis would be going. Why should she be worried? She'd leave at the end of summer and that would be it for her. Her new life in the city would begin. The tears fell faster and faster and her heart crumpled like delicate tissue paper.

Chapter 22

Everyone wanted a piece of Nerissa. The anti-oil drilling protest and her subsequent arrest reignited the debate throughout New Zealand. Her cell rang non-stop. National Geographic wanted to interview her and do a magazine article. Would she come on *Today's Issues Now*, the nightly current affairs show? Greenpeace was offering her a role as the poster girl for their environmental causes.

She answered calls with yes, yes, yes and a whirlwind of appointments and interviews were set up. She didn't even have to go anywhere. Either people came to her or she skyped her TV interviews. And everywhere she looked she was in the newspaper, on the TV or on the front cover of a magazine. She had become an overnight celebrity.

The best thing to come out of it was that it had pushed the issue into the media spotlight and had put heat on the Ocean Resources Department. A hastily arranged meeting between Operation Protect, Nerissa, Chris Rye and ORD was organised.

An embarrassed ORD admitted that they had not followed their own policies and seismic surveying was about to take place without any consultation.

A meeting with the community was arranged for Wednesday to fast track the consultation process. But she left the meeting angered by a poor attempt by ORD to prevent the *Perspeculor* from undertaking its first survey.

She was stuck between a rock and a hard place. The *Perspeculor* unable to do any seismic surveying was good, but if it didn't go out to sea she wouldn't get the opportunity to be an observer.

Jackson rang her Monday afternoon at work to let her know that she still had the green light to go out on the *Perspeculor* on Wednesday if she was still interested.

"Still interested?" Nerissa almost choked. "Of course I am!"

"Thought you would be. We're leaving at 0700 hours on Wednesday. Meet me at the entrance gate to the wharf."

Peter gave her his OK for her to have the morning off.

On Wednesday morning she parked her car and sat waiting for Jackson to arrive. The morning air whispered of anticipation and apprehension. She loved this time of the day. She drew in a deep breath, the salty, seaweed tang tickling her nose. The sun rested above the horizon, shining its brilliance onto the aqua-coloured sea.

Two minutes later Jackson pulled up.

"Morning," he said.

"Morning."

"Great day for a boat ride. I'll swipe us through."

She peered up at the Perspeculor. She estimated the length to about 230 metres. There was a helicopter landing pad above the bridge, a derrick in the middle and various cranes towards the stern. The size of the ship and its equipment rising from the deck was intimidating, throwing black shadows across the wharf.

"I'll need to sign you in," said Jackson.

They walked up the gangway and Jackson led her to a meeting room where he explained the safety requirements and issued her a high visual vest and hard hat.

The meeting room door opened and a tall man entered.

"Ah, right on time. Good. I'm, Captain Shimanski." He shook Nerissa's hand in a strong knuckle-clenching grip. "You must be Nerissa Taylor."

"Pleased to meet you," Nerissa said.

"Jackson. Long time no see."

"Has been a while. We've been doing a lot of ground work waiting for you to arrive."

"Still chasing the pretty ladies I see," Captain Shimanski said, eyeing Nerissa again.

Nerissa watched Jackson squirm and then chastely lower his head. Did his reputation for women circumnavigate the globe?

"Perhaps we could concentrate on what I'm here for," Nerissa suggested.

Jackson threw her a thank you glance.

267

"Now, before we set off, young lady, Jackson tells me that you're an activist and was recently arrested trying to prevent our vehicle from accessing the wharf."

Activist? It wasn't a term she would've used for herself, but given how the recent activities had reached a higher level maybe taking the role of activist was not something she should shy away from. The safest reply would be to be honest. That way she'd gain respect. "That's true, Captain Shimanski, but the charges were dropped."

"I need to be clear with you. There's to be no funny business on my ship," Captain Shimanski said, his voice strong. "Understood?"

"Understood. I know this is a privilege being invited onto the *Perspeculor* as an observer. I just want to learn as much as I can about what you guys are doing here."

Captain Shimanski studied her for a moment and then directed his attention to Jackson. "OK, but you are totally responsible for her actions."

"Nerissa won't be a problem. She'll be on her best behaviour."

Nerissa detected the condescending tone in his voice and fought a resistance to poke her tongue out at him. "Always," she replied back sweetly, and batted her eyelids.

Soon they were underway and headed out to sea. Jackson gave her a tour of the ship and introduced her to some of the crew. The wind and swell had picked up pitching the ship evenly into the peaks and troughs of the waves.

After half an hour the seismic surveying was underway.

"We do what's called a Level 1 survey where the airguns are towed about several hundred metres out," Jackson explained, pointing towards the stern. "The airguns use a controlled release of high-pressure air at regular points which create low-frequency noises. The soundwaves bounce off the ocean floor and are reflected back to the listening devices. This way we can map the sub-surface terrain and this will hopefully reveal if there are any oil deposits."

Nerissa buried her head into her jacket as a large cloud of sea spray blew over the deck.

"Of course the effect of the soundwaves on the mammals is one of the things that you're concerned about," Jackson acknowledged. He licked the salt water off his lips. "Let's move back inside and I'll explain more about what we have in mind." He led her gently by the elbow back to the meeting room. "It's quite blustery out there today."

"The sea can look deceiving from the shelter of Aqua Bay. It's not until you get out here you realise how strong the swell and wind can be."

"Can I make you a coffee?"

"Sure."

Jackson put the jug on and made two cups of coffee. "Taxxoil is currently trialling having observers on our ships so people like you, with a concern about the mammals, can have some degree of comfort that we're not purposefully out to explore at all costs. So you'll remember I mentioned the Environmental Protection Values?"

"Time to give me some more detail." Nerissa blew on the scalding coffee.

"While we're undertaking the seismic survey, the observers would look out for marine mammals and ensure that we're adhering to impact assessments developed by the likes of Aqua Bay interest groups."

Nerissa nodded. This was a great idea.

"We're suggesting that if any marine mammals are detected when we're surveying then we would immediately stop and would restart after the animals have left the monitoring area. Observers would report any non-compliance to, I would presume, your Ocean Resources Department. I guess they would investigate and if we were found to have acted outside of the EPV then we would be appropriately punished," Jackson said. "Biscuit?" He slid a packet across the table to her.

Nerissa bit into the cookies and cream biscuit. "How do we get more involved in contributing to the assessment and the EPV?"

The ship plunged into a trough. Her stomach dropped and a wave of nausea swept over her. She put her hand to her mouth. Cold beads of sweat broke out on her forehead.

"You OK?" Jackson said.

She nodded.

Jackson continued to outline what work had already been done in the development of processes. "I guess we could share that work with you and that would mean you wouldn't have to reinvent the wheel."

She focused on the clock on the wall. If she could just keep her head straight, this moment of unexpected sickness would pass. Jackson's words came at her as incomplete sentences. What was he saying? The ship plunged into another trough.

Jackson looked at her quizzically.

A rising wave of sickness swept over her again. Could she trust herself to say one word? "Bathroom," she managed to say.

"Next door."

Running out the door, she just made it into the bathroom before throwing up the biscuits, coffee and breakfast. She dry heaved a couple of times until her stomach hurt. She leaned back against the wall breathing heavily. What on earth was going on? She had a stomach of steel; she was never seasick.

The ship plunged again, unbalancing her as she pulled herself up to the basin.

She splashed some cold water onto her face and patted it dry.

Nerissa walked slowly back into the meeting room. The pitching and plunging had lessened somewhat as they moved into the more sheltered waters of Aqua Bay.

"Sorry," she said. "I lost everything I ate today."

271

"What a waste of biscuits," Jackson said. His eyes twinkled in amusement.

Nerissa scowled at him.

He poured her a glass of water.

"Thanks," she said, taking a tentative sip. "I've never been seasick."

"I bet you've got the stomach bug I had. We have shared a few things lately."

If Jackson was trying to get her to talk about 'that incident' she wasn't taking the bait. "Katey had it too. I most likely got it from her."

"We're almost at the wharf," he said. "Feeling better?"

"Yeah. Although I don't think looking at that biscuit is helping."

Jackson popped the last biscuit in his mouth and disposed of the empty packet.

"Thanks for showing me how it all works. It's given me a greater understanding of what we're up against," Nerissa said.

"Taxxoil genuinely wants what's best for your dolphins and mammals. We're not deliberately trying to hurt them," Jackson said, peering down at her.

She had her doubts, but she let it go for now.

"If you wanted to we could get together to-work out what documentation to give you guys to help you develop guidelines that you'd be happy with," Jackson suggested.

Nerissa bit her lip. Every time she promised herself that she would stay away from Jackson they kept being thrown together again. She could say no, but that would defeat the whole purpose of what she was trying to achieve. No, they were two mature adults who could put whatever feelings they had for each other aside and work together professionally.

"OK. Sounds good. When?"

Jackson checked the calendar on his phone.

"How about next Friday afternoon?"

"I'll check with Peter. I'm sure that will be OK."

Jackson dropped her off at work just as *Seabird* was docking.

A full tour again. The happy tourists disembarked waving, joking and comparing photos.

Once the boat was hosed down and supplies replenished for the first tour out tomorrow morning, Nerissa debriefed Peter about her excursion on the *Perspeculor*.

"I'm meeting with Jackson again tomorrow afternoon to see what information we can share in developing the EPVs if that's OK."

"That's fine," Peter said, as he put the chilly bins in the kitchen. "You know, Nerissa, I'm really glad you're doing this stuff for us. We need someone like you, with the energy and passion to take this where it needs to go. I know you're upset about us selling, but Mavis and I are confident we'll get a good buyer."

273

"What if no one buys it? What if people are scared off by the drilling?" Nerissa asked, wrapping a curl round her finger. "What will happen then?"

Peter placed a steady hand on her shoulder. "Let's just take one step at a time. It's early days. Who knows what might come out of the woodwork? Don't worry. It'll all work out."

Katey was on her way out the door.

"Hey, Katey. Do you want to go for a drink after work? It would be a good chance to talk about the wedding."

"Umm. I don't know. I don't think so. I've got an assignment due next week. I really need to knuckle down and get it underway," Katey said, brushing a hand across her forehead.

"One night off wouldn't hurt. Why don't you ask your new guy to join us?"

"No, really. I need to study. Maybe after I've finished the assignment." Her parting words faded as she headed out the door.

Nerissa frowned. This was not like Katey. She wouldn't normally pass up the opportunity for a drink or two. Was this a new Katey?

Nerissa spent Friday, the weekend and the following week completely immersed in either work, continued media engagements or negotiations with the ORD.

She burnt the midnight oil researching magazines, books, websites, anything she could get her hands on regarding marine mammal reserves and eco-towns. She drafted up a plan to take to the next Operation Protect meeting. She had spent hours and hours on it and this was just the beginning. This work would take years to achieve. How could she still be able to be involved when, at the end of summer, she would be leaving Aqua Bay?

By the following Thursday her energy levels had plummeted. She couldn't stomach any food in the mornings and twice she had thrown up after she had gotten out of bed. A stomach bug was all she needed. If she wasn't better by next week she'd go to her doctor.

Work had been full on with all the morning and afternoon tours booked out. She'd had hardly any time to chat with Katey, who seemed to be avoiding her. When the two of them were in the tea room alone, Katey found an excuse to leave. As they worked alongside each other on the reception desk, there was a reluctance from her to chat. It was probably either the stress from studying or more man trouble.

Scott had been strangely uncommunicative too. He had not rung or texted during the week and the texts she had sent had gone unanswered. He was obviously busy. It seemed everyone was busy. She had texted him that morning to check he'd still be up tomorrow night and had just received a simple, "Yep". Something wasn't right. She'd make an extra special effort this weekend to devote all her time to him and firm up the wedding plan.

A marathon research session on Thursday night almost left her in tears. There was still so much work to do. It was going to be virtually impossible to keep her crusade going if she wasn't living in Aqua Bay. When her brain couldn't take digesting any more information the desire to hear a stabilising voice hit her. And at the same time she needed to do some more research but from a closer to home angle. She turned down the country music she'd been playing and dialled home.

"Andrew Taylor."

"Dad. It's Nerissa."

"Nessie, honey. How are you?"

Nerissa smiled at her father's pet name for her. Of course, never said when her mother was in earshot. Nerissa was always Nerissa. That was the name you were born with and that's the name you should be called.

"I'm fine."

"You're everywhere, sweetheart."

"I know. It's been a crazy time."

"Your mother would like to speak to you – again, but what can I do for you, honey?"

"You know that trust fund I have, that matured six months ago? How much money is in there now?"

"I'm not sure exactly. I'd have to go and check."

"Perhaps later. Can you give me an estimate?"

"I think it's about $50,000."

Her grandparents, on her father's side, had set all the girls up with a trust fund when they were born. When her grandparents died, they had left a significant amount of money in their will to be banked into their trust funds and maturing when each granddaughter turned 21. Apart from using some money to contribute towards the land purchase in the city she had never touched the money. She had never needed to until now.

"Dad, I need some of that money and as you're the only person besides myself who can authorise a transfer can you pop $20,000 into my bank account."

"Sure, honey. Are you OK? You aren't in some kind of trouble are you?"

"No, dad," she said. She had never been so sure of what she needed to do. "It's just something I need the money for."

"I can arrange a transfer tonight."

"Thanks."

"You'd better talk to your mother."

"It's late. I don't want to disturb her. I'll talk to her later."

"OK, but she won't be happy."

"It's OK. I'll deal with her later." She sighed.

"Thanks for ringing sweetheart. Talk to you soon."

"Bye, Dad."

$50,000. She stared at the photograph of her and Scott taken on the day they'd got engaged. There she was smiling back, so confident and sure of what she wanted, with Scott doing the guiding, the planning. She'd been happy to go along with it then. It had been what she wanted, right?

She'd lost herself with Scott, lost her purpose, swallowed up by his dreams. Her head snapped up with sureness like the sea tides that forever ebbed and flowed. It was time for her to be her and that could only happen in Aqua Bay. She was at a crossroads and about to change the course of her life.

She scrolled through her phone and hit dial. Her hand trembled ever so slightly.

"Hello. You're speaking with Angie from Aqua Bay Homes."

"Angie. It's Nerissa."

"Hi, Nerissa. How's it going?"

"Good. Angie, listen, I want to put an offer in on the cottage."

Chapter 23

Nerissa breathed a sigh of relief. She'd abandoned her morning swim and had gotten through the morning tour without losing her breakfast. She'd eaten a couple of plain cracker biscuits and then biked to the Taxxoil offices in a pesky head wind.

The number of posters on fences and signs had increased. *No, deep sea oil drilling in Aqua Bay* or *Go home Taxxoil*. These had provided a backdrop to some of the news items appearing on TV and the Operation Protect Facebook page. The town was becoming a model for anti-oil drilling protests.

She locked her bike up at the bike stand and as she strolled down the main street, Senior Constable Valerie Appleton was walking towards her.

"Keeping out of trouble?" the constable asked.

"Yes. I've been very well behaved," Nerissa replied.

"I'm glad I bumped into you. We've just arrested the guy who attacked you and he'll be charged with aggravated assault. He'll appear in court tomorrow. He'll work out his sentence and then be evicted from the country."

Her head dropped with relief. Finally, the closure she'd been desperately seeking. Both times. Now she wouldn't have to look behind her every time she went out, worry about being alone in the cottage, fearing that someone would flash a knife at her.

Tears threatened to fall, blurring the two seagulls in front of them squabbling over a discarded sandwich.

"Hey, you OK?" Valerie asked, laying a gentle hand on her arm.

"Yes, I'm sorry. It's just..."

"I know. These things can be quite emotional."

"Thank you for your help. I'm glad you persuaded me to carry this through."

"Sure thing. That's what we're here for."

One seagull conceded, leaving the winner to gulp down its meal in peace.

Valerie's radio crackled with instructions from the communications unit. "Duty calls."

Nerissa put her hands up to her eyes. She'd done the right thing and hopefully prevented another woman from falling prey to an appalling act of crime.

She entered the Taxxoil offices. Mac and Brodie were poring over maps on the big conference table, but Jackson was absent.

"Hi," Nerissa said.

Mac and Brodie looked up.

"Well, it's the rebel," Mac said.

"I think rebel is overstating it somewhat," she said.

"I think she prefers the eloquent Guardian of Aqua Bay," Brodie said.

These guys were just as bad as Jackson. She wouldn't let them rile her up though and she refused to be diverted from her purpose.

"Where's Jackson? We were supposed to be doing some work on the EPV."

"Jackson's working from home today. He had a family matter to sort out or something," Mac explained.

"Oh." She drummed her fingers on the reception desk.

"We'll let him know you popped by. I'm sure he'll be sorry he missed you," Mac said.

Brodie sniggered.

Whatever was that comment about? "I'll catch up with him later." She descended the stairs and walked back to her bike.

Should she text Jackson to see what was up? But he might cancel their appointment and she was dead keen to get all of Jackson's help on the EPVs. Besides what family matter would Jackson be referring to? Was something wrong with Ben?

She jumped on her bike and pedalled down the main road, out on to the highway and down Cottage Row, this time with the brisk wind behind her, and cycled up to Jackson's cottage, propping her bike up against the fence.

The front door was wide open, but the lounge was empty.

"Hello?" she called out.

When there was no answer she walked inside. "Hello," she called out again.

Jackson emerged from his bedroom and walked down the hall. He was half-asleep, his hair was tousled and clothes creased. "What're you doing here?"

"We were going to meet this afternoon and you were going to show me the EPV work. I went to your offices, but they told me that you were here."

Jackson ran his hands through his hair and closed his eyes. "Sorry, Nerissa. I completely forgot. I had something I needed to attend to."

"Everything OK?"

"Oh, yeah, um, I think so."

"If you prefer we could do this another time."

"No, no. It's OK. I have everything here that we need."

"You sure. Is there anything I can help you with?"

"No. How about a drink?" Jackson said quickly, changing the subject.

Nerissa nodded. She sat down at the table and watched Jackson as he poured some OJ into two glasses. He seemed distracted and not his usual self. It dawned on her that here she was once again alone with him. A couple of weeks ago that would have unsettled her. Sure, the physical attraction towards Jackson was strong and at times his eyes lingered on her a moment too long. But she had made clear her boundaries and they had settled into an easy professional relationship.

"Where shall we start?" she asked.

Jackson retrieved some documents from a satchel and spread them out on the table. He chewed on a fingernail as he explained the history of Taxxoil's development of the EPVs and how other countries were incorporating them into their environmental policies. He occasionally stopped in the middle of a sentence. He'd stare out the window, shift in his chair, then clear his throat swinging right back into where he'd left off.

There was definitely something wrong with him. She was itching to ask, but resolved to leave well enough alone.

She took notes on her iPad, asking questions here, clarifying there. Jackson had an extensive knowledge and was willingly sharing it.

"You've given me a heap of stuff here, which is going to be useful for us to use," Nerissa said, getting up. "I've probably taken up more of your time than I should've. But actually, if it's preventing you from going out on the *Perspeculor* using those awful sonar guns then the dolphins have won again."

Jackson chuckled. "Well, the boss might not be too pleased about that. What are your plans for tonight?"

"Scott's coming up," she said, as she gazed out the window.

Jackson collected the two glasses and put them in the sink.

"How about you?"

"Nothing major. Listen, Nerissa-"

Tyres crunched on the gravel outside the cottage.

"Expecting visitors?" Nerissa asked.

"No. Unless it's Mac and Brodie here for beer o'clock."

A car door slammed and footsteps pounded up the path to the front steps and through the front door.

Scott marched straight past her and punched Jackson in the face. Jackson's head snapped back.

"Scott!" Nerissa gasped.

Jackson stumbled backwards, lost his balance and landed on his butt. Blood ran from his nose. He wiped it away, jumped to his feet, and strode towards Scott, whose fists were clenched at his sides, his face contorted in rage.

She couldn't move, mesmerised by the scene that was playing out in front of her in slow motion.

Jackson's fists were raised and ready to strike back, his anger all too clear. But then he stopped and lowered his fists.

Scott's raised fist turned into a sharp, pointing finger. "You stay away from her!" he spat.

Jackson's voice was low and threatening and his eyes flashed. "I bet you've never had to fight for anything in your life, city boy. If you want to keep Nerissa then you'd better fight for her and I don't mean with your fists. Now get out."

Scott glared at Jackson, both of them in a defiant deadlock.

Finally Scott whirled round and stomped out the door without even looking at her. The squealing tyres on the gravel as the car pulled away emphasised his fury.

Her hands shook. The floor seemed to tilt and she was sure her legs would give way. "Oh, God. He knows," she whispered.

Jackson smeared the blood now steadily streaming from his nose across the back of his hand. A pained look whipped across his face.

"Who did you tell?" The pitch rose in her voice.

"Nobody."

Nerissa threw him a doubtful look.

"Honest. I swear. I didn't tell a soul."

"Not even Mac or Brodie?"

"No. Despite what you may think of me I don't share my sex life with my mates."

Who else knew? Nerissa's hand clutched her chest. Katey. Katey was the only person she'd told, and she had betrayed her.

"Your nose," Nerissa said.

"You should go to him." Jackson's voice was barely audible.

She hesitated, torn between wanting to help Jackson and the need to get to Scott.

"Go. I'll be fine," he muttered. He spat blood into his hand.

Her feet wouldn't move, but then the vision of Scott in all his agitation spurred her to grab her bag. She flew out the door, mounted her bike and pedalled down the road. She had to get to Scott, explain. Explain what? What was she going to say?

Scott's car was parked outside the cottage. Nerissa threw her bike down on the lawn and raced up the stairs.

She stopped dead in her tracks. Scott sat on the couch, elbows on his knees, and his head in his hands. His shoulders were slumped forward, the posture of a broken man.

He raised his head slowly and Nerissa's heart lurched. His eyes were red from crying.

She sat down slowly on the chair and waited for him to say something, anything.

Finally, he lifted his head and without looking at her said, "Why? That's all I want to know. Why?"

She didn't know how to answer him. She couldn't even begin to understand it. How could she explain how much she loved Scott, how she'd fought the pull of Jackson that she had tried so hard to fight?

"I'm so sorry, Scott," she whispered. "It just happened." She winced. How pathetic those words sounded.

"When did it happen?"

"A couple of weeks ago."

"Be more specific."

"Friday."

"The Friday I came up?"

"Yes." She bowed her head. She deserved all that she was getting.

"When?"

Flames burned under her skin. "I don't think this is helping-"

"When?" Scott's voice was louder, harder.

"That night."

A horrified expression washed over Scott's face. "You can't be serious."

Slow, fat tears fell from Nerissa's eyes and plopped onto her legs.

"You told me you'd been out with Katey, but you'd been with Jackson?"

Nerissa spluttered.

Scott's eyes widened. "You fucked Jackson and then fucked me, what?, in the space of an hour."

A cry burst from her lips. Scott never used words like that. He made it sound so sordid.

"It wasn't like that," she pleaded.

"The sex we had that weekend was unbelievable. And here I was thinking it was because you loved me, wanted me. You know, it all makes sense now. Your sudden insatiable sexual appetite, finally coming up with a wedding date – because you were guilty."

He had seen right through her. He was no fool. "No. No. It wasn't like that."

Scott rose to his feet. "You bitch."

She wheeled, as if she'd been slapped. She looked up at him. Tears streamed down her face. She was drowning, losing control. "Scott, please. That's not very nice. I understand you're angry."

"Were you going to tell me?"

She stared at her feet.

"So you were going to marry me letting me believe that you had been faithful to me. That's not a good way to begin a marriage – dishonesty."

"It just happened once." Her voice cracked.

"So that makes it all right?"

"No, of course not. But I haven't been sleeping round if that's what you think."

"I don't know what to think anymore. You were the one thing that was true in my life. The one thing I could trust. It's gone. It's all gone," he choked. Tears welled up in his eyes again.

"I'm sorry. I don't know what else to say."

She watched him, searched his eyes, looking for some sign that everything would be OK, that they would get through this.

"Maybe we could-"

"Don't." Scott put up his hand. "I don't want to talk to you anymore."

Did anymore mean just now or forever?

He walked right past her, shoulders slumped, and out the door.

Her hand hovered at her side aching to reach out to him, but it was too late. He was gone.

Nerissa had given up trying to cry quietly. Loud sobbing noises erupted from her as she gasped for air and her whole body shook.

Did he hate her that much that he couldn't even stand to be in the same room as her? Why couldn't he have stayed so they could talk it out? She wanted to resolve it now. She wanted to know there was hope, that they had a future.

She was going to have to wait, but waiting wasn't something she wanted to do right now.

The shadows of the trees lengthened, succumbing to the dusk. Her mind willed her body to move, to shut the doors and pull the curtains closed. Her brain was numb; her emotions spent.

She made herself a Milo, the comfort that she needed and crawled into bed. She threw the sheet over her head so she could block out and escape from the world. One part of her willed herself to fall asleep so she could forget it all, that it was just a horrible dream. The other half strained to hear any noise that would indicate that Scott had come back. But sleep wouldn't come. Every minute seemed like an eternity. When she finally drifted off she woke with a start, drenched in sweat, recalling a mixture of faces that alternated between Jackson, Scott and the man who attacked her; blurring into one so the face that eventually emerged was unrecognisable, laughing a hideous cackle, mocking her. The flash of a knife set off in her indescribable panic.

She reached for her Milo. The mug was stone cold.

Outside a car door slammed and the keys in the front door jangled. Scott was home. She peered at the clock – 2.15 am. Where had he been all this time? She waited in the dark. Would he come and see her, tell her it would be OK, that they'd get through it? Hope evaporated. Scott would make good of his intentions by spending the night on the couch.

Chapter 24

She woke again with a start. An unthinkable dream. But it hadn't been a dream. Scott had found out and now there would be repercussions.

The too-bright sun shone against the curtains as she fought waves of nausea. She ran to the bathroom just in time. This had gone on for too long. She'd make a doctor's appointment next week.

When her stomach had settled she took a deep breath ready to face Scott. Now that both of them had had space and time to think, they could be more rational.

She tiptoed into the lounge and peered over the couch. Scott wasn't there. She frowned as she pulled the curtains open. An empty space where Scott's car should've been.

Had he gone already? Without saying goodbye? Maybe he'd left a note. She wandered over to the table, shuffling papers out of the way, but there was no note. She flopped down on the chair. Was this the way it was going to be? How could they get things back on track if he wouldn't talk to her? She checked her phone. Nothing. The blank screen laughed at her. A whole weekend lay out in front of her.

The man who'd bought Maisie was coming to drive her away today so she washed and vacuumed her. She'd be sad to see her trustful, reliable car go.

She then phoned Peter. "Need an extra pair of hands for tomorrow's tours?

"We're all covered," Peter said. "But there is something you could do. We need to get some financial information to the accountants in preparation for selling the business. If you don't mind spending tomorrow sorting through the archival records that would be of real help."

Anything. Anything to keep herself occupied.

The cottage was too quiet. A walk would perhaps settle her stomach.

Down the road, going away from the township was a popular forest track which gently weaved up the hill offering spectacular views over Aqua Bay.

It took her half an hour to get to the top passing only a couple of people going back the other way. It was a pleasant walk marred only by a rotting dead bird lying on the track. She narrowly missed stepping on it.

The sun glistened on the sea. *Seabird* was on her way out for the morning tour.

A woman, sitting on the only seat, sipped from a water bottle and studied her phone.

"May I?" asked Nerissa, indicating the vacant space.

The woman peered up at Nerissa beneath her cap. "Sure." She moved over slightly. "Nice day."

"Typical Aqua Bay weather," Nerissa replied. She turned her head towards the woman. "Tanya, right?"

"Yep. And you're our guardian."

"It's a name that bears a heavy cross." Today she was the furthest person from being a guardian.

"I'm sure you're up to it. Everyone thinks you're great," she said, without maliciousness.

"Well, I'm not feeling that great at the moment."

"I would've thought you'd be relishing spending time with those hunky Taxxoil guys."

Nerissa clenched her jaw. "I can't say I've noticed."

"Aw, come on. I think every sane woman in Aqua Bay wouldn't mind getting some loving from those guys."

"We don't all have one thing on our mind," Nerissa snapped back.

Tanya squinted at her. "You've been spending a lot of time with Jackson. You must admit he is seriously good looking."

"How would you know how much time I spend with Jackson?" Alarm bells rang in her head.

"You can't escape the fact that we live in a small town. People talk."

God. What were people saying? Did the whole town know? A tight knot formed in her stomach.

"Besides," Tanya continued, "that tone of voice sounds like a denial when there's actually truth behind it."

The knot exploded and with it, tears.

"A-ha," she said. Her mouth turned up in a smirk. "Something's going on."

"I... Jackson," Nerissa stuttered.

"That Jackson has probably broken a million hearts the world over."

"Thanks. That doesn't help."

Tanya cast an eye over Nerissa. "I don't know much about you, but you come across as sweet, maybe a little green but generous. And you have Mr Perfect. You're made for each other. When watching the two of you together it's like the epitome of the perfect couple. He worships you and you wear your heart on your sleeve. You obviously love him. But somehow that hasn't been enough for you."

Nerissa bowed her head. Was she really that transparent? "I would never intentionally hurt Scott." She looked as far as she could to the horizon. If only she could just sail away. But running away from her problems, problems that she had created, wouldn't help.

"Let me see if I can paint a profile for you. Before Jackson arrived on the scene life was predictable and mapped out for you. You were unconsciously looking for drama to spice up your existence. And low and behold Jackson arrives not only threatening Aqua Bay, but your idyllic life.

"He's the complete opposite to Scott. You're attracted to him because he's wrong for you. He represents danger and unpredictability, something you're craving right now. Jackson's a mischief maker. He tests boundaries as far as he can to see what he can get away with. He's charged things up for you. You think you knew what you wanted from life and he's challenged that and you've naively fallen into his web of charm. He's one bad boy with high testosterone trying to channel his aggression in some meaningful way. Sex with bad boys can be adventurous and rough." Tanya laughed.

A hot, fiery flame spread across Nerissa's chest as she shifted uncomfortably on the seat. Was Tanya talking generally or specifically about Jackson?

"How am I doing so far?" Tanya asked.

"You're pretty much on track," Nerissa confessed.

"You're using Jackson to fill an emptiness and when everything you stand for fails to impress him it compromises your values. How long has Jackson been here? Eight weeks?"

"Sounds about right."

"In just that short timeframe Jackson has entered and rocked your world because it's filling a space that you haven't defined properly. It means you're open to anything."

Nerissa brushed back tears. This was like having someone telling her the cold, hard truth about herself. "I've tried to stay away from him, but the harder I try the more I seem to be there in his face and he in mine, I'm not sure which."

"Hey, I'm not going to ask you whether you and Jackson did the wild thing. It's none of my business. But you know there's no future in it. He's opened your eyes to risks you can take. But what ones are you comfortable about pursuing, and getting away with? There should be no doubt about who your true self is."

"How do you know all this?"

"Hey, I've been round." She laughed. "I know the town thinks I'm a hussy. I'm the go-to woman for a good time. But what most people don't know is that I have a psychology degree."

Nerissa raised her eyebrows. No, she hadn't known this. Who would've guessed? She looked at Tanya with a new found respect.

"Anyway, sitting here isn't helping with the flabby belly," Tanya said, tapping her stomach as she stood up. "You used to come up from the city during the school holidays with your family, didn't you?"

Nerissa nodded.

"I remember your sisters. You were the youngest trying desperately to be just like them and obey your parents, do what they wanted you to do. Especially that mother of yours. I think you've finally said enough's enough and you're rebelling. Just channel that rebellion in the right place and you'll be happy. Ciao now." She gave a slight wave of her hand as she headed off down the track.

"Tanya," Nerissa shouted after her.

"Yes?" she said, turning round.

"Thanks. Oh, and um, if you were thinking of popping by Jackson's at some stage to pick up a scarf you might've mislaid, he threw it out."

Tanya laughed. "I wondered where that had got to"

Nerissa stared back out over the bay. The wind had come up, whipping whitecaps on the waves. What Tanya had said was true. It was like she could see right through her. And having it explained like that drove home the truth.

She didn't see herself as a rebel, but maybe she was making a defiant statement against a strict upbringing. She hung her head. She'd fallen from grace and it was now up to her to fix it. Her heart ached from the pain she had caused Scott. He was her priority now.

She stood up with a new determination to make everything between them right again. She would wait until Scott rang her. They would talk and figure this all out together.

Chapter 25

Everything was turning more complicated by the day. Scott, Katey, Jackson. Would the awfulness never end?

On Saturday in an effort to keep her mind off things she grabbed a pair of rubber gloves and a rubbish bag and jumped on her bike. She rode down Craypot Road towards the beach. She parked her bike up against a seat underneath a cypress tree and wandered down the stony path that led out onto a less popular part of Aqua Bay. At this time of the year, more tourists round meant more rubbish.

She made her way down the beach scooping up discarded plastic water bottles, paper, containers and cans. The brisk wind whipped up white caps, spray skimming off the tops.

When the rubbish bag was half-full she made her way back to her bike. She secured the top tightly. Now there would be fewer hazards for animals.

Her mind wandered to the thing that had been bugging her the most - how to approach things with Katey. Not only was she her best friend, they spent a fair amount of time working together. Maybe it was best that she didn't say anything. Pretend she didn't know and just let it pass. Her cell rang. It was Scott's father, Lou. She was ready to deal with it.

She breathed in deeply as she answered. "Lou, hi."

"Nerissa, how are you?"

"OK."

"I'm sorry to bother you but there's um… rather a delicate matter I need to raise with you."

She tightened her grip on the phone ready for what was to come.

"It's about Scott."

"I know I'm sorry. I haven't really had the chance to speak to him yet."

"Did he mention anything about the money?"

"Money?" What did money have to do with it?

"There are some funds that have gone missing at work."

"Wh- wh- What does that have to do with Scott?"

"Well, we did a bit of detective work and Scott has made an unauthorised payment."

"How much money?"

"$10,000."

Cold prickles of fear ran down her spine.

"Nerissa, have you received any money from Scott recently?"

"I have. Well, not me personally. He gave me a piece of paper confirming a payment for $10,000 to help with the legal costs for Operation Protect. I had no idea that it hadn't been through the necessary channels."

"All debit transactions must have two signatories."

"I don't understand what the problem is."

"One of those signatures was Scott's. The other was mine. Except I didn't sign it. The signature has been forged."

Nerissa gasped. "Are you saying Scott forged it?"

"I don't know. And that's what I need to speak to Scott about. I wanted to talk to you first to see what you knew."

"I had no idea. I can't believe Scott would do anything like this."

"Well, I need to get his side of the story. I've been trying to get hold of him all weekend, but he's not answering his phone. I thought he'd come up to see you this weekend."

"He did… He was…" she stumbled. She bit her lip. Lou obviously had no idea the turmoil his son was in.

"Nerissa?"

"Ahhh. He's already left." Yesterday. But why wasn't he answering his phone? "I'm sure there's a perfectly good explanation."

The breeze picked up a notch.

"Nerissa?"

"Yes."

"It might be best not to touch the money until we get to the bottom of this."

"Yes. Sure. I understand."

She rang off, sat down on the seat with a thud and took a deep breath, the smell of the sea filling her lungs. Her hands clenched and unclenched. Her nerves were like tightly strung wire. Missing money? Scott? What was going on? It didn't make sense. None of it made sense.

The perfect image of Scott disintegrated in front of her like someone throwing a brick at a mirror, shards of glass raining down on her.

What about the money? Operation Protect needed that $10,000. How would they be able to pay their bills? Where would the money come from to finance the next lot of activities?

The sea spray cut across the waves, blurring the horizon.

Was Scott avoiding her because he was guilty too? Hope that Scott would ring drifted away.

Chapter 26

Swimming wasn't something she needed to concentrate on. Routine meant that she could do her laps of the pool while her feet kicked constantly, churning up the water in time with the churning in her stomach. She swam like a woman possessed.

Both she and Katey were scheduled on alternate tours and apart from a quick handover between each tour there'd been little time to talk. It seemed Katey had been going out of her way to avoid her. Was she trying to deal with her guilt too?

Scott hadn't rung. Surely he'd had enough time to think. Did he not want to work things out? Was it over? Nerissa couldn't bear the alternative. Enough time had passed. It was clear Scott wasn't going to ring her. Maybe he'd been waiting for her to call first. Why hadn't she thought of that? He had no idea that she still wanted him in her life. Perhaps her silence meant to him that she didn't care. And with Jackson still round his male pride would be severely dented.

Katey phoned in sick on Thursday which meant Nerissa had to do both the morning and afternoon tours. Not that she minded. The one place that truly made her feel at home and forget everything was being out on the ocean and watching the beautiful dolphins.

She left the pool and walked to work nibbling on plain cracker biscuits, the only thing she seemed to be able to stomach early in the day.

She scowled as she peered out to sea. The *Perspeculor* was out working. Maybe the ship would sink.

Tonight she would work up the courage to call Scott.

After the morning's tour she took yesterday's cash to the bank and picked up the mail from the post office. As she walked towards the van someone called out to her.

"Hey, Nerissa."

She turned round. Angie was on the other side of the road, waving.

Angie ran across the road as best she could in her sky-high heels. "Perfect timing. I was going to let you know that the owners of the cottage have accepted your offer. Congratulations."

"Oh. I'd... Gosh." Nerissa had completely forgotten about the impulsive offer she'd made. With things so unclear now, it didn't seem like a good idea any more.

"You don't look all that pleased," Angie said.

"I've just been busy. It'd slipped my mind."

"Completely understandable with all your commitments. You know you're really putting Aqua Bay on the map. Our own little eco-star. You're doing us proud."

Nerissa shook her head. Proud was the last word she'd use to describe herself.

303

"I've got documents you need to sign. Maybe I can pop over during the weekend."

"Sure," Nerissa said. Grey clouds were building up behind the hills.

"Better fly. I've still got some other things to do. Will I see you and Scott at The Crab and Apple tonight?"

"No. Scott can't make it this weekend."

"What?" Angie frowned. "Oh, that's bizarre. I'm sure I saw Scott's station wagon parked down Forest Road."

"No. I don't think so. He definitely couldn't make it."

"Dark blue Holden?"

"Yeah, that sounds like Scott's car."

"Oh, well. Maybe he's going to surprise you." Angie punched her arm playfully.

Nerissa shook her head. "I'm really sure it's not him. I'd better let you go."

"I'll catch you later."

Nerissa walked back to the van. Angie was mistaken. Surely Scott would've let her know if he was coming up. Besides, there was a lot of dark blue Holdens round.

She started up the van when something in her brain chimed like a warning bell. Forest Road. That was the road Katey lived on.

Steered by some automatic switch, she drove down Forest Road. As she got closer to Katey's flat, the blue Holden that Angie had described was still there. And it was Scott's.

She parked the van. What was he doing here in Aqua Bay and without even telling her? And why was he at Katey's?

Her legs were like lead as she climbed out of the van and ventured up the path. She walked round to the back door, which was open. She raised her hand to knock, but stopped. It was unusually quiet inside.

She tiptoed inside. She had been to Katey's flat many times and knew the layout. She had often slept in the spare bedroom after one of their late night drinking sessions. The kitchen and small lounge was empty. Why was her brain telling her not to go any further? Walking down the hall, she was drawn by the sound of soft moaning and groaning. What was she about to discover? Her heart thumped so loudly she was sure the walls would collapse with the vibrations. She swallowed and peered into Katey's bedroom. She was in bed, but certainly not ill like she'd claimed to be. She was sitting up with her back to Nerissa and she was naked. Her head was arched back. A male, grunting, getting louder.

Nerissa gasped. Katey turned round. "Oh shit!" she exclaimed, falling to one side.

"What the..?" the male exclaimed. He lifted himself up onto his elbows.

Nerissa took one look at Scott and covered her mouth. The blood drained from her face. Shock, nausea, fright hit her all at once. A foul taste of bile rose in her throat.

"Oh God!" Scott said. Horror passed across his face.

305

Nerissa bolted down the hall, out the door and jumped in the van her mind screaming in a hundred million directions.

"Wait, Nerissa," Scott called out.

She shoved the van into gear and tore down the street and back to the cottage. Tears swam in her eyes like an overflowing swimming pool.

Inside the cottage she pulled all the curtains shut, flung herself on the couch and rocked back and forth as the tears kept falling and falling.

How could Scott do such a thing? Was this his idea of revenge? It didn't seem like something Scott would do. But did you ever really know someone? She didn't even know herself anymore. And as for Katey. She never wanted to see her again. How long had this been going on? Unanswered questions raced back and forth tumbling over and over in her mind.

Her phone buzzed. She pulled it from her pocket. It was Scott calling, sending her into a new spasm of weeping. She threw the phone on the couch.

When there were no more tears left to cry, an unbearable surge of emptiness, numbness and sorrow engulfed her.

As dusk descended, her phone buzzed again. A text from Scott:

I'm so sorry. Please, please can we talk.

What would talking do now? Perhaps if she had been brave enough to ring Scott in the first place, to make the first move she wouldn't have driven him into the arms of another woman, her best friend.

She ignored the text. She left the phone on the table and stumbled into bed.

***

She craved sleep, for blankness, blackness, but there was only blurry grey. Neither here, there or anywhere. Gloom overwhelmed her. And the tears started again. She swallowed hard over the lumps that formed in her throat.

***

Saturday passed. Sunday passed. She cocooned herself in the bedroom rising only to visit the bathroom to pee or throw up.

One half-hearted check on her cell phone and there had been ten missed calls or pleading texts from Scott.

One instantaneous act of passion had led her to where she was now, drowning in a sea of turmoil. But it had been her own fault, her own doing and she was paying the price. And she had no idea where to go from here.

***

Monday she phoned in sick, cancelled all her media commitments and made a doctor's appointment.

Five missed calls/texts from Scott, each text seemed to grow more frantic.

She missed a call from Angie, something about signing a sale and purchase agreement.

Greenpeace had left messages, but she wasn't interested.

She turned her phone off, flopped on the couch and pulled a blanket over her head, blocking out the world.

***

She lifted her head off the pillow. Somewhere, something banged.

"Nerissa. Open up," the distinctive American voice called out. More banging on the front door.

She wiped her hands over her face. She wouldn't answer the door.

"Nerissa. Come on. I know you're in there."

"Go away," she yelled out.

"Please let me in. I'm worried about you."

Silence.

"I'm not going away."

"I'm not opening the door."

"Well, I'll just keep banging and you'll have to deal with the stories people will tell as they drive past and see me standing at your front door."

God. That would be the last thing she needed. More gossip, more lies.

She struggled up to a sitting position then stood and shuffled over to the door opening it a smidgeon.

She sighed. "What do you want?"

"What's going on? Your curtains have been pulled closed since Friday night."

She opened the door wider taking a better look at him. He had yellowish/brown bruises under both eyes and a sticking plaster across the bridge of his nose. The ends of sutures poked out.

"What happened to you?"

"A disgruntled fiancé punched me in the face, remember?"

She'd been so absorbed over the last week and determined to stay clear of Jackson she'd forgotten about last Friday's punch up. Had it only been a week ago? How things changed so quickly in the blink of an eye.

"I'm sorry. Come in." She opened the door wider.

She drew her dressing gown round her. What a sight she must look. Ratty hair, a face and body not washed for three days, teeth unbrushed. She moved her blanket and pillow off the couch.

Jackson sat down beside her and wrapped an arm round her shoulder.

Once being this close to him would have sent her pulse racing. Now, nothing.

"OK. Spill."

"Scott and I haven't spoken since he flattened you but he came up on Friday, which I didn't know. I found him in bed with Katey," she said. The never-ending tears fell again.

"That wild cat. I knew she was trouble."

"I feel such a fool. I know I did wrong but, this really hurts."

"Have you spoken to Scott?"

"He keeps calling and leaving messages, but I can't speak to him. Not yet."

"What do you think you'll do?"

"I don't know. I'm so confused. I wish I'd never met you," she whispered.

Jackson's arm dropped immediately and he moved away. "Are you trying to blame me for where you are today?" His jaw tightened. "If I remember rightly you were just as willing as me."

She buried her head in her hands. "I don't want to be just another notch in your bed post. I bet you love your reputation of being able to score any chick in any town you arrive in."

"I fought my feelings towards you as hard as I could. I admit you were fun to start with. You were easy bait to tease. I'm not proud that I seduced another man's woman. But eventually I felt something change. I don't know what it is about Aqua Bay and this drive you have to want to protect it at all costs. I guess I see the fierce determination in you that I so often see in myself. You seem to be so sure about what you want – a family, a life here."

"Well, I think I've pretty much mucked that up. What do you want from life?"

Jackson breathed in hard. "I want a family too."

"You have a family. You have Ben, but you're running away from something."

"I have some good news on that front. My mother called me."

"Your mother?"

"She saw the article on the news and tracked me down through Taxxoil."

Nerissa looked at him. "That's good news, right?"

"I can't believe after so long that she finally found me. I had, like, a million questions. Like why she's never tried to contact me before. We talked for hours. She will never forgive herself for leaving me at the hospital, but she didn't feel she had an option. She needed to keep Antoni safe. And there was a mix-up. She went to a refuge for a while and left in a hurry when Old Man Joe's heavies were getting closer. The refuge had left her a message to let her know I was being discharged. She never got the message as she took off to New Mexico."

"How's Antoni?'

"Not well. He has chronic fatigue syndrome."

"I'm sorry to hear that."

"He's ringing me tonight. It will be the first time I will have spoken to my brother in nearly 20 years."

"Wow. This must be a pretty emotional time for you."

"A lot's been going on. But we've diverted. What are you going to do?"

"I don't know."

"Ring Scott. Silence and ignoring him will only make the problem fester."

Nerissa sighed. "You're right."

"And you need a shower."

"Oh, God. Is it that bad?"

"Hey, I've worked in some places where we had to go for over a week without showering. But I wouldn't leave it that long." He jumped up, moving round the cottage and drawing the curtains open.

Nerissa squinted at the assault of the sudden light.

"The weather's packing up. There's a strong southerly on its way," Jackson said.

Nerissa watched the trees wave back and forward in the strengthening wind. The sky was a gloomy gunmetal grey.

Now she had a new found determination, she was anxious for Jackson to leave. "Scott will be back in the city, but God knows what would happen if he unexpectedly turned up and found you here." She hustled Jackson towards the front door.

"I can sneak out the back door if that would please you."

"Don't be silly. Just don't hang about."

"Yes, ma'am."

He walked down the front stairs.

"Jackson," Nerissa said.

He turned round.

"Thanks. And I'm glad you've reconnected with your mum and brother."

His mouth turned up in a crooked grin. "Me too." He tipped his Stetson and walked off, whistling a tune.

After a shower, she stared at her cell for what seemed like an eternity. She drew in a long breath and dialled Scott's number.

Chapter 27

Scott answered on the first ring. "Nerissa. I've been waiting for you to call," he started in a rush.

"I'm ready to talk."

"This isn't something we should do over the phone. I can come over now."

"Are you still here? Why aren't you at work? Where have you been staying?" She paced to the window.

"I've been at the backpackers."

Her shoulders dropped with relief. "Come on over then.

"I'm on my way."

She sat. She paced. She sat down again. Her nerves jangled. Heavy raindrops fell on the roof and the whole cottage creaked as the wind picked up speed.

She jumped up when the front door opened. A cold surge of air followed Scott inside. She watched him as he took off his raincoat and draped it over a chair. He stood with his arms crossed over his shoulders. His pale face was pinched and black circles rimmed his bloodshot eyes. He'd had as many sleepless nights as her.

He reached out tentatively.

She stepped backwards and his face crumpled at the rejection.

"I guess we're in a bit of a mess," he said.

"Maybe I could start. I'll ask the same question you asked me. Why?"

"I have no explanation. I was just lonely and Katey was there."

She had a lump in her throat the size of Africa. "Did having sex with Katey make you feel better?"

"No, it didn't help – at all."

"Well, we're even then."

"This isn't about keeping score."

"OK. So what's this about?" Her voice rose.

The raindrops travelled down Scott's raincoat and dripped on the floor.

"You've changed, Nerissa. I don't know you anymore. You slept with Jackson, you lied to me, and you have no reasonable explanation as to why. And I bump into Angie yesterday congratulating me on buying the cottage. What's that about?"

"I've put an offer in on the cottage and it's been accepted."

"Without discussing it with me?"

"I didn't need to discuss it with you. I'm sick of people telling me what to do, telling me how to think, how I should behave. I want to do something for myself."

"We can't afford the cottage."

"There's no 'we' here. This is about me."

"Where are you getting the money from?"

"I'm using my trust fund. And speaking of money. Your father rang me last week. He wants to speak to you about some missing money."

"I know. We've spoken."

"Did they find it?"

"Yes."

"What happened?"

"I forged dad's signature."

So it was true. "I don't believe you would do that."

Scott's eyes brimmed with tears. "I did."

"Why?" she pleaded.

"I did it for you. I thought we were drifting apart and that giving you the money would help in some way."

Should she be pleased or offended? "Like buy my love?"

"No. No."

"You were spending a lot of time at work. There were three weekends in a row you couldn't make it up here."

"It was not all about my work. Your infatuation with this oil drilling is partly to blame too."

"Infatuation? I don't understand. People just don't seem to get it. You're talking about my livelihood, my life, the place I want to bring up my family, here in Aqua Bay."

"Well, that's news to me. I thought our life was going to be in the city. We chose that land to build our house because it overlooked the sea. Isn't that's what you wanted too?"

"No, Scott. That's what you wanted."

"Why are you telling me this now?"

"This whole business with the oil drilling made me realise how much my heart is here. I don't think I'll ever be able to live in the city."

Scott gave a long, low sigh. "So where does that leave us?"

The gap that had been widening between them grew larger.

In her heart of hearts the words she had to say, needed to say remained stuck on her tongue. The silence expanded. Why didn't Scott take her in his arms and say how much he loved her and that it would be all right?

"Some time apart might be a good thing," she choked.

Scott turned his head away. "If that's what you think we need then, sure, I can give you that. But Nerissa, how did things get this way? I don't understand what's happened to us."

I've had the same thoughts too, but you won't even look me in the eye. How can I believe you still love me? She sighed. "Time apart might help you too," she said quietly. "Will you be going back to the city today?"

"No. I'm going to stay here for the time being. Dad's taken disciplinary action against me." He hung his head. "It's only fair. I have to be treated like any other employee."

"Does he know about us?"

"No. Let's just try and keep this between you and me until things are clearer."

Nerissa nodded. She watched Scott put on his coat and disappear out the front door as the swirling wind and rain gathered momentum. The leaves tumbled over each other down the path.

Well, they'd finally cleared the air, but things were still unresolved between them. What was clear was that she was over Jackson. Tanya had helped her to see why she'd been attracted to him. And somehow the spark that had once been there had died, as if someone had thrown cold water over her.

But Scott? Trust from both sides had been tested and failed. For her to be the wife Scott wanted her to be just couldn't happen in Aqua Bay. Was she strong enough to give it all up to begin a life in a city away from her beloved Aqua Bay? If only Scott had told her face-to-face he was sorry and that he loved her she would be more convinced.

But she guessed that this would be what time apart would prove.

Chapter 28

The next morning she made herself a Milo and nibbled on a cracker. She brought her hand up to her eye and rubbed hard. Every time she blinked it was like someone had thrown fine grit into her eyes. Lack of sleep would do that to you.

Rain had fallen during the night and what had started as a light thumping on the roof had gradually turned into a pounding. The wind had picked up, howling, and screeching like a kea. There was so much creaking she feared the roof would lift right off.

She rang Peter to let him know she'd be coming into work.

"Have you heard the news?" he asked.

"No. I've not had the radio on," she replied, frowning. "Has something happened?"

"There are reports coming in that a container ship, the Pacific Way, has hit the Oma Rocks just north of Aqua Bay. It's not looking good. Fuel oil is already leaking."

A cold chill swept over Nerissa. Was her worst fear of an oil spill in Aqua Bay about to be realised? "What can we do?"

"Unfortunately, nothing at the moment. We'll have to ride out the storm. The ORD is preparing to get absorbent booms set up round the shore."

"I'll be into work as soon as I can."

Driving the van into town was no easy task. The rain pelted down and she struggled against the wind gusts to keep the van in a straight line. The grey sea and sky merged as one in a swirling haze. Road visibility was reduced and she switched on the lights. As she got out of the van, wind whipped up stinging rain, slapping across her face. She pulled her hood over her head and ran inside. She practically flew in the door, pushed from behind by the strength of the wind. Rain water and sea salt mingled on her lips.

"We've cancelled today's tours," Mavis said. "We can't go out in this, it's too dangerous. Besides Katey's called in sick. There is still that awful stomach bug going round. How are you feeling now?"

"Better. It comes and goes," Nerissa replied. She flicked her eyes over the latest marine report.

Katey wasn't sick. She just didn't want to face her. Did that mean she was with Scott? Nerissa didn't even want to go there.

"Any further news on the Pacific Way?" she asked Peter.

"She's stuck fast on the rocks and there's definitely oil leaking." Peter rubbed his eyebrow. "The ORD is about to declare a Level 3 emergency. An animal hospital is being set up next door. They may need some help."

"Good idea."

Nerissa rushed next door. She was familiar with the work of the Marine Mammal Emergency Centre, the MEC, having done a research paper on them for her degree.

Ginny, the manager, spotted Nerissa. "Come to help?"

"Definitely. What can I do?"

"We're preparing for a worst case scenario. Dead and injured birds." Ginny pointed to the rear of the building. "Over here we'll assess the birds. Fortunately, we've got access to a kitchen so we can prepare food for them. This will be our administration area where we'll manage the volunteers and we'll need a heap of them. And over here we'll have the mortuary because we'll be expecting a high proportion of dead birds."

Nerissa gulped. God, how would this affect her beloved dolphins?

"The birds will be tagged and bio test data collected. How about we get you trained up in the incoming area?"

Nerissa spent the rest of the day learning what to do once any birds arrived.

The wind and rain did not let up. The noise was deafening; she needed to almost yell at the person next to her. And in between working, staff and volunteers filled each other in on the latest reports of the stricken Pacific Way. Each update was worse than the one before. A huge hole had appeared in the bow and the ship had listed to port.

The storm continued for another 24 hours and Nerissa spent the next day helping co-ordinate volunteers for what was now going to be a massive clean-up job. All of the time she worried about the dolphins.

When she woke up Wednesday morning it wasn't to the howling wind, but to an eerie silence. Something wasn't right. As she crawled out of bed and opened the curtains, warm sunlight hit her full in the face. The sky was a brilliant blue, rinsed clean of chaos. The storm had finally exhausted itself and had moved on. Today would be the one she had been dreading. The full extent of the Pacific Way grounding would be realised.

She rang Peter who explained he and Mavis would be taking a reconnaissance mission in *Seabird* to evaluate damage and keep an eye on the dolphins. An oil slick could enter their blowholes and they could also breathe in the toxic chemicals that evaporate from the oily surface. All tours for the rest of the week had been cancelled. Did she want to come to?

"I think I would be of better use at the MEC."

She pedalled into town. There was debris everywhere – branches, mud, whole trees, enormous puddles, even a dead sheep. The mess was unbelievable. The slimy stink of oil hung in the air.

When she opened the doors of the MEC, the wildlife emergency response centre was in a flurry of activity; people wearing high visual jackets and clutching walky-talkies strode from one area to another issuing instructions, consulting each other and moving equipment.

She spotted Ginny at one of the tables. "Where do you want me?"

"Our first lot of live oil-slicked birds are coming in. Can you help out in the incoming area again?"

Nerissa joined the incoming group. Her stomach clenched like it was in a vice. Bird after bird – shags, petrels, gulls and shearwaters – covered in a heavy film of black oil were brought in. Her heart almost broke in two when the first of the little blue penguins arrived. She opened a plastic bag filled with dead birds, barely recognisable in the sticky sludge, their beaks buried in each other's feathers. Flies were gathering as the heat and stench increased. She shut her eyes and said a silent prayer.

The surviving birds were triaged, tagged and had blood tests taken. They were then monitored in a holding pen, fed and washed.

Nerissa worked with a group of four to smear the birds with canola oil, which helped to loosen the black oil. Each bird was then washed repeatedly in a mixture of warm water and dishwashing detergent and then sent off to be rinsed by a high pressure hose to ensure every trace of oil and mixture was gone. This was an important part of the process as it ensured the bird was able to waterproof itself again.

Time was critical and they had to work fast.

It was hard not to cry as each bird struggled as it was held - stressed out, worn out and scared.

At midday Ginny came to update the group. "We've got more birds coming in and not enough people to help. The oil has come ashore and everyone's out on the beach cleaning up. The community is stretched. We need more people to help here. If everyone could get at least three more volunteers and meet back here by 1 pm for a briefing."

The group broke up. Three more people. Where could she commandeer three more people? Then it hit her. She took off down the main street and hurtled up the stairs to the Taxxoil office. And as luck would have it Jackson, Mac and Brodie were there doing an inventory of their gear. They all looked up in surprise as she burst through the doors.

"We've got birds covered in oil and time's running out. We're in full recovery mode. We need all the help we can get."

Jackson jumped to his feet. "We'll do all we can."

"I don't know whether that's a good idea-," Mac began.

"Fire me or whatever, but I'm going to help. You two coming?"

Mac and Brodie looked at each other and then without a word they grabbed their high visual jackets.

Nerissa shot a look of relief and a silent thank you at Jackson. "Follow me."

By the time they got back to the MEC a small crowd of volunteers had gathered outside the front.

"It's not enough," Ginny said desperately.

"It's the best we can do for now."

Ginny eyed the three Taxxoil guys. "What are they doing here?"

"I don't think this is the time to be too choosy about who our volunteers are."

Nerissa surveyed the crowd. Some people had come straight from their offices. There was a local fishing crew, a few farmers and some tourists. And standing at the back a discreet distance between them was Scott and Katey. Had they arrived together? Were they together?

"OK," Ginny said. "Thanks everyone. We're going to divide you up into teams of four. Each team will have a leader who will show you what needs to be done. So, Nerissa's team. Let's see... OK... You, you and you. If you can meet over there with Nerissa." Ginny had seemingly, at random, picked three people. But was this some kind of a sick joke? The three people Ginny had picked were Scott, Katey and Jackson. She fought down rising nausea. How was this going to work? But right now, she needed to be the leader.

Nerissa moved over to the side waiting for the others to join her. Would they join her? Scott moved first, making his way over from the back bypassing Katey without looking in her direction. He came up to Nerissa's side. "I'm all yours," he said, looking deeply into her eyes.

The double meaning did not escape her and she smiled at him.

Katey hung back, her chin trembled as Scott snubbed her. She refused to make any eye contact with Nerissa.

Jackson strolled over to join Nerissa, Scott and Katey.

Scott eyeballed Jackson, who stood his ground and glowered back. He had both hands on his hips and his stance was strong.

Scott crossed his arms over his chest. Were the two of them going to flatten each other?

"Sorry. I can't do anything about the makeup of the teams," Nerissa said, looking round her as the other teams had formed and gone inside. "But we'll just have to get on with it." She looked at Scott. "Are you still in?"

"For sure," he said, staring straight at Jackson, his chin defiant.

"Jackson?'

"You bet."

"Katey?"

"I'll do what I can, but I can't stay long. I'm not well."

Nerissa turned her back on her and summoned her team inside.

After she showed them how to treat the birds they settled into a pattern. Jackson and Scott would wipe the canola oil on the birds and Katey would do the washing. Nerissa supervised and once each bird was washed she would take it to the next team to do the rinsing.

There was a lot going on round them with other teams working amongst the organised chaos. Apart from Nerissa delivering instructions in a steady voice, few words passed between the m. They had been forced together by a disaster and what mattered now was saving as many birds as possible.

Nerissa moved between Jackson, Scott and Katey offering advice and encouraging them. Jackson and Scott were working on a shag. Jackson was able to keep a struggling and frightened bird still with a combination of strength and gentleness. Just like when they had rescued the stricken shag caught in the fishing line.

And when she looked at Scott her mind wandered to Chloe's birthday party and how Scott had soothed his niece after she had fallen over. Scott was barely touching the shag, scared as if it would break in two. His touch, one of gentleness too. Here were two different men. She loved Scott. She had-no doubt about that. And Jackson? She didn't love him. But she'd been physically attracted to him. He had been someone who had pushed her out of her comfort zone, opened up her world and had encouraged her to dig deep, to be courageous.

Katey was working alone. Nerissa whisked the shearwater she had been working on off to the next tent. When she arrived back, Katey was removing her gloves.

"I've got to go," she said.

"Thanks Katey," Nerissa said softly.

"You know," Katey said, looking Nerissa in the eye for the first time. "You're a traitor to Aqua Bay, the way you fraternised with Jackson, leading him on. You just use people to get what you want." Her eyes flashed with fury and her words dripped with scorn. "And you don't deserve Scott. He's too good for you." She turned and stomped out of the tent.

The full impact of what Katey had said hit her and her emotions bubbled over. Her knees wobbled like jelly and she gripped the table. A long friendship had just come to an end and she'd also lost a bridesmaid. There would be no more baking cupcakes together, girly sleepovers or listening to the never-ending drama of Katey's love life, which she'd now dragged herself and Scott into. Did she believe what Katey had said? A traitor? Maybe she didn't deserve Scott.

Her bones and muscles ached, her brain was numb and she could hardly think, shell shocked by all the topsy-turvey things that had happened in the last few weeks. But she had to keep going. They needed to save as many birds as they could.

Another team relieved them for a lunch break. Volunteers provided sandwiches, quiche, chocolate cake and fruit.

Nerissa, Jackson and Scott sat inside together munching on their sandwiches as they surveyed the work taking place on the beach. Big oil patches like cowpats had landed on the beach. People dressed in white protection suits were using sieves to pick up the oil.

The tension between Jackson and Scott had eased and small talk now replaced the alpha male attitude.

"Have we lost Katey?" Jackson asked.

"I don't think she'll be back," Nerissa said. She watched Scott. Not a flicker of anything.

They went back to their work again, joined by a German tourist who added a different dynamic to the team. Despite the language barrier he quickly caught on as to what he needed to do and added a respectful, and a welcome, touch of humour. Bags of dead birds kept arriving. News reporters were filming and interviewing and Nerissa spent an hour providing updates to various media personnel pushing her guardian role to the limit.

Ginny relieved the team for the day at 5 pm.

"We'll be back tomorrow," Nerissa said.

She left Jackson to finish cleaning himself up and walked with Scott outside.

"I know that can't have been easy for you," Nerissa said. She brushed her hair off her face.

"I don't like the guy," Scott said. "I did it to help you."

"I appreciate that. I'm sure the birds did too."

A slight smile wavered across his lips.

"And that guy was the first on the scene when I was attacked," she reminded him.

His expression remained blank. "I'll be in town for a few more days. I'm not sure what then."

Nerissa's heart dropped. Hadn't working together today, spending time together helped them to recover from their wounds? But it was obviously too soon and maybe too late. She longed to push him for some kind of commitment, but she bit her tongue. She would give him the space; she would just have to be patient.

"Thanks again," she said and turned to walk back to the centre.

Jackson was standing outside. "You love birds made up yet?"

"I think I've lost him."

"He's working through it. Give him some time. How are you feeling?"

"Empty. I'm trying to push this image of Scott and Katey together out of my mind, but it just won't go away. I don't think he can move past it and I don't know whether I can either."

"Let's go and drown our sorrows," he said, putting an arm round her shoulder. "I've got beer and wine back home. Come and share a drink with me."

Nerissa was past thinking what people would think if they saw her and Jackson together. "My bike is at work."

"Wheel it round to our offices and I'll put it in the back of the Rover for you."

They took off down Craypot Road. Jackson's phone rang and he pulled over to the side of the road to answer it.

"Good to see you've decided not to drive and talk anymore," Nerissa said, when he'd finished the call.

"Hmm. You've been a good influence on me." He grinned at her.

Back at Jackson's cottage he switched on the TV and ordered pizza.

"A wine for you?" Jackson asked.

"How about lemonade?"

Jackson cocked his eyebrow. "That's not like you."

"Anything alcoholic at the moment will make me silly. I think I'm already drunk on emotion and exhaustion."

When the news came on, the full extent of the mountainous task ahead of them became reality.

Silent tears rolled down Nerissa's face as shot after shot of distressed animals being treated were shown. A huge white tarpaulin on the ground was covered in dead birds, their species barely recognisable.

Ginny had been interviewed. "Sixty birds are now being treated at the MEC. And so far we have over 500 dead birds. There'll be a heap more to come. We don't know yet what damage this had done to our paua, crayfish and kina."

The shot returned to the male newsreader.

"This incident has kept the issue of deep sea oil drilling very much alive. Earlier on today Nerissa Taylor from Aqua Bay's Operation Protect had this to say."

Nerissa came on the screen. "We are now facing the biggest oil disaster to ever hit New Zealand. This is a perfect example of what could happen if we pursue this crazy idea of oil drilling. It puts the environment at too much risk and no-one wants to sacrifice that. We need to learn from this unfortunate experience and get the government to develop strong policies that will protect what we have. Once it's gone, it's gone."

Nerissa could no longer watch herself or the heart-breaking images of dead birds. She strolled outside and sank down onto the wicker chair, resting her head on her hand.

A few minutes later Jackson joined her sitting cross-legged in front of her.

"I seem to always make you cry," Jackson said.

Nerissa dug in her pocket for a tissue. "Can't you see now how disastrous it would be if this idea of oil drilling continues?"

"Yes."

Nerissa raised her head.

"I wasn't in the States during the Gulf oil spill. I, like everyone else, saw the photos and coverage. But seeing it first-hand today and those birds fighting for their survival, being not only physically but emotionally involved, puts it into perspective."

A little sigh escaped from Nerissa. "You mean you won't continue to do any more surveying?"

"That's a way bigger decision than I can make. But I'd certainly say after this accident surveying will be suspended at least temporarily." He leant back on his elbows. "Are you sure you didn't rustle up a storm and somehow drive a ship onto rocks to really make your point?"

Her mouth quivered into a half-smile. "I can see now that even though we've a tonne of injured and dead animals, if they've gone through this to help save the future of wildlife then, it will have been worth it."

They both looked up as a car pulled up outside.

"Pizza! Yes!" Jackson said, untangling his long legs. He paid the driver and took the box, chips and garlic bread. "You want to eat this inside?" he asked.

"Might be safer. There's still a distinctive smell of oil in the air. But can we turn off the TV? I just need some time out."

"When have you ever asked for permission?" Jackson cocked on eyebrow at her.

She threw her paper towel at him and it landed square on his nose.

For a while they ate the pizza in silence, but it wasn't an awkward silence. It was one of peace, accomplishment, of understanding.

"You know, after all that's happened between us, I just want to let you know that I don't blame you — for anything," Nerissa said.

He twiddled the paper towel in his hand and stared at his half-eaten pizza.

She waited patiently.

He seemed to be searching for the right words to say, finding them but then changing his mind. "Hey, you know what? I found a stock of DVDs in the wardrobe. I think there might be a couple there we could watch."

"Oh yeah. What?"

"Free Willy."

Nerissa groaned. "Try again."

"Watership Down."

"You'll have to do better."

"An Inconvenient Truth."

"My life doesn't completely revolve round environmental issues you know. Tonight, I need something to completely take my mind off things. What else was in the collection?"

Jackson grabbed another slice of pizza. "I think there was something called *The Notebook*."

"Perfect. A chick flick."

It was Jackson's turn to groan. "Torture. Torture."

Nerissa laughed. At least there was one friendship in her life that was now back on track.

***

Nerissa walked the short distance back to her cottage. The dinner, company and time out was exactly what she needed. That things between her and Scott were unresolved left her unsettled.

There were times in people's lives when firm action was needed. How long would Scott take to decide what he wanted, whether he still wanted her?

What was clear to her though was she couldn't have both Scott and a life in Aqua Bay. The two were poles apart.

As much as she loved Scott and wanted to be with him she had to make a choice.

Her life was in Aqua Bay. Someone was required to keep Aqua Bay protected and pure and she needed to live up to the by-line, Guardian of Aqua Bay, that people had given her. And that could possibly mean that she would lose Scott.

But there was something that she could no longer keep to herself or deny its existence. And this revelation could change everything.

Chapter 29

Nerissa spent the next three days doing 12 hours shifts at the MEC. It was exhausting both physically and emotionally. She had to train three new sets of teams a day as the birds continued to be brought in. However, the number of dead birds being recovered had dropped. Volunteers continued to clean up the beach and the air was not so pungent with oil fumes.

Dolphin Eco-tours would resume business on Monday. As much as Nerissa wanted to keep helping at the MEC, Ginny insisted she have a break on Friday.

After a much needed sleep in that morning, she mucked round the cottage. She had a weariness she couldn't shake. During the week, somewhere in between the craziness, she had signed the sale and purchase agreement for the cottage, which was now unconditional. Her hands had shaken while she'd tried to steady the pen, scared and exhilarated all at the same time. There was no going back now. She was doing this on her own.

She was tidying up papers on the table when her cell phone buzzed.

Scott: Can I come over?

That meant he was still in Aqua Bay.

Was this it? Had he finally come to a decision?

She had to talk to him. She could no longer put off what she needed to say, but what would be his reaction?

Reaching for her phone, she knocked it onto the floor where it landed with a thud on the carpet.

She texted: Sure.

Fifteen agonising minutes passed.

Finally, Scott arrived. She drew in a deep breath and opened the door.

She looked at him, really looked at him. His short brown hair that just touched his collar, his hazel eyes, belying the emotions he'd been struggling with all week. The T-shirt that hugged his muscular chest. He could still make her heart skip a beat.

She offered him a drink and they made small talk about the weather. He was making some point about what an eye-opener it had been for him to help with the storm clean-up, what a mess he'd made of things – everywhere; at work, with their lives – letting things distract him, forgetting what was important.. Words kept tumbling faster out of his mouth, like a freight train that couldn't slow down. He rubbed the back of his neck in short, swift movements. She bit her lip. What was going on? She'd never seen him so agitated.

She couldn't make sense of his words, but when he said her name it seemed to bring them both to a moment of clarity.

"Nerissa, I've had a lot of time to think about things over the last week, to think about you, us, and I wanted to say..."

She swallowed over a lump in her throat that was growing bigger and bigger. His words jumbled together. The roaring in her ears grew louder. She didn't want to listen to him. She was so unsure as to what he wanted.

"Scott, I'm pregnant," she burst out.

Chapter 30

She'd found out a week ago. She'd been certain it was just that stomach bug that had been going round until the doctor had made noises about taking blood tests. She had never had particularly regular periods and although she was on the pill, she'd kept forgetting to take it.

Scott stared at her. His mouth opened and closed, the words lost in the silence. The question he wanted to ask was written all over his face.

"The baby's yours."

"Are you sure?"

"I'm nine weeks. The baby was conceived the weekend we went to the city for Chloe's party."

When the doctor had told her she was pregnant, her whole world had tilted. She could hardly breathe while he did some calculations. *Please, please, let it be Scott's.* The other possibility flickered and quickly disappeared.

"Oh my God," Scott said.

"Whatever it was that you'd come here to tell me, this might change things."

Scott plunged his thumbs into his eyes. "Can I ask you one thing?"

"Anything."

"You're not leaving Aqua Bay are you?"

She shook her head. "I love you Scott, but I'd never be happy in the city. This place means too much to me."

"More than me?"

She gulped. "I can't do both. I can't give this up. I don't know what else to say."

He sat there, stock still, like a little boy lost. "I want to be in this baby's life. I need to be in this baby's life. It's all I ever wanted – you, and a family. It all seems to be falling apart..."

"I'm sorry to have caused you so much pain," her voice broke.

Tears rolled down Scott's face. He rose slowly from his chair and walked out the front door.

So this was it. It was over. This was what he'd decided and a baby wasn't going to make any difference. She put her hand over her stomach, rubbing it. *Well, it's just you and me now.* This should've been a moment of joy shared by two people. In pursuing her cause to keep Aqua Bay protected she'd failed to protect her love for Scott. Was this the price she'd pay?

She stared at the closed door. Her heart hurt and her head floated. Had she just lost the one person who mattered the most to her?

Chapter 31

She had to talk to someone. She grabbed a head of lettuce from the garden and strolled down the road.

He opened the door. "Hey neighbour."

"Can I make you dinner?" she asked, holding up the lettuce.

Jackson smiled his crooked grin and opened the door wider.

After dinner they sucked on a couple of lemonade popsicles, lounging outside on the porch.

"Scott came to see me today," she said.

Jackson remained silent for a moment and then said, "How did that go?"

"Not well. I had some news to tell him." She looked at Jackson. "I'm pregnant."

While Scott's face had been unreadable when she had told him the news, Jackson's was the opposite. The beginnings of a smile crawled across his lips and the dusk caught a twinkle in his eyes.

Her Popsicle stick stuck in her throat. *He thinks the baby's his.* Now she was about to give more news to somebody who'd be disappointed. "Scott's the father."

The twinkle and smile faded in an instant. His shoulders slumped forward.

"Did you want the baby to be yours?"

"I can't even imagine what a brat of ours would look like. Short or tall? Blonde or black hair? Straight or curly? Poor thing. It would look like a creature from another planet."

"Thanks," Nerissa said.

"How did Scott take it?"

"Not as well as you. He'd come over to tell me something, which I never gave him a chance to do. But I had to tell him two things. The first was about the baby and the second was that I'm staying in Aqua Bay. He left without saying a word."

"Do you think you're going to be a solo mom?" Jackson asked, licking the last of the lime liquid off the Popsicle stick.

"It could turn out that way."

"You'll be doing it tough."

"I'd rather do it tough here than in the city." She peered into the darkness. "Petra's a solo mum."

"I know."

"She's probably doing it tough too."

Jackson's head moved slightly to one side. "I got a new photo of Ben. Wanna see?" He flicked through his phone and stopped when he got to the one he wanted to show her.

Ben was looking more like a Jackson mini-me every day.

"My mum flipped when I told her she was a grandmother and she didn't even know. She insisted on seeing a photo and wanting to visit Ben. When I told her I wasn't actually keeping in touch with Ben she was mortified. Mum practically ordered me to contact Petra so she could see baby photos, birthday photos, the works. So I've been back in contact with Petra."

"And...?"

He threw her a tight smile. "We're taking things slowly. She wants Ben to have regular contact with me."

"What are you afraid of?" she whispered.

Jackson cracked his popsicle stick in half and chewed on one end. "I'll mess up like my old man. That I'll hurt him and Petra."

Watching Jackson struggle with his fear made her throat ache. This larger-than-life, confident man, now dealing with what he'd pushed aside for so many years.

"We've had this conversation before. We've only known each other a short amount of time, but what I've noticed about you is that if someone had told me you'd killed a fly I wouldn't have believed them. There are a number of times you could have retaliated physically, but you never did. You never hit Scott."

His face tightened. "Oh, believe me. I wanted to. Don't make me out to be a saint."

"The difference is you didn't react. And that's a big difference. You showed nothing but care, concern and tenderness when we rescued that shag caught in the fishing line. Not just for the shag. You helped me when I was attacked, when I fell off the horse, when I got stung by a bee, then washing oiled birds. I haven't seen anything that tells me you're a violent man. You couldn't hurt your son, or Petra. You and I aren't that different. I want to protect the environment, you want to protect those that can't do that for themselves, like Antoni. You want a family, don't you?"

"Yep I do. More than anything. It's what's been missing in my life. I'm ready to settle down."

"You have a family. Go home and be a father to Ben, work things out with Petra, reconnect with your mum and brother. That's what life's about."

"Yes," he said, releasing a big sigh. "I want that very much."

"You know those times I said I wished I'd never met you?"

Jackson nodded.

"I lied."

He cracked a grin, and she laughed.

Chapter 32

Nerissa stared at herself in the hairdresser's mirror.

"So, what are we going to do today?" Faith asked, running her fingers through Nerissa's hair.

She drew in a deep breath and braced herself against the chair. "Cut it short," she said.

Faith's eyes widened, and she laughed. "That's a bit drastic." She draped a black cape over her.

"I'm serious. It hasn't been the same since I put that fake oil mixture in my hair. It's bugging me and it keeps getting in the way. I can't control it."

"You sound completely frustrated. You sure it's not just your hair that you're mad at?"

"I need a change." She tossed her head.

"OK. If you're sure. Must be something to do with that storm. I had a guy in here today wanting his long hair cut off too."

Faith picked up the scissors and started snipping.

***

That night Jackson appeared on her doorstep for dinner. She opened the door and laughed. "What have you done to your hair?"

Jackson's long black hair was gone, replaced by a neater, shorter cut. The black clothes had vanished. His long legs emphasised by the blue denim jeans and white T-shirt that hugged his chest.

"I almost didn't recognise you," she said.

"Ditto." He pointed at her hair.

She looked him up and down. "I like it."

"Ditto," he said again.

"Oh, and I have something for you," she said. She reached into her handbag and pulled out a small paper bag, which she handed to him.

"What's this?"

"Take a look."

He peered inside and drew out a postcard of the *Seabird* surrounded by dolphins. "Nice," he said, studying it." Who am I sending this to you?"

Nerissa stared at him. She wasn't going to say anything. *I'm sure he'll figure it out.*

Jackson's face was a blank and then the lightbulb went off. "I should send this to Ben?"

Nerissa nodded. "This might in some small way help you build a bridge to Ben."

"It will be a great start. Thank you," he barely whispered.

***

Every night that week Nerissa and Jackson alternated dinner at each other's cottages. While Jackson attempted to revitalise his guitar playing, and many an off-chord and off-key tune was played and sung, Nerissa picked up her paintbrush for the first time in a long while. She dipped a brush into a paint pot. The scene that had been troubling her came to life as she intensified the colours.

They would watch chick flick DVDs and Jackson would roll his eyes skywards.

When it was his turn, he chose a rootin', tootin' and shootin' DVD and she groaned.

But for three consecutive nights Jackson had texted Nerissa to say he wouldn't be able to make it. Something was up and late on the fourth night he knocked on her door.

"May I come in?"

"Sure."

"I wanted to let you know I'm leaving tomorrow."

"Seismic surveying starting up again?" A muscle in her neck twitched.

"Not quite. I've resigned. I'm going back to Texas tomorrow. I've a late flight to Auckland and then onto LA."

Nerissa clutched her chest. "This is very sudden."

"Not really. I want to work things out with Petra and Ben. I don't want to wait any longer."

"What will you do instead?"

"I'm going back to college. I'm going to do some studies in environmental geology."

"Really? What made you change your mind?"

"Being here over the last couple of months. Being with you. You've really opened my eyes to the fact that we are potentially destroying the environment. I don't think I can live with that anymore. I think the clincher was the dead birds covered in oil. It's been playing on my mind for days."

"If I have been able to change just one person's thinking about oil drilling and it was yours, then everything was worth it."

"I'll miss you."

"Me too."

"I wanted to say goodbye now. I need to pack. I'm leaving first thing tomorrow. I also wanted to give you this." Jackson handed Nerissa a small box with a blue ribbon on it.

"What is it?"

"Look at it after I've left," he said.

"Thank you. That's very sweet of you."

"OK then," he said awkwardly. "Better go."

They moved towards each other and Jackson's arms enveloped Nerissa in a big friendly hug. She hugged him right back.

"Take care," she said softly.

"You too," Jackson said. "I'll send you photos."

"That would be great."

"Been nice knowing you, ma'am."

A tiny tear escaped Nerissa's eye as she watched Jackson walk away.

She propped her bike up against the tree and strolled down to the shore.

Dawn was just breaking and strobes of bright-yellow lit a path from sea to sky.

She eased herself down onto the rocks, reached into her back pack and pulled out the box Jackson had given her. She gently pulled on the bow then took the top off the box. Sitting in the box was an exquisite glass dolphin perched on the crest of a wave with her new born calf beside her. Nerissa's hand went to her mouth.

There was a small card in the bottom. She opened the card and read the words:

"For you and the little one. Let all our dreams be free, Your friend, Jackson."

She clutched the dolphin to her heart, the only place it could be, with the promise to keep protecting them stronger with every heart-beat.

***

The Operation Protect team met a few days later to reassess its plans now that the danger to the wildlife had passed. Salvage crews had contained the oil from leaking from the Pacific Way and were now looking at ways to safely get the ship off the rocks. The dolphins and whales had returned to the area and didn't appear to have escaped from harm.

"This is a red hot issue now. We have to make the best of any media exposure and we have to keep the momentum going," Nerissa said.

"We've received heaps of donations," Angie said. "And a rather significant one yesterday. Anonymous."

"How much?" Peter asked.

"$5,000."

"Good grief," said Sam.

Nerissa frowned. "Can I see the bank statement?

Angie handed Nerissa the statement and while the rest of them chatted about their next moves, Nerissa's finger trailed down the statement looking for the $5,000 donation.

Her finger stopped when she saw it. There was only one clue to the deposit. One simple word – Flinty. She had really gotten through to him and her heart gave a little leap of joy. That man was going to be a fantastic father, partner, brother and son who would also leave a small legacy to a tiny seaside community half a world away.

***

Two weeks later, 20 little blue penguins, who had been rescued and cared for until the MEC were satisfied they were 100 per cent fit and could survive in the wild, were released back into the ocean. They had to have swum six hours unassisted and had blood tests taken to prove they were healthy.

The Aqua Bay community had finally found something to celebrate after the previous rollercoaster weeks of anguish and hopelessness.

A crowd of people stood behind safety barriers as the wee penguins were let out of their boxes. People laughed, clapped and cheered as the penguins, smelling freedom, waddled towards the edge of the sea.

Nerissa watched them; a tear fell from her eye as she watched them. They had lost so much wildlife, but these penguins represented the stories of survival. One penguin turned round to take a look back at the crowd lining the beach as if to say, 'Thank you; we made it'.

As the last of the penguins were encouraged on their way, she walked back to the beach car park. The Operation Protect team and other volunteers were preparing a sausage sizzle to help raise money to cover the increasing expenses.

She helped set up, then buttered buns while Sam and Angie cooked the sausages. Soon the smell of the frying meat drew people over to the tent and sausages, buns and money were quickly changing hands.

Nerissa looked out over the full length of the car park and in the distance a solitary figure stood looking out to sea. She narrowed her eyes until her vision sharpened. Scott had turned and was looking her way. She hadn't heard from him for two weeks and as each day passed she grew more certain that she wouldn't ever hear from him again.

"Angie, can you take over for a while?" she asked.

"Sure thing, honey."

Nerissa pulled off her apron and walked towards Scott.

"Hi," she said. Butterflies flitted in her stomach.

"I wasn't sure it was you. What have you done to your hair?"

"I had it cut off."

Scott raised his hand to touch her new shorter cut. "I loved that hair."

"It was time for a change."

Scott lowered his hand.

A lump formed in her throat. "I didn't think I'd see you again."

"I needed some space. The pregnancy thing threw me. How are you?"

"I'm fine. I had some trouble with morning sickness for a while, but that's gone. Now I have a craving for pickles."

Scott chuckled. "Do you want to sit down?" He gestured towards the bench. "I'm not very proud of what I've done over the last month. I've defrauded my father's business, I've decked a guy and I cheated on my fiancée. And then I left her in the lurch while she was probably wondering what the hell was going on."

"You can't take all the blame. I'd not been paying you the attention you deserved and I cheated on you too. I'll always regret that."

"I love you, Nerissa. I can't let you go. I want us to put what's happened behind us, let it die in the past. We can move forward from this. I know we can. We can try again, if you want that too."

It was going to be a day for tears. She completely broke down. Scott wasn't abandoning her after all.

"Aw, babe," Scott said, wrapping his arm round her and pulling her close to him.

"What about Katey?"

"I've not been in touch with her since... since..." He couldn't finish the sentence. "Katey has a way of drawing you into her web. Initially I was flattered by her attention. And I was weak. She means nothing to me."

"I love you too Scott, but I still can't see how this would work. Our goals are too different."

He searched and found her hand gripping it tightly. "Ah, well, that's where you're wrong. I'm going to move to Aqua Bay. To be with you and the baby. I want this baby. I want you... I want us to be a family together."

"You'd move to Aqua Bay?" Her heart thumped against her chest.

"I've given it a lot of thought. I'll do this if it means being with you. We'll sell the land at Surfboard Point. Invest part of the money in the cottage. We night need to add a couple of rooms on, though. You create mess and a baby will create even more mess."

She playfully swatted at his arm.

Scott's tone changed from light hearted to serious. "I've been making a few enquiries round here. Peter and Mavis tell me Dolphin Eco-tours is up for sale. Why don't we buy it? We could use the rest of the money from Surfboard Point. We could own the business and you'd still be round your beautiful dolphins and do all the work that needs to be done on getting rid of those pesky Taxxoil people. Plus it makes sense for me to lay low for a while from the city. I could start a branch of Maindonald Jones Crowley here in Aqua Bay."

"Wow! You've really thought this through. Are you sure?"

"Never more so. And you know you're right. Who wants to raise a family in the city when we have all of this beauty here?"

Her mind was spinning. Scott back with her, living here and possibly owning her own eco-tour business. It was perfect!

She threw her arms round Scott's neck and hugged him fiercely. "I couldn't have asked for anything more." She drew back and looked into his eyes. The same look of love he used to have for her had returned. She leaned in and pressed her lips against his. He responded with an eagerness she had not felt in a long time. He tasted of desperation, regret and a need of her. And she reciprocated right back.

When they finally drew apart, Scott said, "Who else knows about the pregnancy?"

"No one." Now was not the time to mention she'd told Jackson.

"I hate to be in the same room as your mother when you tell her you're having a baby before we get married."

Nerissa laughed. "I'm not worried about her anymore. It's not going to be a shotgun wedding."

Nerissa reached out for Scott's hand. He took it and squeezed it tightly.

As they strolled back towards the car park she looked out over the dazzling teal-blue waters. Aqua Bay. She was home, where she belonged. There was still so much more work to do, but with the dedication of a community fiercely committed to protecting its untouched world and a new life inside her, she could face whatever challenges the future threw at her with strength and courage.

Acknowledgements

So much goes on behind the scenes of writing a book. These are the people I need to thank who contributed in so many different ways:

Lesley Marshall – thanks so much for your editorial input and comments on the first draft on how to make Aqua Bay even better. Your insight was spot on.

Lynn O'Shea – your talent for taking the vision I had for what I wanted on the cover and coming up with the final result was outstanding. I'm so impressed!

Kristen Keiffer for the wonderful resource of Well Storied www.well-storied.com and building the supportive and close knit community of Your Write Dream. Thanks for being so supportive and answering those pesky questions I had on writing in deep point of view.

Mollie – Thanks for all the suggestions you gave on how to make Jackson a real Texan. I hope I did OK. You're obviously a very proud Texan!

Lindsay Carlton – Thanks for beta reading again. Your suggestions made me look at things I hadn't even thought of and I valued the personal experiences you shared. Best wishes to you and your new family!

Bob Boze – A huge thank you for being a fantastic beta reader. I can never thank you enough for the time you gave to help me, and your patience and understanding. Your suggestions on how to make Aqua Bay better were invaluable and given with thought and consideration. Your generosity in so many other ways still leaves me lost for words.

VB – you asked me every day how my writing was going even if you did get the title muddled up a couple of times. How did Aqua Bay become Blue Lagoon?! And for also understanding when I would daydream, staring out the window and you'd comment that I'd gone into 'book land' again.

And to my readers. Hope you enjoyed it!

About me

Casey Fae Hewson lives in sunny Marlborough, New Zealand. She loves to write young adult and contemporary romance fiction. When she's not reading, she'll be mountain biking, walking, gardening, travelling and listening to music.

Connect with Casey
http://caseyfaehewson.com
Friend me on Facebook: http://facebook.com/caseyyaauthor
Follow me on Twitter: http://twitter.com/@caseyfae
Follow me on Pinterest:
https://nz.pinterest.com/caseyfaehewson/
Instagram: https://www.instagram.com/caseyfae8917/

Love to read? Love to write? Be the first to read about my latest book release and my reading and writing life. Sign up for my newsletter for romance readers, The Romantic Heart when you visit.

Coming in 2018!

Misty Springs

Emily is hurting from a broken engagement. Can she trust Ricky with her broken heart?

Light My Way
(co-authored with Bob Boze)

Can Ciara recover from the devastating loss of her husband, Logan? Can Aidan, the firefighter who desperately tried to save her husband, open her heart and help her love again?

Available Now

Haven River

Sixteen-year-old Luke Conway is in his last year of high school in the harbour-side town of Haven River.

Writing is Luke's life. All he wants to do is be a journalist and write stories about storm chasers.

But Ryan, Luke's protective older brother and guardian, has other ideas.

When Luke meets newcomer to town, the mischievous Jamie Pascoe, his world is turned upside down.

Tragedy strikes and Luke is catapulted down a path of self-destruction.

Can Luke overcome the odds pitted against him? To make Jamie proud of him. To hold on tight to his family. To follow his dream on his own terms.

Reviews for Haven River:

"A delightful story – which in my case – rekindles the delicate and precarious path of young love. The narrative explores a love of books and writing and overcoming major events in life, all skillfully woven into the plot.

A Satisfied Reader, Wellington, New Zealand

A warm, well written romance story that should be added to your "want to read" list. 5 stars!"

Bob Boze, USA

Available on Amazon, Barnes and Noble and iBooks.

www.ingramcontent.com/pod-product-compliance
Lightning Source LLC
Chambersburg PA
CBHW060352260626
47160CB00006B/2280